For Gavin and Brooke

Acknowledgements

To Kelly Smith for your ruthless logic and clear-sightedness: You make me a better writer.

To Kym Neck, Erin Culver, and Lillie Petrillo for reading 25-page serials: You kept me honest.

To Carole Boswell and Steve Capellas for thorough, invaluable procedural advice.

To Bett Norris for encouragement in the clutch.

To Caroline Curtis for dots and crosses and keen insight.

And to my family, for every exquisite meal.

Some of the places named in this novel exist—including Spokane; this is a work of fiction.

Of all the mushroom guides, I referred most frequently to the slender volume *Common Mushrooms of the Northwest* by J. Duane Sept because of the lovely color photographs.

Part One

If you don't get it, then you've got it

One

Sailing small boys

The boy had fallen into the water. Usually, Liv stood within easy grasp of him, but she'd stepped away to crush her cigarette, and as she'd turned, Simon slid right off the bank and into the water. His head hadn't submerged, but his eyes went wide. She grabbed his shirt at his chest and heaved him out.

"Are you OK?"

He nodded, gasped. Nodded again.

She hugged him against her, both their hearts raging. Afraid. She'd been afraid. In the moment he'd slipped, she'd seen him dragged away into the current and lost. She'd seen him disappear. With the child pressed against her, she ran toward the house, up through the brush and the larkspur and the ugly meadow scrub toward Claire.

"I'm sorry," she said, handing the child to Claire. All of them drenched now. "I'm sorry. He just slid right off the bank. He just slid. He was on the bank, then right into the water. He didn't do anything wrong. He just slid right off."

Claire undressed him, asked Liv to grab her a towel from the bathroom. Liv dashed into the bathroom and back. "It was surprising," Liv said as she gave the towel to her. "He just slid right off."

"It's OK," Claire said to Liv. "You're OK."

Simon hadn't cried or shouted. He shivered now as his mother toweled him dry.

"Bath?" he asked.

"Would you like one?" his mother asked.

He nodded, hurried naked from the room.

Liv walked out to the deck, her shirt and pants cold against her, and wanted to scream. Her heart wouldn't quiet. First the girl last night, shivering so hard that Liv thought maybe it was a seizure, and finally realized the girl was sobbing. When Liv stopped, and tucked around her, the girl clung to her and cried into Liv's chest and kept apologizing, "This is so embarrassing. I don't know what's wrong with me."

They were related, the girl last night and Simon this morning. Simon, only three years old, and drenched rather than crying, but they both needed her protection. They both needed Liv to help them. Now, in her sopping clothes, she felt herself crying and was paralyzed by it. She stood on the deck and wept.

In the house, Claire put Simon down for his nap. Comforter pulled over his head, he stilled almost at once, and she went outdoors, stood on the rapidly appearing deck, and waited, as Liv hammered slat after slat at a furious pace. Claire shielded her face with her arm, the buttons of her shirtsleeve pressed against her hair, and watched the woman on her knees. Claire kept looking for reasons to interrupt. Over the past month, she'd volunteered to help transport loads of wood, or roofing shingle for the garage, or wallboard and insulation; something always needed hauling. Claire kept asking the woman working for her to put her to work. She'd rather be out here, with Liv, than in that office alone.

Just this morning, she'd discovered that the last of her aunt's research was missing. She'd riffled through all the papers in the office, frantic that she might have misplaced it. That she might have lost something else.

Barely June, still cool enough in the mornings for Simon to wear socks with his sandals, and already Liv was dark, her cheeks lightly colored with freckles. Claire imagined she could see those freckles now, though Liv's head was bowed toward her work. Both women were small and dark-haired, athletic and quick, with remarkable definition along their arms, Claire's from hefting Simon.

When Liv stood to grab more wood, Claire dropped her arm at her side. "He's OK," Claire said quietly. "He's sleeping and he's fine. Things like this happen. It's not your fault. Neither of you did anything wrong."

Liv didn't speak.

"You've almost finished," Claire said, looking at the deck.

"Yes."

"Then you'll start on the house?"

"The kitchen, yes."

"I like that you're here. I'm glad." Claire turned and went back into the house.

When Simon came outside, after his nap, he squealed and ran around the deck. It had a railing now, like a little ladder, which he immediately clambered up. He could crow from here. He could drive his trains along the railing; it was like a high track, a mountain track. All Liv's tools were gone, and in their place, recliners with cushions. Stretched on the largest recliner, he leaned back and stared into the sky. The cushion's buttons pressed into his back. Near the railing, a butterfly fluttered like lint in the air. She'd built this. She'd built it for him. He scrambled down and walked through the fields, searching for Liv, but her yellow truck was gone.

Later that evening, Liv returned in time to watch Simon help his mother stack charcoal on the grill, and then the child climbed onto the railing while Claire lit the lumpy black hill.

"He asked for hamburgers," Claire said, "and to eat outside, on the deck. Like a picnic."

Liv handed him a long wooden dowel. "A sword," she said.

The boy's eyes lit. He ran into the yard and whirled around with it, smacking shrubs and the deck and the air until he was called to dinner.

"You can play with it after you eat," Claire told him.

Simon laid the dowel on the table beside his plate, but kept his hand on it.

Liv took in the slices of tomato, onion, pickle, and the potato wedges, everything laid on plates like an offering. Simon dunked his quartered hamburger into the ketchup, and murmured as he ate.

As Liv fixed a burger, she asked, "How's your work?" Still unsure what Claire's work entailed. For several weeks, since the beginning of May, Liv had been living on the property, in her ridiculous pink trailer, building a garage to replace the shed and carport, and this deck, and could only say that Claire sat every day in front of her computer.

"Oh," Claire said, and grabbed Simon's glass of milk before it toppled. "I need to take a research trip, I think, west of here. I'll camp and hunt. Take a few notes. My aunt's notes are incomplete, or I've lost some."

"Camp and hunt," Liv repeated. "Tell me about your book again?"

"It's a mycology field guide."

Right. Mycology. Claire was a beautiful geek, Liv understood that much. At first, Claire had seemed evasive about her work, and her aunt, but tonight, maybe because of Simon's calamitous plunge into the river, in an effort to reassure Liv that she wasn't angry with her, Claire had answered a question about her work with more than four words.

Raised on his knees, Simon squeezed another pool of ketchup onto his plate, and Claire, in what appeared to be a single motion, stoppered the bottle before he flooded his plate, and righted his milk before it tumbled off the table. Liv loved these moments: the constant diverting of disaster. "I don't know that word," she admitted, dragging from her beer, "mycology. Your aunt was a doctor of some kind?"

"A mycologist studies fungi. My aunt specialized in mushrooms." She stood abruptly, and said, "I forgot the watermelon."

Simon ate two pieces of watermelon, and kept holding out his hands to be wiped.

"I missed the summers here," Liv said, trying to remember the name of the pink flowering tree by the drive. Crabapple?

"Did you grow up in Spokane?" Claire asked.

"South Hill. We moved to Portland when I was in junior high."

"I used to play on the hill. Rode my bike around Cannon Hill Park, played soccer at Manito, waded for coins in the pond at the Japanese Gardens."

Liv nodded. "So you too?"

"My parents lived in Seattle, but I spent summers here with my aunt."

"You were close with her." Liv understood this was not a question, though it baffled her. Her aunts made quilts, went to craft fairs and Bible studies.

"Yes. We were close."

Liv sipped her beer, asked, "What about Simon? Will you take him on your research trip?"

"Of course," Claire said, "he loves camping: all those rocks to throw."

If Claire took Simon, it would be easier to work in the kitchen, no one underfoot. Minimal cleanup. No little boy crouched over his trains, running them through the grass as Liv worked. No walks to the river with his hand in hers. No picnics on the deck.

While Claire put Simon to bed, Liv had started a fire in the ceramic backyard fireplace. Now, as Claire approached, her wine glass in one hand, and a plate of cookies in the other, she watched firelight play off Liv's skin like tongues.

Extending the plate, Claire asked, "Do you want any?"

Liv ate her cookie, periodically flicking Simon's sword against her pants' leg as though it were a riding crop. "You worked as your aunt's assistant?" Liv asked.

"That's right."

Her assistant, yes, Claire thought. Yet that word was wholly inadequate. It didn't begin to explain this emptiness. Claire's aunt had died suddenly in January: a heart attack during her morning run. Snow on the roadside had hidden the body for hours. Claire had driven along the road several times before she'd seen the tread of a sneaker. Simon, strapped in his car seat, pressed his boots into the back of her seat, munching on pretzels while Claire sat, willing herself to get out of the car.

"And you're finishing the book from her notes?" Liv asked.

Except that some of her notes were missing. But Claire couldn't think about that. "Yes," she said.

"What will you do after you finish?" Liv asked.

"After I finish?" Claire drank her wine, held the deep tang a moment before swallowing.

"After you finish the book, what will you do?"

A fair question, Claire knew. The sort of question everyone asked. She'd contemplated modifying her field guides to other subjects: field guide to dynamic lunches, featuring the cheese sandwich, the peeled carrot. Especially popular with toddlers! A field guide to clearing out your dead aunt's study. Denial and procrastination will help draw this pleasure out. You can move piles from one surface to another for months, and make absolutely no headway. After fourteen years, she had come to love her work, the mapping of their discoveries had become thrilling to her. Mushrooms, for god's sake. Mushrooms had become thrilling. "I don't know," she said. And then to deflect the issue, she added, "Maybe you'll keep giving me jobs."

"Sure," Liv replied. "You can be my assistant, working with you is like working with myself. I can't even tell us apart."

Claire grinned. Visitors to the house had mistaken Liv for Claire, then asked, after the confusion was sorted, if they were sisters. And Simon, upon meeting Liv, had stared back and forth between them as though it were a wondrous magic trick.

Claire thought Liv an unusual girl, quiet like Simon, contained in her movements and watchful like the child as well. She still hadn't decided if she found their resemblance eerie, or if she were more disconcerted by the ease with which she and Liv moved around one another. The improbable simplicity of a stranger among them, in this house in particular, shielded always from external examination. Later Claire would marvel at that thought.

"How did your aunt like Simon?" Liv asked.

Claire started laughing. "You know the first thing she told me? 'Please tell me you've scheduled an abortion.' She thought I'd gone completely mad. My entire pregnancy she grumbled at me about how I'd ruined my life. And then he was born, and she cut the cord, and held him, and never wanted to give him back."

"And has he asked?"

Claire stared at Liv, then looked away at the hover of mosquitoes, the darkened meadow beyond them. At first, she had been afraid that Simon wouldn't remember Dee, that all of their adventures together would be lost to him, but now she was afraid that he remembered too clearly. He avoided Dee's room just as his mother did. "In his way," Claire said, "he still asks."

"I have a canoe—stored at a friend's," Liv said, lighting a cigarette. "I'd like to take him out. Along the river here, or for a float on the Little Spokane."

"Simon in a canoe." Claire imagined his delight, his rapturous little face.

"He'll love it."

"Yes," she said, and then, "Could I come too?"

Liv blushed, dragged from her cigarette, nodded. Wind through the trees hushing around them. In the meadow, two deer ambled through the scrub, down to the river, pausing often, wary.

Two

The Ramones are punks

Simon woke and began running his trains along the side of his bed by the railing. Edward and Henry had slept with him, their wooden engines chipped of paint, worn down by Simon's furious love. Through the window's shade, light splintered. Simon hummed his warrior song. Engines were always going to war. Simon's engines especially.

When he finally climbed from bed, he opened the adjoining door to his mother's room and watched her sleep. Her arm tossed above her head, a furrow between her eyebrows. His mother's long, thin nose, her shiny face. Simon tossed his trains onto the bed, and climbed up beside her. Before Dee went away, he would get up in the morning and visit her room; she was always awake and propped against the pillows, her hair wild like wolf man. They would eat Cheerios with raisins, and sip warmed milk.

"Simon?" his mother asked as he scrambled over her, and slipped under the blue down comforter. She curled into him. He placed his palm against her face, covering an eye.

Then he remembered they were going sailing. Liv was taking them on the river. Simon kicked his bare feet into his mother's belly. Mashed his face against her face, his hands cupped around the back of her head.

"Simon," she said again, and strained her neck backward.

Last night, Liv had brought him a special orange vest and let him wear it until he went to bed. It would make him float on the water just like a ship. She said he could wear it whenever they went to the river from now on. His mother had laughed.

10

The door from the hallway opened and Liv's dark head appeared in his mother's room. "Come on," she whispered to him. "Don't wake your mother."

He scurried from the bed and took Liv's proffered hand.

"Cereal?" she asked. "And milk?"

He squeezed her hand and hurried along to the kitchen with her. Liv was not Dee. But she was like Dee, even her wolf-man bed-head.

Liv let Simon carry two bottles of water. She had the cooler, packed with sandwiches and fruit, in the truck already, and towels, paddles, flotation vests, a change of clothes for Simon. Coffee, ordered from a stand, would be pure joy.

The previous evening, when Liv had stopped by for the canoe, Bailey wasn't home. Her housemate, Sophia, had let Liv into the garage and helped hoist the boat onto the roof rack. While Liv tied the boat down, Bailey drove into the driveway.

"You, my friend, have a reputation already," Bailey said, leaning through the window. Snug against the collar of her chef's jersey, her hair wound into a bun.

Liv looked her over, secured the last knot. "How's that?"

"You've forgotten this is Spokane. Small town life is all I'm saying. Just keep that in mind, right?"

"Sure."

"You need any more paddles?"

"No," Liv said, "I'm golden. Thanks."

"Yeah. Have fun." She reversed to let Liv through. Hollered after her, "Don't fall in."

If Claire weren't up soon, she'd have to let Simon back in to wake her; Simon had mastered the wickedly effective pounce/ululation combo—as she herself could attest. Each time she'd been stalked and shrieked awake, she regretted teaching him to open the latch to her trailer. He hugged the water bottles to his chest, then solemnly handed them over when she asked. He was already wearing his life vest.

"I'm sorry to be so late," Claire said behind them.

Liv jumped, dropped the bottles, Simon giggling.

"Sorry," Claire said again. "Usually Simon wakes me at dawn. I brought your monkey hat." This last to Simon as she pressed the hat over his untidy hair.

Claire wore short black trunks and a red camisole. Her brown eyes looked larger in the morning like a marmoset's. They latched Simon's car seat into the truck. When Claire squeezed between them, her thigh pressed against Liv's. In a moment, the engine roared, sputtered, and died. Liv pumped the gas pedal, turned the engine over.

"Your stereo," Claire said, tucking some of the wires back into the cracked console, "is supposed to go here."

"We'll just have to sing instead," Liv said as the truck roared, vibrating so hard that the windows rattled as she reversed down the gravel lane. "Know any Ramones?"

" 'I Wanna be Sedated' would certainly be fitting. Or we could just shout at one another."

"Like a proper family outing. Now you're talking. Say you want coffee," Liv said, her mouth nearly against Claire's ear as the truck shifted them.

"Yes," Claire said over the tumult. "Oh god, yes."

They slid the green canoe into the water. Liv held the rope and dragged the boat back toward shore. Hopping from foot to foot, Simon looked apprehensive, swallowed by his orange vest and Capri-length swim trunks. His mouth O-shaped.

"You're in first," Liv told Claire. "I'll hand Simon to you."

Claire nodded. An adventure at last, she thought, and nothing to do with field guides. Between Liv's thick black belt—barely holding her plaid shorts at her waist—and her sports bra, Claire could see Liv's belly tattoos, and a little thrill she thought she'd forgotten rushed through her.

To steady herself, she took Liv's hand, and stepped into the boat. Simon exclaimed behind them, and rushed forward as though he might be left on shore. Liv dropped the rope and caught the boy as the canoe shot forward with the momentum of Claire's boarding.

Claire fell forward into the canoe, had to right herself and determine how to paddle back to shore.

Simon was crying, his eager little body restrained against Liv's hip. "I'm OK," his mother called to him. Paddling ineffectually, frustrated at her gracelessness, she suddenly realized that this was their first adventure since Denise's death, and found herself near tears. She considered climbing out and walking the canoe back to them.

"Just lean into your strokes," Liv encouraged.

Watching the girl on shore, and the small grasping boy, Claire felt a sudden, wild laugh climb through her body, and sang, Hey, ho, let's go, as she leaned forward, dug the paddle downward, and moved the canoe infinitesimally closer to shore.

"Yes," Liv said. "Look at Mommy, Simon. She's coming. Look at Mommy."

He stopped crying and looked: his mother's face tight with strain; her arms muscled and fluid; the paddle deep in the water and suddenly airborne. In a moment, the canoe rushed toward them and he retreated as though from a monster.

Liv caught the canoe and grabbed the rope. Reluctantly Simon came forward and allowed Liv to hand him into the canoe. He gripped the rungs of his seat while Liv pushed off the bank. The Little Spokane River, narrow and sleepy, meandered through reeds and heron nests; the air dense with insects. Simon listened to the strokes of the paddles, watched his mother's shoulder muscles flex as though they might launch wings.

Liv leaned forward to give him a drink of water. When he refused to relax his grip on his seat rungs, she braced his back and held the bottle to his mouth.

"Water?" she called to Claire.

And they glided: dragonflies sailing past them and skirting the water's surface; occasionally the startling screech of a heron, its wings thrown wide as if in greeting; and the great looming trees. Simon held a stick over the canoe, adjusted its wake at will.

A field guide to floating, Claire thought. Remember to launch with spectacle. Anyone can push off a dock. Mosquitoes from the

Pleistocene period—roughly the size of bats—will aviate along the river with your canoe. They will influence your velocity. Then Claire stopped rowing, took another swig from the bottle, enjoyed the soothing, umbilical tug through the water.

He fell asleep in Claire's arms. Hiking back on the trail to get to the truck, she and Liv took turns shouldering the heft of him. On Liv's upper arm, a thick scar in the shape of a star. Contemplating Liv's large tribal tattoos, earth brown on her belly and shoulders, Claire wanted to ask the origins, but fought herself and kept walking. For the first time, she felt intimidated by this woman: the skill and silence and markings of her.

"Thank you," she said, finally. Liv smiled at her, offered to take the boy.

Three

Bailey investigates

The band was ghastly. All three men dour and topless: the singer with his guitar, shuffling to the high hat as though he were a tightly wound child's toy; the bassist condescending; the drummer a sprawling, hectic pinwheel. In the narrow, frenetic bar, Bailey leaned against the wall, her legs drawn the length of the booth, the unlit cigarette in her mouth masking her lips' natural pout.

"They're so earnest," she said; her eyes were brown beneath the hooded boredom. Her loose blond hair snarled around her shoulders.

Liv shrugged, took another sip of beer, watched the door. Her anxiety to be elsewhere clutched at her like one of the sorry drunks huddled at the bar. She needed to alter her routine. As undergraduates, Liv and Bailey had been friends. In the past six years, they'd both managed a brief escape, but had returned, for varied, unnamed reasons to the town they despised. Over the past few weeks, she had come to regret that decision. She'd forgotten how annoying Bailey could be.

"Why are we here again?" Bailey asked. Her shirt had ruffles at the sleeves, like an aristocrat, or a buccaneer.

"Don't stay for me."

"Ha. You're killing me." Bailey sipped her shot of whiskey and eyed Liv. "So this woman does something with mushrooms? She, like, studies them or something, am I getting that right?"

"Yeah, she studies them."

"Why?"

"I don't know." Liv wished she could say it was important work, but she wasn't sure.

"Does she sell any?"

"It's not like that."

"Like what?" Bailey asked.

"You know. It's not like that. She's a scientist. A researcher."

"Oh, a researcher. Wow."

"Let it go. She's nice. She's had a rough time."

Liv thought about leaving—making an excuse, any excuse—and trying another bar. She couldn't decide which she liked less, the band or Bailey. Across the table, Bailey smirked. "Oh, you like her. I didn't get that at first."

Liv flicked her lighter closed. This was bullshit; the bars had become just another obligation. This wasn't even fun anymore. The spazz of a drummer hit everything within reach.

"So you want to fuck the mushroom researcher," Bailey said. "Wow. Your standards really have fallen. She's into fungus, dude. Fungus. What the fuck is wrong with you?"

"You're boring, Bailey," Liv said and finished her beer. She stood up and crossed to the door. The girl on her way in stopped and looked at Liv. Tilting the pack toward the girl, Liv asked, "Cigarette?" Her voice sounded tired, even to herself, but the girl turned and followed Liv outside anyway.

In the truck, the girl reattached her bra. Liv lit another cigarette, handed it to the girl, and tried not to be impatient. These girls made her tired. Twenty-eight wasn't impossibly old, but still, these girls exhausted her. Why did it feel like she wasn't moving forward anymore? Was it Spokane—back in this town, in the same holding pattern? Or was this what it felt like to be a pioneer: wearying instruction and encouragement? Virgins: the last frontier.

"Can I have your number?" the girl asked.

"Sure," Liv said, and wrote seven digits on the girl's arm. "Give me a call."

Liv dropped the girl back at the bar and cruised out of town. Did they need her, the girls, or did she need them? She felt a little sick now in the aftermath; she felt like a cheater. Even her wrecked console, the pathetic hole where her stereo used to be, made her think of Claire.

16

On Government Way, the road wound like a riddle, and Liv remembered the way Claire held Simon on her hip in the morning as she picked plates up from the table and set them in the sink. Her loneliness in that house with that silent child, her reticence, the way she sang to Simon as she bathed him. At night, before bed, Claire read to him for an hour. "One more book," she'd say, though she kept going when he brought another. And Liv stood in the hallway, rapt and waiting.

She couldn't remember the last time she'd been on a date, had a conversation about hometowns, favorite books. This was how it was: random connections. These girls didn't seem to want more. Liv had stopped looking deeper than that. They were habit now, the girls—a necessary habit, like cigarettes—something to occupy her mouth and hands. She couldn't remember the last time she'd enjoyed it.

Liv crossed the little bridge and took the next right on the gravel road, tucked into an inconsequential opening between Douglas-fir trees. Gravel crunched beneath the tires as her truck crept forward. A light in the stone house blinked out.

How did Claire occupy her time? Liv would have been surprised to learn that Claire spent most of her time grieving. That Claire stood now, in the dark house, thinking of Simon.

That morning, in the office, beside his winding train cars, Simon had stretched as though he were a gliding engine as well. Feet bare, hair mussed, he still wore pajamas. Claire had realized that she'd missed him. Unaware, until he lolled upon the floor with his trains, how much his presence soothed and sated her. Jealous? Was she jealous of his time with Liv? Or was it simple loneliness?

Field guide to a silent child: how to parent by Thomas the Tank Engine and Friends. Ensure you have a track in every room, and enough engines and freight cars to populate the tracks. Listen for the knock of magnets, and the rattle of the wheels on the tracks as though to your son's own heartbeat. His little wooden consciousness rolling before him like a silent play you will only ever interpret.

Her screen saver had flashed a pomegranate across the monitor, and disrupted her meditation. She might have told, of course. She might have told her aunt's editor the truth. Her aunt was simply a researcher: though an intuitive hunter of mushrooms—one thought of ballet as one watched her scour the forest litter—her writing was wretched and stilted and tiresome. Denise Bernard's reputation was founded on her field guides, of which Claire had written every vibrant word. The two women had lived together in this same house for fourteen years, since Claire had come to Spokane at twenty, seeking refuge.

It didn't have to be a scandal; after all, her aunt had done all the research, and supervised the writing of each book. Perhaps her editor could arrange for Claire to work with another researcher, to continue producing field guides. They could keep it quiet. Maybe no one would ever spot the similarities—move away from mushrooms, and write wild flower guides.

Simon's trains had derailed in a horrible crash. He'd looked up at his mother and grinned. She'd as likely slit Simon's throat as expose her aunt, to her editor of all people, a man whose opinion Denise had revered.

"Is James hurt?" she asked.

The boy nodded.

"Does he need a kiss?"

Simon carried the train to her for comfort, flat in his palms as though it were an injured bird, and claimed a kiss for himself as well. Field guide to the medicinal property of kisses. He returned to the track to stage another tragedy.

In the dark office now, the child asleep, the house quiet, Claire dreaded her impending research trip, another first without her aunt. At some point, she'd quit counting firsts, wouldn't she? First canoe ride on the Little Spokane, first stirring of desire in years, first time she'd stood at the opened window to watch Liv, seated on the hood of her truck, light a cigarette. The night around them swollen with the sound of crickets.

Four

The howling fence

Liv stained the deck. For cigarette breaks, she made herself walk down to the river as though this were any day: their absence not a howling inside her. We'll be back midweek, Claire had said. Simon had a little mummy sleeping bag that he'd carried out to show her, the most blinding shade of orange she'd ever seen. At the riverbank now, she smoked her second cigarette, imagined the boy sailing his boat in the little eddy just there, a step from her.

On the deck, she worked barefoot and topless, the scent of the stain igniting the dense summer air. Brush strokes were too subtle; she wanted some heavy, painful work. She wanted to demolish a wall, or pour foundation, or dig a trench.

At three, she left and hit several bars before she finally found one.

The howling woke her in the night. For a moment, she panicked and had to grab her own throat to keep from shouting out. Beside her, the girl sweated. Liv threw her pants on, and sneaked out. Before she made it to the truck, she was crying.

In the morning, she drove to Windsor Plywood and bought load after load of wood. She'd build the fence while they were away: digging holes, and dragging posts, and pouring cement. In the garage, she unloaded the wood, went back for more, and did the same.

She dug and imagined Claire pregnant: her face fuller; her breasts like clutching beasts; leaned backward, her hand on her hip; the tremendous pouch of her belly rocked by his mutant kicking. She dug and imagined Simon nursing: his fingers kneading at Claire's skin; his little shark-mouth seeking; his eyes on her face. She dug and

19

begged the imagining to stop. She saw herself cut the cord. Felt the weight of the newborn in her arms. Heard his wailing, touched his glossy, swollen eyes. Please, she said. Please. She dragged rocks the size of a toddler from the earth, and kept digging.

That night, at the bright fire, she thought herself obscene. She'd been afraid to try the bars: afraid of the howling, afraid she wasn't in a holding pattern so much as a tailspin. What has happened to me? She drank another beer. Refused to consider the question. Fell asleep on the recliner on the deck, and woke in the dark, trembling with cold.

Two days later, Liv's hands were bleeding. She'd finished the run along the driveway, and now had only the front of the property left to fence. At the riverbank, she lay on the grass, held her hands in the water, and squinted as cigarette smoke burned her eyes. Suddenly he was on her back, heavy and painful, with his knee in her spine. She rolled over and clutched him to her, her cigarette flung away. "Simon. Simon."

Claire had grilled asparagus and fish with lemon and butter and roasted garlic. She hadn't noticed Liv's hands until they were washing up, Simon asleep under the table.

In the following flurry, Liv found herself seated at the kitchen table, her hands deep in a basin of warm water and Epsom salt. Claire's lecture was magnificent. It had a thesis and sub-points and a magnanimous conclusion: "We're taking the weekend off. You and I have been working like slaves, and it's over. We'll hike and eat and play with Simon. No research or tools or mending of anything. Promise me."

"I promise."

"You're not allowed to injure yourself again. Promise."

Laughing now, this woman so beautifully earnest, Liv said, "Yes. I promise." She couldn't stop grinning—high—poisoned maybe, by lingering fumes from the stain, or some toxin in the fish, or the river water.

Claire lugged the child from beneath the table, carried him away to bed, and then returned to pour each of them another glass of wine.

"Tell me about your trip," Liv said.

20

Claire had thrown rocks into the river with Simon, and walked along the trails, watching butterflies. They'd collected sticks and roasted marshmallows, and she had avoided mushrooms by focusing her considerable attention on the child. At night, she'd told him stories about the stars. When he fell asleep, she wished for Liv. Pressing her jacket tightly around her, she'd wished she weren't alone.

I missed you, she wanted to say to this woman soaking her hands in Epsom salt. I missed you, and I don't know what to do with that. "I haven't taken a research trip without my aunt, ever."

A fly had gotten into the kitchen; she could hear it buzzing against the screen door. After she let it out, she said, "Fourteen years." She might have been talking to the fly, or the door. She sat and added, "practically my entire adult life. I worked with her, and lived here in this house, and obsessed about mushrooms for fourteen years. She's dead and the work is five chapters from over, but I'm still here." Water sloshed in the basin as Liv shifted; they watched until the water stilled. "The normal, daily parts are hardest: meals, and grocery shopping, and reading to Simon. All the things that haven't changed."

Twenty when she agreed to work as her aunt's assistant, Claire hadn't expected to keep the job long, had accepted her aunt's proposal only because she thought no one would ever search for her in Spokane. Spokane: where the world ended.

"Look at this place," Claire said, and swept her arm back to take the entire L of the house in. "I missed it. I missed this sad refrigerator— that shade is called pimento, if you can believe it—and the wood paneling in the basement, and that shitty linoleum in the bathroom." She shook her head. "I was only gone for three days."

"Just imagine how much you'll miss it when we gut the place," Liv said. "Maybe we should leave one room completely intact as a shrine to seventies décor."

Claire laughed, put her feet in Liv's lap, and leaned her chair back. When Liv didn't object, Claire laughed again. Enough of shrines, she thought.

Five

An intrusion in the dark

Claire woke, alert and listening, just as she had during Simon's infancy. Had he cried out? She crept to the doorway and peered into his room. He lay perpendicular to his bed, his arms dangling. She tucked him in properly, listened to the depth of his breathing.

Three in the morning, she guessed. She wandered to the kitchen for a glass of water, heard the whir of the refrigerator, and something else. Strangely watchful now, as though she expected an intruder, she tiptoed into the great room. No one here. She paced through the last of the stately furniture—soon to be replaced by comfortable, plush sofas—and walked along the line of photographs documenting the construction of this stone house, and stepped over several bins of toys. A thief would break his neck. In the dining room, Claire checked beneath the walnut dining table, in the corner by the hutch, and finally the lock on the sliding door.

What had she heard? At the top of the stairs to the basement, on the metal strip that edged the carpet, she stood and listened. Ridiculous. A grown woman frightened—her pulse rapid—at the thought of descending. She even considered flipping the light on. In the end, she dashed down the basement stairs and stood in the dark, gasping, as she tried to decipher her sense of alarm.

When had she last been in Dee's study? She touched the desk, remembered that she hadn't yet searched through this room for the missing research. Probably dusty—the papers, the books, the window-sill—probably everything in this room had dust on its surface. Or worse, centipedes, and poisonous spiders, and if they were here, they could be

22

in the rest of the house. She'd have to clean. Now. The entire basement. She'd vacuum first, and obliterate the worst of the infestation. Mice—maybe mice had woken her with their skittering.

In the utility closet, she grabbed the duster, and started with the windowsills. She vacuumed, and scrubbed, and emptied the garbage cans, and ran back upstairs to make pancakes when she heard movement above her, and then left Liv and Simon to their sticky devouring, only to run back downstairs, to stand in the middle of the shag carpet, and contemplate the paneled walls. It looked like a country lodge down here. There should be mounted heads of horned creatures.

"Hey," Liv called from the basement door, "you're not allowed to do any work. Remember?"

Startled, Claire turned toward Liv as though toward laughter.

Liv came down the stairs, "What's going on?"

"I don't know what I'm doing here. There's something—something I'm supposed to do, but I have no idea what. I'm just standing here, waiting for an answer."

Liv considered the disarray in the sad, paneled room. "Maybe it's the book. Maybe you feel guilty about playing hooky."

"Maybe."

"Maybe it's the décor in here."

"I know. It's so grim."

"Or maybe you just need to be outdoors. Let go a little."

"Let go?" Claire asked.

"It's what all the kids are doing."

"Right, the kids. I nearly forgot."

"Don't worry," Liv said, "I'll help you remember."

"Now why would that worry me?"

They drove Claire's car to Riverside State Park, played Norah Jones to appease Simon; he'd decided no other artists existed. After crossing the swinging bridge above the river, they picked up the trail, rutted and loping and easy enough for Simon. Pockets filled with treasures, Simon would dart down to the river to hurl stones, then catch the women up again, gasping for breath, his face euphoric. Liv collected stick-swords for him and they battered rocks as they passed. Cyclists hurled through, their bikes wrenched by stones and roots on the pathway. And dogs, off lead, sprinted down the trail and into the water, the light around them smoky.

In her backpack, Claire carried water bottles, and spicy jerky. She had chocolate Sundrops for Simon as well. Ahead of her, Liv walked in sandals, her calves flexing during quick scrambles, her shoulders browning, unprotected by the thin straps of her orange tank top.

"Maybe it's grief," Liv said.

"You mean this morning?"

"Yes."

Claire ignored this. To their right, the river tore past in frothy pitches. Why should having a child make her feel so much more alone? But it was true, Simon put her solitude into relief and it hurt her now. Her solitude hurt her.

From the front of a raft, a woman screamed as the raft shot down the rapids beyond them. They heard the scream bend.

"Fun," Claire said, the brim of her hat pulled too low to see Liv properly. Away from the house, she'd expected to outdistance the strange nagging, but she could feel it out here too. Liv's interruption bothered her, called her mind into focus.

"I've rafted here," Liv said. "It's too short, over too quickly."

The trail wound through a stretch of burn. Claire watched Simon jump over a charred log. Grief, her stubborn mind said. Maybe it's grief. She had never worried while her aunt was alive. Never thought she'd be alone with a three-year-old. How did this happen? A morning jog, and you're dead: a body in the snow. Among the burn, dozens of saplings poked through the litter.

Simon slept on a towel from her pack; Claire and Liv reclined against a log. Along the little beach were smooth white stones of various sizes, and pieces of driftwood. Liv's feet were bare; her shirt bunched behind her head.

"What do your tattoos mean?" Claire asked.

"Nothing. They're just designs."

"Are they Polynesian?"

"That's right."

"So they're symbols without meaning?"

"They aren't symbols, just designs."

"I think maybe it was grief," Claire said.

Liv looked at her. She tore into a piece of jerky and passed the bag to Claire. Claire had meant to say more. From the trees: birdsong. Light dappled the water.

"How is it you're in Spokane?" Liv asked.

"How is it anyone's here? Isn't that really the question? It seems like people end up here on their way someplace else."

"So, how is it you ended up here?"

Claire pushed her hat up, and said, "I came here when I was twenty. Working for my aunt was just this temporary thing that lasted for fourteen years. Why are you here?"

Liv lit a cigarette, stretched her body out, "I have no idea really. I was living in Portland and then I thought it wasn't good for me. One morning, I packed my shit and drove here."

"You have family here?"

"Not anymore. Most of my friends have moved away."

Claire drank water and swatted at a mosquito. "Why wasn't Portland good for you?"

Beyond Liv's feet, the water snagged. Pine trees leaned overhead.

"Portland is too close to my family," Liv said.

"That's me and Seattle."

"But with Simon, wouldn't it be worth the trouble?"

"Not for either of our sakes. Dee was the only family I ever got along with." Claire grabbed a handful of rocks, and skipped them across the river, four five six times.

On the shag carpet in her aunt's study, Claire sat cross-legged, chin in her hand, and fumed. It was two in the morning, and she'd felt that nagging alarm again. Why was she awake and in this room? What was she meant to do? She would finish the bloody field guide. She'd find the notes and finish, and no one would ever guess there had been entire days when she'd stared at her keyboard and not written a sentence. No one would ever know.

25

This room was a hideous beast. Brown in every direction, like being buried alive. Maybe instead of starting with the kitchen, Liv should gut the basement. Would the nagging—and this sense of claustrophobia—vanish with the paneling? Claire waited, listening, and still nothing came to her.

In the dark, she climbed the stairs, walked through the cold stone rooms, and stood on the deck. She could hear the river and the rustle of leaves. As she debated whether or not to give sleep up, and work for a while, headlights cut through the night. Liv's truck crawled down the gravel road to her camper. For a moment, Claire considered calling out, but remembered she only had on boxers, so withdrew, instead, to the house. Her curiosity about Liv deepened with every step.

Just before dawn, she dreamed the money. The room with the broken cupboard, her aunt seated in a rocking chair, knitting something irregular in degrees of brown.

"You've come back," Denise said.

"Back?" Claire asked.

Her aunt pointed to the bag Claire found in her hands. "Have you come to take the last of it?"

"Yes," Claire said.

"Then hurry." Her aunt looked at her opened palm as though the time were written there. "It's late."

Claire woke to the smell of bacon and coffee. Simon, wearing a helmet, bounded into the bedroom, yelled, "Eat!", and bounded back out. Cotton-brained, Claire squirmed into her robe, and wandered down the hall to join the fray. Piled in the sink and on the counters were pans and cookie sheets, mixing bowls and Simon's trains, utensils of every description, several pairs of socks, and a couple of glasses of milk.

"Simon and I cooked breakfast. Do you like monkey bread?"

Claire, uncertain whether or not this was imaginary bread, answered, "Yes."

"And we have eggs and bacon and coffee."

Simon sat at the table, his short legs metronome kicking, his helmet pushed back from his forehead as he ate chunks of cinnamon-glazed bread. Liv handed Claire a large plate, piled with food, including a tiny citadel of monkey bread. Simon had finished his and was scooping more from the funnel-cake pan on the table.

"This is a superb surprise," Claire said, several bites in. She would not think about the dishes.

"Don't worry about the kitchen," Liv said as she joined her. "I'll load the dishwasher before we go."

"Go?"

Liv pointed at Simon's helmet.

"Rock climbing?" Claire hazarded.

"We're riding bikes on the Centennial Trail today."

"Ah. Of course."

"If we bike through the Valley, I know a cool little spot where we can swim."

In the cold, sandy-bottomed pool down from the trail, Simon dunked his whole head in the water and swam about his mother and Liv.

"You're like a river rat, Simon," Liv told him.

He dunked himself again and floated past them on his belly.

"How's Simon's trailer?" Liv asked Claire.

"Heavy."

"Do you want me to have a go on the ride back?"

"Are you worried I'm too old and infirm to pull it both ways?"

"Yes."

"Shall we race?"

"Oh, Claire. You can't be serious."

"Loser buys dinner."

"You are so on."

Claire's legs burned along the muscles, her wrists hurt, and her neck and her ass. Still she pedaled; Simon behind her, cawing. As the wind teased through her short black hair, clouds of bugs spattered her face and sunglasses. She rode like terror itself kept pace with her. She'd lost track of Liv and the time and everything but her heart and her legs. Along her back and shoulders, her muscles pushed against her skin.

So she was alone. Alone with a three-year-old. Unplanned, yes, but she'd be fine. She'd always been fine: a girl who landed on her feet. Her aunt had employed her, but she hadn't saved her. Claire didn't need anyone to save her. She leaned forward and pedaled harder, her breath roaring through her like a dragon.

They waited for Liv at the truck: Simon sprinting around, kicking pinecones, and Claire on her back in the grass, her legs boneless as jellyfish. She'd just remembered her dream when a shadow blocking her light made her aware of him.

"Hard ride?" the man asked.

Claire opened her eyes, tilted her head sideways, "Clearly."

The man chuckled, stepped back; his enormous black poodle licked at Simon. "What's your name?" He asked the boy. Simon patted the poodle. "I'm Dave," the man said. He wore the dog's leash across his torso like a girl-scout sash. "Dave," he said again, this time to Claire.

"Yeah, Dave, my girlfriend's just coming. Excuse us, will you?" Claire had said this as though it were true, and found herself standing, keen and relieved, as Liv tore into the parking lot. Her hair awry, sweat from every pore, her breath coming in dashes.

"Oh, that hurts," she said, grinning at Claire.

They ate at Thai Bamboo, the mango smoothies thick and rich; Simon slurping Pad Thai noodles; Liv and Claire exhausted and blissful.

"How is it you're so fit?" Liv asked, trying to understand being beaten by someone's mother.

"Yoga."

"Oh, right," Liv said, uncertain whether or not Claire was teasing.

"There's no shame in it."

"Oh, it's like that, is it?"

"When you're older, you'll understand."

"Right. Well, I appreciate the lesson anyway."

"No bother," Claire laughed.

That night at the bar, Bailey scowled across at Liv. They were drinking beer; both in tank tops, Liv watching the troupe of college girls march up and down the stairs. Sitting on the upper level of the Mercury Café with a clear view of the door, the first floor, and the bar, Liv thought the gay bar overwhelmed with straights.

"So I've been promoted," Bailey said.

"Yeah?"

"I'm head baker now."

"That's swell, congratulations. So, more dough?"

"You're cute. And yes, now I'm salaried."

"Next round's on me."

"Thanks," Bailey said. "Can I ask you something?"

"Yeah."

"I've been back in Spokane a year-and-a-half, right? And I haven't met anyone—not anyone—that I'm excited about. I've met some nice people, some sweet girls, but I haven't met anyone I'm really into." She bent her coaster, smoothed her hair back from her forehead. "So I don't get it. You're back like ten minutes and picking up chicks all over the place. I know pickups aren't relationships, but they're sex and that would be OK too. You know?"

Liv sipped her beer, waited.

"I just, I just want to be happy here. I know it's Spokane, but I want to be happy here. I've got a job I'm psyched about and I love my house, and I can't meet a single person that I'm into. Why is that?"

Bailey in all her honest desperation: her tank top and jeans ironed, her hair curled and styled, her nails polished. They both knew she was pretty, and that that was not the problem. She was really asking, though, and this made it painful for Liv; she was embarrassed for Bailey.

"I don't know," Liv said. "It's tricky."

"So like with you; I mean, you don't even think of me like that, right?"

Liv debated sprinting from the building. "I don't sleep with my friends."

"Right. Because that would be messy."

"Bailey, what is it that you want?"

"Jesus, you're like talking to a guy. I want you. You're what I want."

Liv rocked back in her chair, held her breath.

"Not a relationship—I know you. Just sex. Light and uncomplicated."

Uncomplicated. Liv nearly laughed. "Bailey, I don't sleep with my friends. It never goes well."

"But we're not friends. Not really. We hang out, but we're not friends. Not if you're honest."

"Bailey—"

"Is it because we're not strangers? Is that what it is? Does it have to be anonymous?"

Liv watched the beautiful gay boys dancing by the jukebox. This was the worst conversation ever. Bailey's eyes were red when Liv checked back in. "I can't do this with you, Bailey. I can't even tell you why, but I know that I can't. And I'm sorry."

"Don't let it worry you," Bailey said, standing. "I know I'm a little older than you're used to." She threw some money on the table and walked away.

In the truck, the girl rammed her head back against the window, grabbed at the strap of the seatbelt. She lactated into Liv's mouth. Astonished—the thin milk sudden and sweet—Liv looked up at her, murmured; the girl's hands fluttering; Liv sucked harder.

At night, the river had a different tone. Liv sat on the hood of the truck, the metal warm beneath her, and smoked.

She thought of the girl in Portland who'd come to her parents' house. Seated in the kitchen, eating a bowl of soup with Liv's mother one evening when Liv came in from work. Afterward, her mother had said that word, the one that wounded her, the one she refused to consider, "predatory". And Liv had started up, yelling: declared they'd met at a bar, convinced she'd been of age; no one victimized; inappropriate, prejudicial, to trot that word out as though it applied. "Chivalry never did me any favors," she'd said. Like a slap. She'd said it to her mother like a slap. The next morning she'd given notice, and left Portland for the nearest place she knew.

Liv dragged her sleeping bag and bedroll outside to the deck and planned to sleep there, like an old dog, sentry to the house. In starlight, the stone looked elegant and cool, the cedar shake roof almost foreign, as though one had stumbled on a manse here in the wilds.

Six

Outpace this

Simon used his trowel to dig carefully into the earth as Liv had showed him. Moving the dirt, slowly slowly, he poured it over Toby and the Troublesome Trucks. Six feet away, Liv plunged the post-hole digger and squared off the hole. Another three days to finish the fence line along the front of the property.

Claire had sent them out with a thermos of lemonade and some crackers. Magpies blitzed a cherry tree in the field beyond them. As they arced and quibbled, Simon thought of planes. Poor Toby, another scoop buried him.

Wasps in the blossoms, and the sun like a wicked parent, Simon lay back and listened to Liv digging, each thrust like a striking clock. His mother was happy again: singing and patient and laughing. Simon wanted Liv to stay with them forever. Like Dee, only never go away.

In the office, Claire kicked her chair, tore some credit card offers into coin-sized pieces, thought about abandoning her pretense—she'd spent the last hour sharpening two boxes of pencils, and separating those irritating little paper clips from the larger ones—for a run along the road. Quickly thought better. Sat down, fidgeted, stretched her fingers like a pianist and attacked the keyboard.

Five more chapters, and two months to finish them; she had this well under control. The anxiety, then, was inexplicable. She thought of Liv's hands, the taper of her fingers, the nicks to her skin. Claire stood so suddenly that her chair pitched backwards. She yanked on her running shoes and fled outside.

Liv and Simon, barefoot, lay asleep on the recliners. The umbrella covering their faces and torsos, the afternoon a thick, wavy dream, Claire watched them while she stretched. Her shins ached from the pavement. She decided on ribs for dinner, buttered corn, baked beans, and peas. She bent over, palms in the grass, and felt her hamstrings protest. Running. Not her best plan ever. She'd just shifted the ache to a different set of muscles.

Simon woke first, sneaked peas from the bowl on the table, while Claire grilled. They had to wake Liv for dinner; even the smell of ribs hadn't done it, Claire basting on her father's dense tangy sauce.

"All afternoon?" Liv asked.

"The entire thing," Claire answered.

"I'm so sorry."

"As punishment, you'll do dishes."

"You can't think of anything worse?"

"Give me a little time."

"Anything," Liv said. "Anything at all." And then she gasped, "Deer!" and ran to the railing of the deck, motioning for Simon to follow her as she clambered up. Five large animals, thirty meters away, ate from the molasses lick Claire had left in the meadow. "What do you think?" Liv asked the child.

"Ride on them," he said.

"You'd have to catch them first."

"Let's go," he said, and jumped down.

"No, no." She laughed, and waved him back. "They're having dinner. Let's just watch them."

After their own dinner, Simon brought all the Sandra Boynton books down to Liv to read at the table. His mother drank wine, watched the blond head beside the black one. Liv looked leaner than she had even six weeks ago. Her body tanned and spotted, her hair winged out a bit over her ears. She read playfully as Simon turned the pages.

"Will you read one to me, Simon?" Liv asked.

He nodded, opened a book, and began to read, mimicking perfectly his mother's own reading voice. Both women held their breath.

"Simon, can you read another?" his mother asked.

He read them all. They sent him inside to get more, and he read those too. At the end, they gave him a small bag of chocolate-covered almonds for a prize.

"Did you know he could read?" Claire asked after he'd been put to bed.

"I had no idea. Except he turned the pages just as I finished reading, so I knew he was following along."

Later, into a second bottle of wine, she asked Liv if she'd considered having children. Liv laughed, shook her head, "I don't sleep with men."

"I didn't either."

"Didn't?"

"Artificial insemination."

"Promise?" Liv asked.

"Promise."

"Did your aunt know?"

"No. I told her I got drunk and met someone. She always loved a brawling story."

Liv's eyebrows knitted together. "Can you afford all this—the house, the kid, this place—on your own?" She stretched her hand out as though to cover everything.

"My aunt paid for this place years ago. I have savings, and she left us money; we're more than fine."

"Do you want a cigarette?"

Claire took one, knelt against Liv to have it lit. She could smell her, the musk of her body. Inhaling, she cocked her head back and glared at the stars.

"Where do you go at night?" Claire asked quietly.

"I drive around."

"Do you pick up girls?"

"Yes."

"Does it make you feel better?"

"Not yet." Liv stared at Claire's thighs. Her nipples were hard,

34

her breathing irregular. Claire dragged from her cigarette to have something in her mouth.

Through the dark, noises carried, too heavy to be wind or leaves. They couldn't see the deer anymore, but they knew they were there.

Mushrooms could look like blown glass: violet or brilliant orange. They could grow up through asphalt. Some were hula skirts carved from the meat of a coconut. Some were golden martini glasses. Tender, as various as sea creatures, mushrooms oozed and blossomed. In a basket, they might be mistaken for candies. A bouquet of mushrooms, a colonizing fungus: they were delicate, dangerous, ancient, and frequently delicious.

Claire had not typed a single word of text. Instead, this morning, she'd flipped through the file of labeled photographs studying the samples. They might be alien. They might be poisonous. They might make the world a bold, psychedelic dream.

Her head ached. Uncertain which had ruined her most effectively— Liv or the wine—Claire had left the deck with the spins and sat on the edge of the bathtub, willing herself not to be ill. Dee had called mushrooms sea angels. In the photographs, Claire thought most looked like they were melting, and a moment later would be gone: the vanishing Witch's Hat, the drawn Alcohol Inky.

Why did Liv pick up girls? Claire hadn't asked, but she'd wanted to. She wasn't even certain how she had known to ask about the girls at all. As soon as the question formed itself in her mouth, she had known the answer. Does it make you feel better? What had she meant? And why had Liv answered? Claire couldn't understand any of it.

Claire stopped at a photograph of Dee: wild grey curls framed her face as she crouched on the ground beside the spined sphere of the Dusky Puffball. And in the next, Simon beside her, hands on his knees, concentration in his gaze. Abandoning the file, Claire sat at the computer and began to batter away at the tedious identifying descriptions: markings, measurements, coloring, seasonality, habitat, range, edibility. The tiny, trod upon kingdom of mycology, the devil's toenails, her aunt's renown closing around her more tightly with every tap of her fingers.

Simon kept his hand on the side of the wheelbarrow. Against this load of fencing, Liv yanked and drove. How had it happened? Claire pressed against her, voice no more than a sigh, and Liv tells her she drives around at night to pick up girls. Dear god. You king fuck of all time. Liv stopped to spit and heard Simon do the same.

"Nice one, buddy," she said encouragingly.

He waited, hand still on the wheelbarrow. Red monkey hat blocking half of his expression from her. She pressed on, smothering curses. And more violent hammering, her back and shoulders raging, a desperate fury roused in her like a creature surfacing from some incomprehensible depth that cannot re-submerge.

Simon handed her nails, and held the hammer while she grabbed more wood. Already, she had pissed away possibility: she had torn the petals off. Does it make you feel better?

"Oh, Simon, I've spoiled everything."

He handed her another nail.

Claire had baked potatoes for dinner. They ate in silence. Each fork set down on the plate like a white flag. Bees hovered about and had to be thrashed with rolled magazines.

Seven

Murdering mother figures

Liv had had a letter from her parents, recycled from the pad in the kitchen—the back of each sheet had phone numbers, cryptic messages, and lists for cottage cheese, salad stuff, luncheon meat. As always, her mother wrote the body, and her father added a postscript. They were well, had stayed with Liv's sister for several weeks, and—wait for it—fallen even more in love with the grandkids. You wouldn't believe, her mother wrote, how precocious they are. Her father had scribbled a note about a sports team she'd never heard of, or possibly something to do with golf. Before she folded it away, Liv read it three times. A lot of words to say so little.

She and Simon had taken their shoes off to soak their feet in the river. It was a shame, Liv thought, that they didn't have a dog. If she could see him now, Liv's mother would have called Simon towheaded, but Liv thought golden-haired whenever the sunlight struck him. The child glowed.

The fence, finished at last, and praised in detail by Claire, had done much to improve diplomatic relations. Liv had not left the house at night, not even for a supply run. She would never have vocalized her rationale for this, nor would she have needed to.

"Simon, I think we should get a present for Mommy. Do you want to get her a present?"

"OK," Simon said and stood up to go.

"What should we get?" Liv asked.

"Ice cream."

"How about something that won't melt?"

37

He grabbed his shoes and socks, and waited for Liv to put them on.

"Maybe something for camping." Liv said, wiping his wet feet off with her shirt before shuffling on his socks.

They went to REI and found a new camp stove. "Something that melts, after all," Liv said. She let the idea man pick out some Haribo gummi bears. On the way home, they stopped for strawberry milkshakes.

Claire actually blushed when Simon handed her the REI bag. She looked up at Liv and then took out the stove and squealed almost exactly like her son. They put the stove together and heated some hot chocolate to be drunk from tin mugs as though they were already on an adventure.

Simon ran inside and dragged the tent out to them. They set it up in the meadow, inflated the pads, and unfurled the sleeping bags. Simon kept zipping himself in and out, a headlamp around his neck like a rugged necklace.

When Claire put him to bed, he noticed the tent had only two sleeping bags.

"Three," he told his mother.

"Three what?"

"We need three of them," he said, anxious, pointing at the bags.

"Honey, Liv doesn't want to squeeze in here with us."

"Three." He was crying now. "We need three."

"But it's so small," Claire said, pointing to the walls of the tent. "We'd be sleeping on top of one another."

"Three," he cried again. Repeating the word in a rapid wail.

"Simon," his mother said, almost angry. "Stop it this instant, or you'll sleep indoors."

He went on crying, and she left him to it. At the ceramic fireplace, Liv had heard everything. Claire's face burned, and her skin felt too tight, but she walked toward the deck as though it didn't cost her anything to breathe, to walk, to ask, in as even a voice as she could manage, "Do you want a beer?"

Behind her, Simon's crying stopped abruptly. Then he shouted Liv's name and wailed on.

"Jesus," Claire murmured. There was nowhere to go to escape this woman, this tether Claire felt taut between them. She couldn't look at Liv, couldn't bear to know what she'd see in her expression. If it would be something besides desire, something incredulous or bored or reluctant. Claire needed more time. A drink, and more time, and then maybe she could toss off some nonchalant proposal. Feel like squeezing into a two-man tent with a little kid who thrashes, and a woman who grinds her teeth? If you think just standing here is awkward, how about we all pile into a tent? "Do you want a beer?" she asked again.

"No," Liv said. Her voice wrong, the word jagged.

"No?" Claire repeated, not understanding. Liv left through the scrub, the stalks grabbing at her bare legs. Claire thought to call her back, but couldn't somehow, and stood instead beside the unlit kindling, her body as still as the ceramic fireplace, as still as Simon now in the tent, and then, the truck kicking gravel.

"Wait," the girl said, and leaned over Liv to pull something from her glove compartment. "I want you to wear this."

Surprised, Liv almost asked where the girl was from. Reminded herself it didn't matter, and snapped the glove on.

In the bar again, she found another one, like a perky cheerleader, the girl's skirt flared at mid-thigh. Liv followed her to the bathroom and braced her against the sink to screw her.

From the street, Bailey's house looked asleep, the porch light off like everything else. Liv lit another cigarette and breathed. She felt worse now than before, sex a failing palliative. Go home, she thought. Give this up and go home. She saw Claire stepping from the tent, embarrassed. Embarrassed! The kid's scream approaching the frequency of bats, and Claire just pretended like nothing was happening, like they could have a beer, and chat, when Claire couldn't even look at her. Couldn't even say something like, "What a sweet kid," or "How crazy is that?" or "Do you want to sleep in the tent with us?" No. I don't want a beer. Liv slammed the door to the truck. No. That's not what I want. She turned the engine over. No. The roar of the truck drowned the word as she accelerated, and raced out of town, and across the bridges, and down the snaking road to the Douglas-firs. She ran along the gravel and dirt and grass and wood and stone to Claire's room. The bed empty, she threw open the door to Simon's room, where his, of course, was empty as well. Both of them asleep in the tent in the backyard: an adventure inspired by a new stove.

Claire could hear the saw even from the office. Though Liv had cordoned herself in the garage with the doors shut, the saw blade shrilled through the property. Another paragraph and then she would take Simon to swim at Comstock. For a moment, she considered an extended trip. Take the laptop and finish the book in Seattle at her parents' condo. That actually appealed to her less than her current living situation.

"Simon," Claire called, still typing, "let's go to the park."

They swam together and had ice-cream cones afterward. In no hurry to go home, Claire rented some movies, shopped for groceries, let the day slip away. Simon, fractious and hungry, made for an un-pleasant companion.

Field guide to a particularly trying day: Hooray for the heroic mother of tantrum boy. Way to keep birthrates down.

On the drive back, Claire considered having a sitter come to give her a night off. And then what? Troll the bars like Liv? She realized with amusement that she was furious. Liv had left just in the middle of something—the beginning really—and she had torn away like some impetuous and spoiled teenager. Intolerable behavior that Claire found herself wishing she could describe to her aunt: she stalked off before I could explain anything. I'd actually decided to sleep with her, instead, she runs off without saying anything, and stays out all night, picking up god knows what. I don't know what to do with her.

To which her aunt would have replied what, exactly? Claire had no inkling. Just what you need, another destructive self-loather. In all probability, Dee would have laughed and said, This is getting good. Tell me more.

Claire put Simon to bed and walked out to the garage. During a break in the sawing, she knocked on the door and called for Liv. In a moment, goggles and gloves still on, sawdust light over her entire body, Liv poked her head out.

"We should talk," Claire said.

Liv pushed the door wide and stood back. Stacked against the back of the garage by the riding mower were the finished pieces, and on the sawhorses, several long sheets still to be run through the table saw. She'd covered most of the garage with tarps to simplify cleanup.

Field guide to a completely mystifying courtship: if you don't get it, then you've got it.

Perched on the riding mower, Liv took off her gloves and pulled the goggles down around her neck. She wore a thin, white tank top and belted shorts. Her silence, Claire realized, made this more awkward.

Claire had prepared a speech, a sort of romantic declaration. It included a comparison between Liv's eyes and a certain unique mushroom. But right now, Claire couldn't remember the speech, not a word of it, not even the name of the mushroom shaded Liv's particular brown.

"Come here," Claire said.

Liv came toward her without hesitating. Claire pulled the goggles over her head, and then brushed the sawdust from Liv's forehead, along her jaw, away from her lips. She slid Liv's tank top and bra down her torso, traced each tattoo. Topless now, fine sawdust over Claire as well, Liv remained motionless. Claire unfastened Liv's belt and let her shorts drop to her boots.

The booted knight! That was the mushroom. Brown rimmed with amber, like these eyes. Claire touched Liv's eyebrows. "You built this garage," she whispered, as she pushed Liv backwards toward the shelves. "You made a place for me. Here. You made this place." Claire pushed against Liv's pelvic bone and kissed her mouth. At first Liv submitted, until finally, when Claire bit harder, Liv rent her shirt and bit back.

Claire wrote out the check to Liv and met her in the kitchen. On a chair beside the sink, Simon filled her plastic water bottles, while Liv packed oranges and a bagel in her day bag. Her father had left a voicemail on Liv's cell: her mother had breast cancer and was having two malignant lumps removed. Her surgery was scheduled for Tuesday morning; he just wanted Liv to know. She'd been trying to reach them all morning, calling intermittently, but no one picked up at home or on her father's cell. She'd called her sister, and left messages there too.

"I have to go," she'd told Claire, her face sallow, her eyes incapable of concentration. "A week, maybe less. I don't know."

Claire handed her the check now, and picked Simon up. He clung to his mother, in that way Liv found magical and ancient and simian. Both faces drawn and strangely haggard as though the grief were theirs rather than Liv's. She kissed Simon, and looked at Claire, and fled from the kitchen.

Eight

Doppelganger

In the courtyard of the Mercury Café, a pudgy, inept fellow spun dance music, and groups of lawyers, drunk and argumentative, still in their court suits, lounged at tables. Amidst the myriad tables, sat two large contingents of lesbians, in their softball gear, emptying pitchers of beer. Back by the fire door, the gay boys stood with cigarettes. Claire wound through the tables, and along the wall where more girls leaned, and a kind of hiss had started, then finally inside the bar. Three lines for the bar, all of them long and surly, Claire chose the one that looked a little less teenybopper. A girl approached her almost instantly: "I was hoping you'd be here tonight."

Claire stared at the girl, trying to place her, "How have you been?"

The girl looked like she might cry. "Oh. Right. Sorry." She walked to a table by the jukebox and muttered something to the two girls sitting there. Claire ordered a gin and tonic, but the bartender wouldn't let her pay for it.

"Your drinks all night are covered," he told her. "I'm not allowed to say who."

Claire had picked the Mercury to be left alone. With just three chapters left, she'd phoned Agnes, Simon's favorite sitter, and asked if she were available Friday evening. Now, baffled, she moved through the tables, aware of being watched from every direction, and headed upstairs. She sat on a stool by the pool tables and sipped at her drink. It was stiff.

"Hi," the girl said.

"Hi," Claire answered.

43

"We should go."

"I just got here."

"The bathroom locks, remember?"

Claire sipped her drink. Despite her confusion, something fierce was stirring; she could feel its weight shift, almost like a fetus, inside her.

"I don't think so," Claire said. The girl's face pinched and reddened. "Right. Gotcha. Enjoy your drink." And then she, too, was gone.

There were two more of them before the blond sat down on the stool across from Claire. Claire braced herself.

"I'll bet this is all a little confusing," the blond said. When Claire didn't answer, the blond went on, "They think you're someone else. You look a lot like her actually; it's kind of marvelous."

Claire considered this as the blond smiled, drank her beer. The woman was slender, long-legged to spectacular effect in her black Capri pants, and artfully made up. More than anything, though, she was not like the girls before her, and this, Claire realized later, allowed Claire to relax, pick up the conversation politely, and hand it back to the blond.

"I'm a little less confused now. I appreciate your telling me."

"Oh," the woman said, and waved the sentiment away, "I should have done it earlier, but I was enjoying myself too much."

"Ah, glad to amuse."

"No, no. It's not like that. Liv has been an ass—my friend, your twin, Liv—and this little parade is proof of it. I've been enjoying myself at her expense, not yours."

Claire felt the fetal shift again. She took another drink to avoid speaking.

"Sorry," the blond said. "I'm Bailey. I've been kind of an ass myself tonight. Let me buy you a drink."

"No bother," Claire said. "Let's forget the whole thing."

They ordered more drinks, and Bailey began to tell Claire a story about the first time that she'd met Liv in an Early American Literature class as undergraduates. "We had the most bizarre professor—beady little mole eyes, random lectures—but he could recite anything. It seemed like he had all of literature inside his head. We were afraid of him.

"Anyway, he had us write a daily response, only a page, to our reading assignments and picked someone to read every class. The first time Liv read, I thought I'd been struck with something. She was talking about how a particular essay gave her a sense of yellow, about how the sentences felt like butter when she read them. I'd never heard anything like it. I thought, listening to her, that she was some kind of genius."

Bailey finished her drink. She looked at Claire, and blushed. "It's funny. I've never said that to her. And I can only tell you because you aren't her. Isn't that strange?"

"Let me buy you another drink," Claire said. And Bailey agreed, smoothed her finger across her lower lip as though she were applying gloss.

"I've been back in Spokane," Bailey was saying, "for eighteen months and I can't meet anyone. I've got a great job and I love my house and I just can't seem to meet anyone."

"It's easy to be isolated here. I think this is where people come to be left alone."

"Too alone. People here are too alone. It's not good for people to be so alone."

Claire thought of her own loneliness, and agreed.

"I'm almost thirty years old," Bailey went on, "and I thought my life would mean something by now. No, don't look at me like that; I'm talking about real meaning. Let me tell you something. My grandmother lived in a retirement home on the South Hill and I used to go up there in the afternoons to sit with her. We'd read or talk or whatever. And one day she tells me, 'Love, Bailey, love is a collision.'"

Bailey took another drink. "Wait, I'm telling this wrong. My grandmother was married for sixty years when my grandfather died of liver cancer. Fucking horrible. He lost half his body weight before he finally died, in constant pain. Horrible. And my grandmother, she was made of steel then. That whole time he was sick, she took care of him.

"So this day in her apartment we're talking about my grandfather, and how she met him and when she knew—you know—knew that he

45

was the one. She tells me, 'Love is a collision. It blows out the glass, and bends the fenders, and wrecks the engine, and it moves you. My god, it moves you. It shifts you from one spot to another. Simple. Easy. You're there and then, in a moment, you're here. Live here. Exist in this space. Be brave enough to stay.'

"I wrote it down in my notebook in the car. The whole thing. It fucking shook me. The way she said it as much as anything. I memorized it and I say it to myself sometimes like I'm saying a prayer. It hurt me. Her saying that hurt me, it was so beautiful.

"And it's true, what she said. It's true and I want my crash. I want to be moved like that: shifted from one spot to another." Bailey smacked her palms together.

Claire found herself trembling. She couldn't articulate why, even in her own head, but she was shaking. She thought of the money in the broken cupboard; she had taken it without a moment's hesitation. She had not considered even, had simply known that she would take as much as she could carry, and then return for the rest. Simple. Easy. You're there and then, in a moment, you're here.

Love was like that, yes, but so was freedom.

"I'm sorry," Bailey said. "I'm talking too much. I just met you. You're like Liv and not like her all at once. It's intoxicating." She laughed, shook her head like an apology, and drank again.

"I'm interested," Claire said. "I don't mind."

"Would you have wanted any of the girls that came up to you tonight? I mean, on their own account, would you have approached any of them?"

Claire thought of the girls: young, almost foolishly young, and more than a little helpless. "No."

"I keep thinking of Liv as that genius I met in school. The quiet one, the unassuming one, and now she's going through girls like they're heroin. How do you reconcile that?"

"You're in love with her." Claire knew this was true, yet it startled her: the thought as well as the statement. Across the table, Bailey nodded.

"Yes. I'm in love with her."

"What will you do?" Claire asked. She worried for Bailey's love. For the weight of it on the table between them, and inside Bailey, for the despondency of this love, she worried.

Bailey shook her head. "I've no idea. What about you?"

"What about me?"

"Have you had your collision?"

Claire's mind brought Simon forward in answer to Bailey's question. Surprising and true, she realized. Simon was her collision. "I have a three-year-old. He changed everything."

Bailey looked confused a moment, her hooded brown eyes suddenly wholly open. "But it's not the same. I mean, parental love is more definite, isn't it. Clearer."

"Yes, but no less moving."

Bailey shook her head. "No. Too easy. A child isn't a collision. For one thing, you choose to have one, don't you? Can't choose love, though. Can't choose a wreck. Just fucking happens, doesn't it?"

Claire agreed. She liked this woman across from her. She liked her vulnerability, her obstinate mind.

"Have you never had a collision either?"

"No," Claire said. "I guess not."

"Fucking Spokane." She pushed her hair back from her forehead. "But a kid, that's something. Some meaning anyway. Did you have him on your own?"

"His father was in a band. It was all stupid really, that part. And then Simon, and it didn't seem stupid at all. It was supposed to happen, exactly like it did."

"In a band?" Bailey seemed affronted by this. "So you slept with some drummer or something?"

"Bassist, yeah."

"So you're not a lesbian?"

Claire laughed.

"Let me guess," Bailey said. "It's complicated."

They agreed to walk to a diner for coffee and breakfast. It was nearly two in the morning, and neither able to drive. On the dark streets,

47

the stoplights flashed, and rain drizzled. Bailey walked with great concentration.

"I love summer nights," she said.

July was a balm for these two women and the night itself, determined to comfort them. Claire felt that too, their need—hers and Bailey's—for comforting. That day in the garage with Liv, sawdust in their mouths, hard metal surfaces behind and beneath them, even that day, Claire remembered with disquiet.

"Where's your son now?" Bailey asked, after stabbing her eggs so that the yolk spread over her entire plate.

"He's in the car, sleeping, I hope. I left his baby monitor."

Bailey, startled, and quite instantly terrifying, had just begun her tirade when Claire held up her hands, apologized, explained about Simon sleeping over at the sitter's house. "He loves it. He gets to sleep in a bunk bed with her little grandson."

"Sure, I had a bunk bed. Loved it. Like being on a ship."

Tears along the purple vinyl of the booth scratched at Claire's legs. Below the photographs of men racing cars, paint bubbled on the walls. Bailey used her toast as a spoon for her eggs and hash browns, asked, "What do you do, for work, I mean?"

"Well, I write field guides, actually."

"Nature guides?"

"Yes."

"That's interesting." Bailey poured two little plastic thimbles of milk into her coffee, stirred, and smiled at Claire.

Nine

Just like paper

Simon sat on the steps, crying. He'd spilled his milk in the office and his mother was furious. Scolded him and sent him away. He threw Murdoch in the grass, scowled at him a moment, and then quickly retrieved the engine. Bees flitted about everywhere and he walked along the field, keeping back from the high grass, until he came to the fence line. He ran his train along the fence as though it were a rail.

He had not said her name once. He had not asked his mother where she was, or when she was coming back. Liv had told him that she would be quick. With a present, she had said. "I'll be back with a present." Simon stared down the gravel road and said her name once like a magic word. He looked for a long time, but no yellow truck.

At dinner, they had spaghetti. Simon twirling the strands in his fingers, sucking them hard so they squirmed as he ate them. Claire gave him extra cheese, rubbed his head for a moment before she handed him a second toasted roll.

"Is there another plate for me?" Liv asked behind them.

Simon sprang from his chair and was at her. Liv scooped him up and kissed him repeatedly on his face. His hands were fists at her shoulders, holding fast to her shirt. Liv walked forward, and then he was pressed between them.

She'd bought him a small plane with a motor and a remote control. It flew and Simon could direct it. Mostly he ran beneath it while Liv controlled its flight. Claire, sipping at her lemonade, sat on the rail of the deck and watched them. She'd forgotten, in seven days, how young

Liv looked. Lithe in the field with Simon, both of them bright with laughter: immortal. That word came to her as she looked on, immortal.

At bedtime, they both read to him. He gave books to each of them and sat between them, on his knees, turning the pages. Liv brought him Edward and Emily and kissed him goodnight. His mother knelt by the bed and then they closed the door, and stood a moment in the hallway, savoring.

Liv kissed her, finally, there outside Simon's door. A tender kiss, new and hopeful, and Claire's eyes closed heavily as she leaned into Liv. Their bodies entangled, afflicted, soft as vellum.

They sat on the recliner, wrapped in a blanket, and Liv told the story. Her mother's surgery, how they'd removed a breast, but thought they'd found it all. Her mother's anger volcanic, destroying in all directions. Her father at the sink, frightened, baffled, washing the same plate over again. Liv administered pills, took any assault, returned with soup and water and another dose. Ugly. Mean and ugly and frail.

"My mother," Liv said. "My mother's in tremendous pain and I'm bringing her soup. Everything she ever wanted."

Claire thought of herself in the car on the roadside. Her aunt's body in the snow. Impotent. A scared child left behind, incapable of climbing from the car. You cannot be broken. You cannot be broken while I am still alive and needing you.

"Can we get drunk?" Liv asked.

"Sure. Come and see the pantry. Any poison you like."

Claire does not mention Bailey, or their night out. She does not mention the Mercury Café or Liv's disappointed disciples. After that night, she found herself a reluctant stone thrower—unwilling to cast judgment.

"Are you close with your parents?" Claire asked.

"Before I moved back to Spokane, I lived with them for a while. That's not something I would recommend." Liv picked Tanqueray, and tailed Claire to the kitchen for tonic and limes.

"I rarely last a conversation with my parents," Claire said, worrying for her mother's breasts. For the illness that must be inevitable. "Get a kid. Simon deflects a lot of their energy, and doesn't seem to notice that they're insane."

50

"My mother's usually got four million questions she wants answered the first half hour. She didn't talk much this trip. I kind of missed the endless cataloguing of minutiae. Anything's better than your mom on the couch, sobbing for two days straight. I spent most of my time there trying not to call you." Liv held up her glass. "Anyway, here's to tumblers." She lit another cigarette, then grinned at Claire: "At some point, we're probably going to have to discuss what all this means."

"You mean how I'm paying you for sex?"

"Yeah, you totally lowballed me." Liv flicked ash off the deck. "We don't have to talk about it now, I'm just saying that I know it's coming."

"You make it sound so dire, like you're preparing for a siege." Claire tried to laugh, to sound as though Liv's tone hadn't troubled her, as though she hadn't wondered each night if Liv would return at all. "We're dating, aren't we? It's intense because you live here and we're isolated and Simon loves you. But it's just dating."

Distracted by the rail of the deck, Liv had looked away from Claire. "You're right." She stood and took her glass to the kitchen before coming back out to finish her cigarette. "It's late," she said. "And I'm tired. Sleep well." She kissed the top of Claire's head and left through the field.

Sensitive, Claire thought, and was immediately ashamed of herself. What did it mean—all this? She could see the girls in the bar, an endless line of them in bathrooms, and alleyways. A city of girls with their arms wide, and their faces eager. Cold now, even with the blanket, she went inside to bed.

Ten

Hives

Bailey ordered for both of them. "You're going to love these crepes," she said. "They're marvelous."

Bittersweet Bakery, high-ceilinged and classical, had the most welcoming atmosphere. Claire thought of Hansel and Gretel and the gingerbread house while she drank her latte. Bailey split the croissant between them, her fingernails plum-colored, hair swept back elegantly from her face.

"I love this place," she said. "Eventually, I want to open a little bakery like this."

"I can see it."

"Can you?" Bailey, pleased, devoured her croissant.

Claire wasn't sure why she'd come. She'd had to ask Liv to watch Simon. Bailey's enthusiasm on the phone, her chattering, the delighted delivery of the invite; Claire had agreed, she thought, to have a respite from silence.

"I have a confession," Bailey said. "I know who you are."

Claire, sanguine, looked across at her. "Who am I?"

"You're the woman employing Liv."

Claire nodded. "Yes."

"It was one thing that first night, but not saying now would just seem, I don't know, less somehow."

"Less?" Claire asked.

"Devalued or something."

"Yes." Half of Claire's coffee was gone. She was hungry and wished for her crepe.

"Do you mind if I tell you? Do you mind talking about it?"

"No," Claire said, rocking her flip flop rhythmically with her toes. "I don't mind."

"Liv came back three months ago. She'd been living back east with family, a cousin, I think, and then Portland for a while. She came back to town, and was harder or something, more aggressive anyway. We'd go out and just stare. It was so strange. I'd known her for ages and then I didn't know her at all.

"And then she starts with the girls. Subtle, at first, she'd say she was tired and heading home. You know, like that. And then later ..." Bailey waved her hand.

A woman brought their crepes with little side salads and fans of cantaloupe. Claire bit into the sausage potato and shut her eyes to hold in the pleasure. Miraculously, the second bite was more expansive than the first.

"I told you," Bailey said, smiling. "Anyway, I had this thought recently. I think Liv hates herself. I think she's doing this because she doesn't know what else to do. Her behavior is a kind of manic self-loathing. Do you see? A way out of thinking about anything, a way to be only physical. She's made everything physical: her work and her play. There's no time left to think—no place for the brain at all."

"No," Claire said. "The brain doesn't shut off when you're physical. If anything, it ranges more widely, especially if you're doing something you're adept at, like Liv with construction. She knows exactly what she's doing, so she'd have a lot of leisure to think while she's working."

"Then why?" Bailey asked. "Why is she doing this?"

"Have you asked her?"

"No. She'd think I was judging her. I've hinted about people being upset, Liv getting a reputation, but she doesn't care about that." Bailey fidgeted a moment, leaned across the table. "I think if you asked, she might tell you. I think she's smitten with you."

"Smitten." Claire arched her eyebrows. "No. I'm not going to pry into her personal life."

"But what she's doing is crazy and reckless. I don't want to say dangerous, but I think it is. I think it's dangerous. She's not twenty anymore."

Liv fell off the ladder, straight backwards, and hit the deck. She'd fallen eight feet: the breath had knocked out of her and she'd nailed her head and back. Unconscious for only a moment, she woke to Simon pulling at her, terror on his face.

"I'm OK," she said, moving her hand to touch his chest, to reassure him. "Simon, I need you to bring me my phone. It's on the kitchen table." The boy couldn't seem to move. "Simon, can you get my phone, on the kitchen table?" Liv looked at the clouds and felt sick. For a moment, she closed her eyes.

When she came conscious again, Simon had the phone in his hands.

"Good boy," she said. "Good boy, Simon. Let's call Mommy."

Stretched on the recliner to brace the bag of peaches against her neck, and the mixed vegetables to her shoulders, Liv held the frozen clown fish to her head. Now that she was upright and talking, Simon found the frozen bags draped all over her to be quite amusing. He ran Toby up her bare leg, and down again.

When Claire and Bailey ran up, Liv said, "I must have hit my head even harder than I thought."

"What were you doing on a ladder?" Claire demanded.

"A bee hive. I was trying to dislodge it with a broom handle."

"Why didn't you use a hose to blast it loose?" Bailey asked. For a moment, they all looked at her, thrown by her unsuspected resourcefulness.

"I didn't think of it," Liv said.

"That sentence could be shorter," Claire said. "You didn't think."

"Your appointment was with Bailey?" Liv asked.

Claire ignored this, said to Bailey: "So you'll stay with Simon?"

"Sure. Hey, kid, you'll love this." Simon hovered over her purse, inspecting each item Bailey removed. "Ever played with nail polish?"

During the distraction, Claire helped Liv to the car. On the drive to the house, Claire had considered letting Bailey take Liv to urgent care; in many ways, that arrangement would have made more sense, but Claire knew she had to control the information, the back story, about her connection to Bailey. She drove too fast. Angry, unaccountably angry: Liv's fall from the ladder felt like a ruse to smoke out Claire's deception.

"Your appointment was with Bailey?" Liv asked again.

"Yes."

"How did that happen—you two meeting?"

"Last week at the Mercury Café."

Liv adjusted the clown fish on her head, and turned to stare out the window. They were both angry now. At Claire's speed, the drive to the hospital took six minutes rather than fifteen.

Bailey went through the cupboards systematically, taking down various items as they appealed to her. She handed each selection to Simon and he made a pile on the counter.

"Your mommy's a good shopper," Bailey told him as she rooted through the refrigerator. She let him wash all the vegetables, and eat anything he wanted. "You like couscous?"

They had painted his fingernails and his toenails. He'd stayed perfectly still for her. She was blond like Cinderella, Simon thought. Afterwards, he'd shown her his trains and they had walked to the river. Then he had shown her his airplane, and Bailey had flown it while Simon ran underneath.

She chopped so rapidly he was mesmerized, as though this were a card trick instead of vegetables. "OK, I need a large pan and a small one. Right, good. We're going to bake the fish. Do you like fish? I can do quesadillas for you as well."

She talked a lot. Sometimes just to say what she was doing, and sometimes to ask questions, but rarely stopping either way. She showed him how to set the table after the fish went in the oven. They set for four, reverently. She hadn't asked about Liv falling from the ladder, but she had taken the ladder down and rested it in the grass on the side of the house.

She put many different foods on his plate, in small portions. The colors bright and the smells complex, Simon held his fork and watched her eat. He smelled everything before he tasted it; then bolted his food like a stray cat.

At midnight, Claire's car cruised down the gravel road with Liv—her mouth opened, head bent—asleep in the passenger's seat. Inside the house, the kitchen light glowed. Claire helped Liv to her camper, and laid her, fully clothed, on the bed before covering her with a sleeping bag.

In the house, Bailey had fallen asleep on the couch, left a note asking not to be woken since she had to be to work at 4 a.m. Claire crept through the house, peeked in at Simon, slipped off her clothes before sliding into bed. Asleep and dreamless while overhead the fan hummed.

Liv woke with the headache still very much in residence. She took her time about sitting up, reflected on the grueling hospital gauntlet, all to discover that she had a concussion and some wicked bruises—and to obtain the prescriptions, of course, muscle relaxants and Hydrocodone. She and Claire had not spoken for hours. Each flipping through the stale magazines, or watching the grumpy children and short-fused adults as though preoccupation could stave off their fury. Fury was exactly what it had become. Fury distressed by the tedious wait and the confined space and the silence between them.

Why had Claire gone to the Mercury Café? To pick up someone? It had never occurred to Liv that Claire might—might, what? Have sex with someone else? Date? Liv pried the caps off her bottles, took two of each, then wished she'd eaten first. In her bag, she found a Clif Bar, and choked it down as well. Her back and shoulders were stiff. Her mind unfocused, and she fell asleep.

Bailey walked up the deck and poked her head in the doorway to the kitchen. "Hey," she called, "your favorite guest." In a moment, Claire came down the hallway, Simon trailing behind her like a tail.

"Hey," Claire said.

"I thought I'd make dinner." Bailey had a bag of groceries with her. "Shrimp and oysters and clams, and I brought a steak in case anyone's anti-seafood."

"Because you haven't helped out enough around here?" Claire asked, clearing a workspace for her.

Bailey dragged Simon's stool over to the counter, and began to hand him ingredients as though they'd had this routine for years. Claire sat at the table, and admired them.

"Well," Bailey asked, without turning around, "how's the patient?"

"Still sleeping. I've checked on her a couple of times, left her a sandwich and fruit, but she's slept all day."

"What did the doctor say?"

"A concussion and bruises, no breaks. He said she could expect to be slow-moving and sore. And then he gave her a lecture about smoking. She loved that."

"Smell this, Simon. It's lemongrass; you're going to love it. Well, who wouldn't love a lecture after they fell off a ladder? Nearly as useful as being told you're going to be sore. Tell me you love white wine."

"I do."

"Simon, I'm going to need those pans again, and that cutting board. Yes, perfect. Right, Claire, how hot is too hot for you?"

"I don't like coughing while I eat."

"So, just a couple of peppers. Good to know. I didn't hear you come in last night. Simon, why don't you start rinsing these, and we'll just set the strainer here, and, yes, that's perfect. Claire, if you'll start the grill? Right, good. OK, I'll chop chop these. And then we'll need butter, vats and vats of butter. Simon, say 'butter is delicious.'"

"Butter is delicious."

"You are the golden boy. Right, now I'm going to give you kale to rinse. Perfect. Exactly so."

Claire was sent to the camper to retrieve Liv. Since she hadn't helped with dinner, she had no argument to avoid this. Again, she was struck by the Spartan arrangement of the camper. Surfaces clean and clear, clothes folded or hidden away, only a faint suggestion of patchouli incense, and the seemingly naked girl on the bed, striped by the sleeping bag.

"Hello?" Claire said, easing into the camper. She left the door opened, crept toward the supine girl. "Hello?"

"Hey."

"Would you like to come up to the house for dinner? Bailey's cooked a beautiful meal."

Liv, her face blank, stared back at Claire.

"Oysters and shrimp and kale and some kind of exotic potato."

"I'll follow you back," Liv said. "I just have to get dressed."

"I shouldn't have brought wine," Bailey said when Liv joined them. "You can't have any on your meds. Well, you and Simon can have mango Odwalla. You'll share, won't you, Simon?"

Liv's mouth tasted metallic; she'd taken another couple of pills before she left her camper. Her brain stretched and retracted like silly putty around Bailey's monologue and the hot, bright evening and the robust food. And Simon, glowing beside her, biting into a shrimp with relish. And Claire dressed in a purple tank top and short pale shorts. Claire, for whom all fury had drained away, like Liv's headache. Liv blinked slowly, fought herself not to giggle. She noticed, perhaps for the first time, how much Simon resembled his mother: their thin, angular faces, and bold marmoset eyes, pianist's fingers, and small, beautiful ears.

The table was quiet, and Liv focused on each of them. Waiting.

"Headache gone?" Bailey asked, a bit slowly, Liv thought, dramatically.

"Quite gone." Liv beamed, and ate an oyster. Remembered a trip to Pike Place Market, the men in their aprons, the crowded stalls.

Bailey talked for the entire meal. Next to Liv, Simon kept Murdoch beside his fork, and studiously ignored both his train and his utensil. Claire and Bailey drank the bottle of wine, and opened another. Strips of steak, sweet peas, sautéed kale, Liv feasted on every dish Bailey served them.

"Bailey," Claire said, "this food—I can't even describe it. I feel like I've never really tasted anything before. There's taste beneath the taste, if you know what I mean. Does that sound crazy? I mean it as a compliment."

"Then I'll take it that way," Bailey laughed.

There was coffee, of course, and a dessert of pineapple, cream cheese, and toasted almonds whipped together and plated hot.

Liv let her mind boomerang around the meadow like Simon's little plane. She thought of the first time she'd worked demolition. Paired with a baby dyke from North Portland, they'd been unleashed on three rooms with sledgehammers and no restrictions. At the end of the day, when the crew chief returned, they'd been dirty, bleeding, and joyful. She could smell those rooms, and feel the tears to her skin, and the grime.

For a moment, Liv's mind became so lucid that it leaned forward and kissed her lightly on the mouth, and she understood that along the way her joyfulness had been lost. And her sense of wonder, wonder as an effortless bliss, the kind that Simon carried with him everywhere, Liv had dropped at some past moment, in some place she could no longer even recall. She wanted that delight back, to carry on her shoulders, or cradle to her chest.

"Yeah," Liv said suddenly, the fingers of her hand elastic, blossoming here at the table as she reached for her coffee cup. "Wow."

Eleven

Claire in bed

Two days after her slip, Liv, stoned on the recliner, rolled the tobacco Bailey had brought her. Swirling the beer in her bottle, Bailey glanced again at her watch. Claire had disappeared three-quarters of an hour ago to put Simon to bed.

"Here," Liv said, handing a cigarette to Bailey.

"Thanks."

They smoked. Liv watched the smoke pillow into the night. "So, you met her at the Mercury?"

"Yeah," Bailey said, "you'll laugh when I tell you how."

"Make me laugh."

"They thought she was you, all those girls you fucked. They came one after another trying to hook up with her and she's just sitting there all confused, trying to drink her gin while girl after girl approaches, and stomps away a second later pissed or disappointed. Fucking sad, dude. I had to intervene."

Liv flicked her lighter awake, asleep, awake. Claire and the girls in the Mercury, one after another like some marathon job interview under Bailey's observation. A psych experiment, a case study, and Liv could see them, all their hopefulness, and their youth like a sword they'd fall on.

"That's hilarious."

"Dude, I told you this was a small town. Fair warning and all."

"Bailey, what is it you want? Claire, do you want Claire? You signing on to be the personal chef here?"

Bailey laughed. It sounded hysterical to Liv.

"You hit your head super hard, Liv. Just keep mellow and watch the pollen blow or the grass sway or whatever the fuck."

Liv inhaled something bitter, held it a moment, and let it go. It hovered above the trees like a dazzling helicopter. Wow, she thought. She knew already, not to say it out loud.

In Simon's room, Claire had grabbed a thin blanket from the closet and uncovered a box of Denise's papers. Cross-legged on her bed now, she riffled through the box, and found, mixed in with legal documents and tax forms, the sketches of Amanita varieties that she knew to be her aunt's missing research. How had this box ended up in Simon's closet? She set the research aside, and emptied the box onto her bedspread. More documents, a photograph of Claire's parents, a brochure from a lecture series, and then she read the following, typed letter: *We admire what you have taken on. We are grateful. Claire will always hold herself apart. She is steadfast without loyalty, and loving without demonstration of feeling. She is, always, patient and controlled. You may find her difficult. We believe that she is difficult. We hope that you will understand her better than we. We hope she will thrive there with you.*

Her mother had signed the letter for both of them. Claire read it until the words shuffled together, meaningless. A harsh letter, wasn't it? Not untrue, certainly, but unkind. Laying the letter aside, she flipped again through the sketches. It wounded her, that letter. She felt as though she might be bleeding.

Bailey would still be out there, prattling on. So Claire stayed in her room, re-packed everything but the sketches, and ignored the box—particularly the letter. She wished for Liv. Much later, she wondered if her aunt had answered, and if so, what she'd written.

Claire crept into the camper. Stood, trying to quiet her breathing, her heart. Spooled in her bag, Liv slept on. Looking about her, Claire considered dropping a water bottle, or slamming a cupboard door, anything to rouse the girl. Instead, she climbed into bed and put her hands on Liv's bare torso. Even then, the girl only groaned and curled into Claire.

61

"Wake up," she whispered. "Please. Wake up."

It hurt to speak. It hurt to have her hands on Liv. It felt like pressing bruises. It hurt as she bent lower and kissed Liv's mouth. It hurt to pull the girl into her and kiss her and cling to her and weep. God, finally to weep, and that hurt worst of all. The tears covering both of them and still coming, and Liv had woken; her arms flexed around Claire and brought more tears yet. And then the noise began, guttural and ragged as though it came from Claire's very cells, some ancient voice from her conception; it shook through her viciously, and left her shivering harder.

Liv had reared up on her knees and braced herself against the wall of the camper to hold onto Claire. They were wedged too tightly in the narrow bed to rock, but Liv sang, the way she would have to Simon, and Claire felt herself cradled as the noise, almost a possession, drained away from her. Everything drained away from her. Liv held fast, sang until the shivering stopped, kissed Claire's damp face.

Twelve

A kind of awareness

Paint spattered Liv's hands. Chronically incapable of painting without mess, she'd worn her grubs, and reveled now in the tangy smell, the texture of color on the wall, the feel of the brushstroke along her entire arm. She'd promised Claire, no power tools until she was off the meds, and so they'd spent the morning choosing colors for the basement. Mauve and a kind of husky blue—not as accents—but as unique colors for the downstairs rooms; accents would remain white, but be repainted in the spirit of newness. It had taken the better part of the week to dismantle the wood paneling, and clean and patch the walls.

All the downstairs windows thrown open, overhead fans whirring, and the rooms lightened by the removal of the paneling, Liv could almost convince herself she were in an outbuilding, in the garage perhaps, or her father's workshop. She applied a first coat, and thought of her father at his table, gluing together crafted pieces of wood to create trains and planes and racecars for the grandkids.

She should ask for a train for Simon. Why hadn't she thought of that while she was there? Anyway, now she had a reason to call her father, something to ask about besides cancer. Claire had helped to tape the room, and then taken Simon to get some clothes. He'd had a spurt that made him clumsy and ravenous and impossibly long-limbed.

Liv's body just felt sore now, no longer immobile and alien. She'd kept taking her pills, though, just in case. Paint dropped on her forearm and she gazed at it, unwilling to wipe it away. A fly lifted against the window screen, settled, twitching. Resonance everywhere. That was the gift falling from the ladder had been.

Sex used to be like this. Give this kind of clarity; make her feel like more than herself. With each brushstroke, she felt her skin move and her muscles stretch and her breath come and go. When Claire lay warm against her, Liv knew she could chart the flow of blood through arteries. That was how aware she was. She could see thoughts. Could feel the air move around matter. Liv: alive and aware and keen.

She finished the first coat, and hurried to the camper to change before they returned. Simon's first expedition to swim at Fish Lake; Liv had pitched the adventure to Claire that morning, and described the old Steam Shovel at the turnoff, and the wooden dock, and the idyllic, calm water. In the camper, Liv took four pills, had her trunks on when she heard their car pull up.

Claire drove them to the lake; the windows opened, the oppressive July day sitting heavily in the car, their bodies sticky. Indeed, Simon found the Steam Shovel as mesmerizing as Liv had predicted. He wanted to drive it. They climbed from the car and let him marvel at its hot, rusted metal. Farther in, they parked the car and walked through the pine trees down the trail toward the lake. Needles crunched beneath their sandals. Simon stopped to collect rocks, and again, when he saw the snake; alerted to its presence by a spider scurrying across the snake's flesh, or because he'd thought it was a stick and then realized suddenly that it wasn't. Liv had taken a step beyond the child, and put her hand on his back to press him forward when she nearly stepped on the snake, and it shot forward into the litter.

She screamed, "Snake!" Grabbed Simon. Screamed, "Snake!" again and ran with him through the trees. Though he'd been calm a moment before, staring at the surprising creature, now he thrashed and shrieked for his mother.

"Liv," Claire said, trying to reach them. Their towels left on the trail like wrapping paper, she chased behind. "Liv, stop it. Stop. Liv!"

And just as suddenly as the snake had bolted, Liv stopped, set Simon down, and stared about her. The day a smudge in her head, blurred and baffling, she stood on the pine needles by someone's mini-van in the tiny parking lot. "I'm so sorry," she said to the inconsolable child, and his mother. "Wow. I'm a little thrown. Did you see it? The snake? Did you see?"

Thirteen

Doses

Claire was scary when she was mad. Her voice, restrained and icy, seemed to insinuate itself into Liv's brain so that her lecture came from without and within simultaneously. In the camper, standing by the doorway, she held both pill bottles in her hands. "How many of these have you been taking?"

"Two." Liv was slick with sweat. Low in her belly, a spasm flicked on the right side. She imagined an ovary swelling inside her like a balloon.

"From each bottle?"

"Yes."

"How often?"

Liv wasn't entirely certain. She'd taken them several times a day, but wasn't sure if she'd actually timed the doses. "Every few hours," she said.

"How many pills a day?"

"I'm not sure."

Claire stepped closer and Liv felt herself recoil, and lower her eyes further, like a cornered dog. She reached her arms around her belly to keep it from bursting.

"Liv, don't fuck about. How many pills are you taking a day?"

"Sixteen, probably."

Claire relaxed. Liv felt it—the hardness—drain from the room. She glanced up at Claire and back at her shoes. Her stomach felt twisted and sick. She wanted to vomit and shower and sleep. More than anything, though, she wanted Claire to set the pills down, turn, and leave without slamming the door. Liv didn't want the pills anymore. She still felt bewildered. In the parking lot, the sobbing child, his angry mother, and nothing. She didn't know why he was crying, or where she was exactly. When she thought about the snake, it seemed like something from a story, something she'd read to him. She wasn't even afraid of snakes. Why would she have run from one?

"You're only supposed to take two of each of these twice a day," Claire said. "You've been taking four times the prescribed dosage."

"Oh," Liv said. She knew she'd vomit any moment, maybe into the sink, or on the bed, but definitely any moment. Shut up, she thought. Shut up and go away. Liv closed her eyes, breathed hard through her nose, but nothing could stop it now: the sickness, the wave of it breaking over both of them.

"Liv?" Claire said, her voice entirely outside Liv's head now, and muffled as though she were calling to Liv from outside the camper. Liv vomited. Choking, horribly painful, and it wouldn't stop. She couldn't catch her breath. Pulled then, from the bed, and the camper, out into the grass, where she could only retch and sob, and then slowly across the field toward the house. Slowly, with great care, the grass prickly on her skin; shivering and clammy in her damp clothes; and more retching, nothing left to expel except her own organs. Finally they were indoors, and Claire laid her down on the mat while she ran the bath.

"You're like a rock star," Claire said, not unkindly. And Liv almost laughed, vomit in her hair even—rank and filmy. Claire eased her shirt over her head. Liv couldn't help, could barely hold herself upright. Then the shorts and boxers and Liv heard Claire grunt as she lifted—lifted!—Liv into the bathtub. In the bath, her spasms stopped, and hollowed now—her body a sieve—she slept.

She woke alone in Claire's bed. The sheets white, and roped around her naked body, she rolled toward the window where the light strained, and closed her eyes. Voices, from outside, only murmurs, and Liv felt thick-tongued and zombie-headed. She fell into sleep as though it were a well.

Bailey smoked, twirled her cognac in the snifter, and regarded Claire.

She'd brought Simon back to the house with her. Claire had dropped him off earlier in the evening, said she had to run some errands and would have dinner ready for both of them at seven.

"Where's Liv tonight?"

Claire took a bite of chocolate, chewed slowly. "She's sleeping. Overdid it with the painting."

"I see," Bailey said. "You look like you could sleep as well. I won't stay long. How's the book?"

"I'm finished."

Bailey sat up, nearly dowsed her brown camisole with cognac. "What? You finished? When?"

"Two days ago."

"Why aren't we celebrating? We should be out somewhere, having champagne or something, shouldn't we? Why don't we go out tomorrow night? The bunk-bed lady can watch Simon, and you and Liv and I can celebrate. What do you think?"

"I'm so exhausted now I can't even think about celebrating."

"Don't worry, I'll handle everything. Where's Liv? I'll chat with her about it and we'll arrange the whole thing. We can even schedule the sitter if you want. You won't have to do anything."

Bailey stood up as though she meant to organize this very moment.

"Liv's sleeping, remember?"

"Oh right. I'll just phone her tomorrow. Just leave this to me. It's so exciting. I had no idea you'd finished. After all this time, aren't you pleased? How do you feel?"

Claire considered. "I feel like spoiling myself."

"That's the spirit. Spoiling how?"

"A trip. Maybe to the Oregon coast. Dee and I used to go every few years. We'd talked about going this summer."

She crushed a mosquito. Claire wanted to curl against Liv. She wanted to hibernate. If she took them both—Simon and Liv—they'd walk the beach and Simon could throw stones while Liv recuperated. They'd visit the aquarium and the Sylvia Beech Hotel; Simon could play in the Dr. Seuss room. And she and Liv ... Claire looked up at her bedroom window and wished Bailey gone.

"I should go," Bailey said, not moving.

"Yes," Claire said, and stood. "I'll call you tomorrow. Thanks for watching Simon."

"Thanks for dinner. Tell Liv, well anyway, I'll phone her tomorrow." Bailey handed Claire her drink, hesitated, walked slowly away.

Claire left the drinks on the table, moved barefoot through the house, her clothes peeled away. An ache deep in her, a kind of tether, between herself and Liv, drew her without thought, or consideration, to Liv's body. In a foreign place, Claire knew she could track Liv by smell and impulse alone. They were like bats, some sonar reckoning in the dark.

"Are you sleeping?" she asked Liv.

"No." Muffled.

"Can you?"

Liv rolled into Claire, her skin clammy, her muscles trembling down her back and legs. Tucked against Claire's chest, Liv seemed to shiver harder, and then Claire understood, she was sobbing. Both of them children, orphaned, seeking succor from each other. That word, "orphaned", rang through Claire like memory. I will be your mother too, she thought. Your mother and your child. Twining her legs through Liv's, she bound them both to this place.

Fourteen

Simon sees

Simon ran Murdoch along the wall beside his bed; the engine's wheels made a satisfying rumble. He had dreamed of the Great Pumpkin. Liv was in trouble with his mom. He knew this, although Claire had said nothing. And the snake. Simon had wanted to touch it. He had been afraid, and thrilled by it as well. Fast on the ground, slithering. Slithering, he said aloud. He thought of his body with no arms or legs, gliding through the pine needles like a ghost.

He did not see Liv until he stood by his mother's bed, both of them asleep. Liv's face moon-pale and almost bruised. Simon reached his hand out slowly as though to a large dog, and touched the marks beneath her eyes. Her eyes opened, in a moment she smiled.

"Hello, you."

"Hello," he said in a whisper.

"Come on, then."

And he nestled in between them, Murdoch clutched in his fists. It was alright, he knew, whatever had happened.

"O Great Pumpkin, where are you?" he said to the ceiling.

"I love Linus," Liv said. "The only one who believes."

He turned on his side to face her, and ran Murdoch along the space between them.

"I'm sorry about the snake," Liv said. "I'm sorry about the lake too. You'd like swimming there. If you want, I'll take you again. If you want."

Against his back, he could feel his mother's body, warm and curled.

"I'm hungry," Liv said. "Would you eat a banana?"

"Let's go," he said and sat up.

"You're staying in bed," his mother said.

"Let me try a banana," Liv said. "If I keep it down after an hour, I'm going to paint."

"You're going to stay in bed."

He knew this voice, and so did Liv.

"I want to try a banana," she said again. Simon held his breath. His mother sat up; the bed shifted with a creak.

"I'll bring one. You and Simon can have breakfast in bed. Cereal?" This last to Simon, who nodded.

Liv piled the pillows and they reclined against them, hands beneath their heads, awaiting breakfast like pharaohs.

"I have to finish the second coat in the basement," Liv told him. "You can help, if you want. I have extra brushes."

Claire brought trays: milk, bananas, toast, applesauce, cereal. She sat, cross-legged, at their feet.

"I'll paint," she told Liv.

"You have your book to finish."

"My book is finished." The strap from his mother's white tank top had slipped from her shoulder.

"What do you mean?"

"I mean it's finished."

"Since when?"

Simon stared at Liv. He held his breath again.

"A couple of days."

"And you didn't tell me because?"

Claire glanced at Simon, and back at Liv. "Eat," she said.

Liv took another small bite of banana. His mother shifted, pulled her strap back over her shoulder.

"Why didn't you tell me?"

"I wanted to be happier, when I told you I'd finished. I wanted to feel like celebrating."

"Instead?"

"Liv." They looked at him.

He bit into the buttered toast, watched Liv tear the banana into little chunks.

71

"It wasn't to hurt you," his mother said. She hadn't eaten. Just held her mug of coffee in her hands as though she were cold.

"We can talk about it, or we can't."

"You're right," Claire said. "How do you feel about the Oregon coast?"

"Holy random. I love it. How do you feel about it?"

"I feel like visiting—the three of us—Simon's never been."

"I'm supposed to be working on this house, remember?"

"Yes."

Liv finished her banana, leaned back against the pillows, and regarded Simon. He'd eaten his toast and most of his cereal. He wanted one of the big paintbrushes.

"We should talk about this later," Liv said.

"I'll make a list: suitable topics for another time."

Beside him, Liv shifted. She wore one of his mother's t-shirts inside out. They were making faces. He laughed at them. Claire and Liv, grinning now, threatened to take away his tray, and tickle him. He kept laughing, daring them on.

Claire and Liv painted, Simon had a brush and a smock and newspaper beneath him. He'd been allowed a small tub of blue, and the middle portion of one wall. Paint smelled. The brush was heavy. He wanted to go to the river.

"All done," he said. And they took the brush, washed his hands, and sent him upstairs to play with his trains.

"You found the missing research?" Liv asked eventually.

"In Simon's closet."

"How'd it end up in Simon's closet?"

"I think maybe I put it there," Claire said. She'd remembered finding a pile of Dee's papers on the kitchen table, sometime that first week, and stuffing them away in a box. "After the funeral." Probably crammed the box into Simon's closet to avoid going downstairs; at the time, she couldn't brave her own office, much less Dee's study.

"Why didn't you tell me?" Liv asked.

Because I wish I'd never found that box, Claire wanted to say.

Never seen those last sketches; never read the letter. I wish I didn't know. I'm tired. I want to come to the end of this. "I've already told you, I wanted to be happier when I told you."

"Why aren't you happier?"

Claire painted along the tape, then stood and stretched. She could hear Simon singing from the floor above them. "Because," she said, "I thought—I actually believed—that if I finished the book, I'd feel better. I believed that. But I feel exactly like I did last week, and last month. Exactly how I'm going to feel next month and next year. It never lets up."

Liv smiled at her, said gently, "I'd hug you, except I think I pulled a muscle painting this trim."

Claire grinned in spite of herself, and flicked Liv's arm with the paint stirrer. "I tried to tell you to stay in bed."

"You're very good at being right." Liv set her brush down and rolled her shoulders. "I need a cigarette, and someone to hold it for me."

"You are so sad." Claire flicked her again.

"Stop, you're getting paint on me."

"I have to exploit your injuries," Claire said, darting just out of reach, "Get you now while you're too weak to retaliate."

"Stop, I'm serious," Liv said, laughing. "I think I pulled a muscle in my back. For real, it hurts every time I raise my arm above my head."

"Then you, my friend, are officially back on bed rest," Claire said. "Come on, we're done for the day."

Simon came outside with them, threw off his clothes, and ran through the sprinkler. Afterward, they blew bubbles, and chased around the yard after butterflies, and laughed until they were out of breath. Liv played as hard as Simon, as though she didn't have an injury at all; she'd pay for it later, of course, but that hardly mattered.

At the river with Simon that evening, Liv held her phone away from her head. Bailey was a loud talker, and Liv had a headache that seemed to reach the length of her spine.

"I want to throw Claire a party," she was saying, "for the book, and everything."

Liv inhaled her cigarette, watched a dragonfly angle toward Simon. So Claire had told Bailey about the book being finished. This shouldn't be surprising. It shouldn't be. "Yes?"

"How do you feel today? Claire said you overdid it yesterday painting."

She wished her phone would cut out. Maybe she could get Simon to throw it in the river. Considering this, Liv sat down in the grass, and dug her heel into the sand at the riverbank.

"Liv? You still there?"

"I'm here."

"How's it going? You feeling OK?"

"What's your idea for this party?"

"We can talk about it later if you want. Or I can handle the whole thing? I don't mind. Actually, I'm perfectly happy to handle everything. I know you have a lot going on."

"Why are you calling me?" Liv asked.

"What?"

"Why did you call?"

"I wanted to talk to you about the party. I wanted to tell you what I had planned."

"Bailey, since when do you need to discuss any of this shit with me?"

Simon, at the edge of the water, looked over at Liv.

"I just thought you'd be interested in helping. She's your friend too. This is a big deal for her. She deserves—"

"Please talk to me about what she deserves."

"What's going on? Why are you so hostile? What's the matter with you?"

"I'm going now, Bailey. Bye bye."

Liv lay back in the grass. Bugs everywhere. Her body in open rebellion now, spasms in her belly, her back, her shoulders, and the cigarette had made her nauseous.

Two days later, they pulled up the basement carpet. Simon held the door open for them to drag the rolled sections outside. Rain pelted down. Hefting the sections into the truck bed, Liv gritted her teeth

74

against the sharp pain in her back beneath her shoulder blade. Coffee was enough now to lick the headache. As the muscle spasms dissipated, and her diet included more interesting food than bananas and toast, her sanguine temper returned.

They had the new carpet for the basement propped in the entryway. Already the basement breathed again: the walls striking, the rooms larger and brighter, the nasty carpet rapidly depleting, and the new anxious to sprawl in its place. Claire worked like she exercised, focused to the exclusion of conversation and impediment. Without plotting, or dialogue, or any delay, she could be relied upon to complete this task and prepare for the next. Liv admired Claire's drive, and was pleased that they worked so well and easily together.

While Liv and Simon swept the basement, Claire made sandwiches. Tonight they'd celebrate Claire's completion of the book with a dinner party at Bailey's. Something grand, Bailey had promised. Liv would have given anything to decline. She'd offered to watch Simon, but Claire had refused to go without her.

Bailey couldn't just go out for dinner and drinks like normal people. Everything had to be an event. It felt a little dramatic since she'd only known Claire for a month, but Liv would go and enjoy herself. She expected the food to be exquisite.

"What?" she said to Simon. He'd stopped sweeping and was standing beside her, his broom discarded. He pointed at the desk and dragged Liv with him.

"Mama," he said, pointing at the desk.

The desk was tall enough that Simon couldn't actually see the photographs; he'd only remembered that they were there. Liv had never noticed them at all. She lifted a series up now, and crouched so that Simon could look as well.

Four photographs, and in the first, Claire with her hair long—it had a wave to it long—a barrette pinning it back from her face, and braces. In another she had pigtails, and might have been three, in a green gingham dress. In one she wore a blue hospital gown, the IV still in her arm, and a swaddled infant with a knit cap cradled against her chest.

"Is that Mommy and Simon?" Liv asked.

"Yes."

"Is that Dee?" Liv pointed to the heavier woman, her grey curls unruly, her smile gap-toothed; she carried Simon on her shoulders.

Simon smoothed his hand across the glass covering the photographs. "Simon," he whispered.

"Yes. Dee and Simon." He looked at the photos a long time. She rested her head against his, and stayed.

Fifteen

The dinner party

Claire dropped Simon at Agnes' house at six, and came home to climb in the shower with Liv.

"Don't," Liv said, "We'll never leave."

"I'm helping."

Liv laughed. "Go on, then."

They wore jeans: Liv's with a light blue, long-sleeved button-down shirt, and Claire's a sleeveless purple v-neck. Claire drove, her hand on Liv's thigh.

"Is it just me that thinks this is absurd?" Claire asked.

"The party or Bailey?"

"I have to choose just one?"

"She overdoes. It's her thing."

"How long has she been in love with you?" Claire asked. She'd rolled up the window, and was wishing now that she'd worn long sleeves.

"I think you're my replacement."

"No," Claire said. "Bailey is in love with you. I'm just another opportunity for her."

"How's that?"

Claire tugged on the hair at the nape of Liv's neck. "So far I'm not one of your fuck-and-run girls."

"And that gets her what exactly?"

"Maybe I'm the field guide."

"The field guide to what?"

"You, Liv." At that moment Claire envisioned herself writing it— the field guide to a girl: You're studying the girl as though she were a butterfly. Sketching the musculature and wingspan, charting the range and season as though you'd discovered a new species.

Could you hunt them like mushrooms? Is that what Liv did, hunt girls? Claire wound down Government Way; the pines sunburned, cheat grass tall as Simon, and billowing.

You observe unobtrusively. And the more you watch, the more apparent the patterns become: the proclivity for a certain flower, the skills employed to evade predators, mating. In fact, you want to believe that the throbbing flicker of this creature in-between your thumb and forefinger is your discovery, previously unknown, and unknowable.

In the passenger's seat, foot propped on the dash, an unlit cigarette in her fingers, Liv was mid-sentence. You want to believe yourself scientific, a researcher. What, after all, is your objective, but the furtherance of knowledge? They drove along the cusp of the city.

"What," Claire said softly to the steering wheel, "is your objective?"

"You know, I'm really OK staying in the car," Liv said as they parked in front of Bailey's house.

Some chick named Marjorie opened the door. "Hi, I'm Marjorie. Come in. There's been an incident with one of the pies. We only know it involved a paper bag and a fire. But that's all we know. I'm Marjorie. You guys are twins, right? I used to have twin neighbors when I lived in the Valley. They were not identical, though. They didn't even look like twins, really. It was disappointing like that. Which one are you?"

"I'm Claire."

"Oh happy party, Claire! Bailey's so excited. She said you're a really important artist and you had to be celebrated. So yay, you! Have I seen your art? Are you at like a gallery or something?"

"Sort of," Claire said, and gripped Liv's arm.

"Cool. So which of you guys is older?"

"She is," Liv said, smiling her brightest smile. "We have to go see Bailey. Excuse us." And she propelled Claire through the entryway and into the living room. There were eight trays of appetizers on the coffee table and three people sitting on the same side of the sofa, concentrating on their napkins.

"Hi," Liv said and kept propelling.

Bailey wore an apron around her vintage red dress. She'd worn stockings and red glimmer shoes and had pitched her blond hair atop her head like a diner waitress. At the kitchen doorway, Liv smelled cinnamon and yeast, and remembered riding bikes through her grandparents' neighborhood on a rainy afternoon, and a treat of fresh baked bread with apple butter. On the counter, a platter piled with ears of corn, grilled and still in husks, brought back her first ride in the back of a wagon. The aroma of hazelnut chocolate from a cooling torte, gave her a scene with her first girlfriend on a cross-country skiing adventure.

"This smells like my childhood," she said now.

"Good, you're here. Liv, I need you to open the wine. Those bottles on the counter. Claire, relax, enjoy; go have a seat and eat something. I think the crab cakes are pretty good. And the stuffed cabbage rolls are maybe the best I've made ever." Claire withdrew as though she'd been sent away from the campfire. Bailey went on, oblivious, "Liv, have I ruined my oven? Look at this fucking mess." She opened the oven to reveal ashes, the drenched remains of a pie and a charred paper bag.

"What happened?" Liv asked.

"Paul threw a glass of water on it."

"Why?"

"Because he's an ass," Bailey whispered. "And it was on fire."

"You put a brown paper bag in the oven on purpose?"

"Keeps the pie moist."

"And extra flammable."

Liv grabbed the trash and tossed the mess in. Water and ashes had pooled at the bottom of the oven. "It'll be fine once it cools. Self-cleaning and all."

"Stupid ass ruined my pie."

"So we'll just have seven desserts rather than eight."

"Don't try to cheer me up."

"OK," Liv said. "Who the fuck are these people?"

"Associates of mine."

"From the baking underworld?"

79

"Bring the wine, smartass."

They gathered around the table—beautifully laid with china and place cards—as Bailey introduced each to the rest, and most particularly to Claire, their guest of honor. Claire sat on Bailey's right, and Liv had been placed on the other end, next to Sophia, Bailey's housemate. In the middle were Marjorie and many others like Marjorie in proclivity for vacuous exchange.

But the food merited such a party: pork tenderloin with porcini mushrooms; whipped parsnip potatoes; goat-cheese stuffed chicken breasts; roasted baby red potatoes; cranberry marmalade and balsamico; seared ahi, crusted with fennel, coriander, and pepper; sun-dried tomatoes and fruit compote; grilled asparagus and corn on the cob; Caesar salad and Hazelnut greens.

"The woman can cook," Liv murmured to Sophia.

Sophia nodded, her mouth full, another bite ready to be launched. On Liv's right, sat Paul, the ass.

"What do you do, Paul?"

"I'm a drafter for architects and intellectual property attorneys."

"Interesting work?"

"Not remotely. What about you?"

"I'm a builder."

"Now that sounds interesting. What's the weirdest thing you've ever built?"

Liv wondered if he'd consider a harness weird. "I built a mock-up of my childhood home for my folks when they sold the place. It freaked me out how accurate the little rooms were. I wanted to be small enough to sleep on the tiny couch in the family room, or sneak out my bedroom window."

"Like those mice in that story. They ransack the dolls' house."

"Yeah, like that. I'd built the place and it was so accurate and so wrong all at once."

Paul handed her the basket of bread. Sophia paused eating long enough to ask for more potatoes. They started in on movies seen, and rendered opinions. Down the other end, Claire swallowed her wine and winked at Liv.

"Do you know Claire?" Paul asked.

"I work for her actually."

"Oh," Paul looked up at Liv, clearly impressed. "And she's a well-known artist, is that right?"

"In her field she's quite famous."

"What's her field?"

"Mycology."

"Oh, right," he said and looked down the table at Claire. "Impressive."

Claire had been writing her field guide all evening. A roadmap to Liv, as she'd come to think of it. Begin with intrigue and a proposition; a woman who adores your child; leaves on mysterious excursions; is wholly unpredictable. Ensure that this woman works for you. Keep her vulnerable.

At this last, Claire looked down the table and winked at Liv. She wanted to tell Bailey about her field guide. They could write up a synopsis and sell it at the Mercury Café to all the dejected twenty-two-year-old girls propped against the jukebox or pool table. Claire drank more wine to keep from laughing. This party was worse than a farce.

Knickknacks crowded every surface of the place; they lived like old ladies. Even the elaborate dinner party felt bygone and overstuffed. Bailey talked on and on to everyone around her, who talked on and on in turn. Parakeets, Claire thought. Her neighbor filled her wine glass again.

"Do you like the tenderloin?" Bailey asked Claire.

"It's all marvelous. I've never eaten anything quite like this dinner."

"Oh good. I'm so pleased. You've earned it."

Claire set her wine down carefully. "How?"

Bailey had turned to answer her neighbor.

"How?" Claire said, louder.

Bailey looked back at Claire, nonplussed. "Sorry?"

"How have I earned it?" It was the clarity with which she asked this question, rather than the volume, that silenced the table.

"Well," Bailey said, glancing at Claire's neighbor and back at Claire. "The book. You wrote the book."

"I wrote the book."

"Yes. And we're all proud of you. Proud of your accomplishment."

"Claire," Liv said, at her shoulder. "Will you give me a hand a moment?"

"Keep her vulnerable," Claire said to Bailey.

"What?" Bailey stared from one to the other.

"Will you give me a hand?" Liv asked again. "With the desserts?"

Claire stood up, and followed her lover to the kitchen. Bailey, the consummate hostess, asked her neighbor about his new puppy.

"We'll brew coffee," Liv said, opening the appropriate cupboard and handing Claire coffee beans while she plugged in the grinder.

"How do you know where everything is?" Claire asked.

"I used to room here."

"You lived with her?" Claire hissed this.

Liv stopped, turned slowly around, and told Claire: "You will get hold of yourself this moment. The melodrama is over."

A sullen child, Claire glared, swallowed her response, and crossed her arms. Liv returned to the grinder and its shrill mechanism. Before long, the coffee stoked, and the room changed perceptibly. Another scent, another road to another memory, and both women followed, one to a German restaurant with her aunt, the other to Seattle years before, at the end of a sorry weekend.

Liv handed Claire the first mug, and took the second, sitting on the windowsill. The dinner party forgotten, Claire's hostile buzz overthrown, she drank to keep from speaking, afraid she might attempt to explain. Sick of the confusion—the blur between the woman people interpreted her to be, and the woman she was. Claire wasn't even certain, anymore, which was which. Did dead women have secretaries? What was she exactly? Not a writer; the book was finished. What was she supposed to do now? She held the mug to keep from reaching for Liv. Claire felt herself overboard, desperate, clinging to any object in the water, anything to keep from drowning.

"Keep her vulnerable," she said again. Drank the tepid coffee and wished it were scalding, that it could burn her tongue and the roof of her mouth and bring tears. Liv walked over, hooked her arm around Claire's waist, and tipped her head to Claire's.

"What comes next?" Claire asked.

"We go back in there," Liv said, "and eat until we're sick." She kissed Claire, and then let her go.

Another road, then. Another road, and Claire, no longer in the water, near-drowning forgotten, followed obediently behind, with a torte and a mousse.

Sixteen

Errand girl

Her second trip to Home Depot in as many hours, Liv threw the tail-gate closed like a dirty punch. Sweaty enough to be in an equatorial jungle, she slid into the truck, its windows already opened, and turned the engine over.

"Where you headed, stranger?" The girl was blond, in a white t-shirt and jeans, filthy and lank as a runaway.

Liv started to reverse. The girl reached her arm out, and said, "Liv."

The truck idled and the girl leaned through the window. "You don't remember me?" She sounded injured.

"I remember. I have to be someplace."

"You can't give me a ride?" She smiled, reached her hand into the truck, and slid a finger along Liv's breastbone.

"I have to be someplace."

"I already heard that part. Let me in, will ya? You can't leave me stranded in a parking lot."

Liv took her foot off the clutch, swung the stick shift back and forth, told the girl to climb in.

Seventeen

Bailey investigates, part two

"You hated the dinner party," Bailey told Claire. They sat in the recliners on the deck, drinking iced tea, watching Simon whack a plum tree with a stick.

"No."

"You did. It's OK to be honest. I'm just sorry you were disappointed or unhappy or whatever. I really meant for you to be, you know, honored. You've finished a book and it's an incredible achievement, and I wanted to honor your work, and you. I meant to honor you."

Bailey's red sleeveless blouse looked fine on her. Since they'd met, she'd grown thinner and more sculpted, softened somehow, her lines more fluid and lissome. Claire herself felt years older, washed out.

"Bailey, can we agree to let the whole thing go? I didn't behave very well, and I'm sorry. I appreciate everything you did. It was too much and perfect and I'm grateful. No, don't say another word about it. Not one."

Bailey lit a cigarette, pouted her lips between drags. "Fine, let's talk about something else. How long have you been fucking the help?"

Claire reached over and slapped Bailey, hard, on her bare thigh.

"Ow, Jesus. Don't be so sensitive. I didn't read you as the chivalrous type. How long have you been making love to the help?"

Claire laughed, and hit Bailey again, harder this time.

"That's enough," Simon hollered at them from the plum tree. "No more."

"Busted," Bailey breathed. "Sorry, Simon, honey." Bailey waved to him, then muttered at Claire, "You vicious thing. You made me drop my cigarette." She lit another. "So how long?"

"I haven't kept strict account."

Bailey blew smoke through her nose. "You know what you're doing."

It wasn't a question, but she was asking. Claire understood that. She understood because her answer was Of course, and Never, and they were both true, and both false. Liv was unbridled, audacious, and Claire knew herself to be beyond recall: the trough to Liv's crest, and both in motion.

"Where is she anyway?" Bailey asked, craning her head as though Liv might be hiding nearby.

"Supply run."

Bailey drew her long legs up to her chest, rocked forward and back like an egg. She'd been quiet so long that Claire thought maybe that was all she had to say, when Bailey asked: "What happens at the end of the summer, or the end of the project, whichever comes first? Liv seems hard, she wants everyone to believe that she's hard, but she isn't. And you know that, as well as I do. If you injure her, it'll be intentional, because you know she's vulnerable. So any wound you give her will be deep, and on purpose."

Claire had felt stabbed at the word "vulnerable"—a sharp prick to the heart. She resented Bailey's speech, its mode as well as its intention. Sipping her iced tea, calm and introspective, Claire wouldn't engage. Not with Bailey or anyone, what happened with Liv would happen, and talking never changed a fucking thing.

They had quinoa salad, chilled and improbably filling, for dinner. Liv didn't make it home until almost seven, and Simon, having eaten, sat on her lap, rested against her chest, while she devoured her salad and edamame.

"You're filthy," Bailey remarked, while Claire fetched ice cream from the kitchen.

"Well spotted."

"And fun, Liv. You're fun too."

"Do you live here now?"

"I hear your camper's empty; looking to sublease?"

Liv set her fork down, and emptied her glass. Claire had made sundaes with cherries and whipped cream and hot fudge. She brought bowls for each of them, and rubbed her hand through Simon's hair as he murmured delightedly.

"What?" Claire asked Liv, as she sat down to her own bowl. She turned to Bailey, "What happened?"

Bailey shrugged, and twirled her spoon.

"Has she been telling you," Claire asked Liv, "that you're soft?"

Bailey stood up then and told them she had to go. "Have a swell night, ladies. Don't be too thoughtful. You might develop bad habits."

"Bye, Bailey," Simon called, ruining her exit line, whipped cream on his nose.

"Bye, Simon," she said, and was gone.

Liv set her bowl on the table, the sundae spoiled: the ice cream tasted bitter. "I need to shower," she said, and went indoors.

"Let's go for a walk, Simon." They'd finished their ice cream, and the evening had cooled enough that they'd stopped sweating. He held her hand as they picked up a trail, and walked toward the road. The air smelled of fire, distant and to the north.

Eighteen

Dismantling the kitchen

At the Imax, they watched a movie about sharks, and then took Simon to ride the carousel. He disliked the horses, but loved the giraffe and the goat and the tiger. Afterward, they let him slide down the giant Radio Flyer Wagon and all three of them went to the bookstore.

Browsing along the tables, Liv contemplated her irritation. She'd snapped at Claire repeatedly several days running. Since the girl at Home Depot, there had been three others. Something brutal inside her kept grasping at her throat and she wanted to lash out, to kick something, to throttle her own throat until whatever it was submerged again inside her. And what was all this for exactly? Liv hadn't even enjoyed it: the girls pushy brats who came in a rush and whined for more. Tired. Liv was tired of sex. Tired of their bodies and the begging. Tired of all their transient expectations. Tired of her inability to keep away. Liv was tired of herself. And Claire. She was tired of Claire and her perfect life. Her glowing child, and her money, and her beautiful, secluded house, and her goodness, her tedious, reliable goodness.

"Do you need help?" the clerk asked. She was young, and small, and had pale, piercing eyes. "A recommendation?"

"Sure. Hit me."

"Fiction?"

"Yeah."

"Have you read *Jesus' Son*?" The girl handed Liv the book, and went on around the table, to pick up another book. "*Motherless Brooklyn*. Inventive and unpredictable, this book is hypnotic. Trust me."

"Sure," Liv said. "I trust you."

The girl smiled. "You've read them, haven't you?"

"Yeah."

"I'll bet you haven't read Ali Smith?"

"I've never even heard of her."

"Then you're in for a treat." The girl led Liv down the fiction aisles, and pulled *The Accidental* from the shelf. "Her voice is unreal. She won the Whitbread for this one." She handed the book to Liv reverently as though it were a sacred text.

"Thanks," Liv said, and grinned at her.

"Anytime."

"Found something you like?" Claire asked behind them. Simon, with a Thomas picture book and a small Curious George doll, held her hand.

"Yeah," Liv said, and maneuvered herself around Claire and Simon, to herd everyone toward the cashier.

Whatever had clasped at her throat had released its hold, and she felt buoyant, elated even. She paid for their purchases, and lifted Simon to her shoulders, walking ahead of Claire to the car. "We should go to the Japanese Gardens, yeah, Simon? Want to see the fish?"

He did, of course. He asked about them as they drove up the hill, and turned into the gravel parking lot. From the slats in the bridge, he watched the tremendous koi, sleek and sinuous, propel through the water. And Liv strolled through the trails and waterfalls where light broke and shimmered. She hadn't waited for Claire, and now when she looked for her, couldn't see Claire anywhere, couldn't even recollect what she had worn. Liv checked the bridge for Simon, but didn't find him there. In a panic, she imagined a kidnapping, and moved quickly through the grounds searching, then out to the parking lot and found them, Simon crouched beside his mother, playing with two black Labrador puppies.

Liv slowed instantly, not liking this tug-of-war with Claire, this lesson about running off disguised as an impromptu play date with puppies, this silent lecture about the effects of neglect. Stalled against a tree, she lit a cigarette and imagined the next girl. Free, free of

Claire's attitudes and postures, free of Bailey's insistent interference, and free of her own inevitable withdrawals. These girls did, in the end, have meaning. They meant Liv wasn't Claire: housebound with a child and money and property; entitled and presumptuous and needy.

Simon looked up. "Puppies!" he cried. "Liv. Come see. Puppies. Come see them."

As Liv crossed to them, she saw hurt, as clear as a sunburn, on Claire's face. Need would be their undoing, Liv thought. Need and disappointment. She crouched beside Simon and admired the puppies—biting, thrashing little creatures. They kept climbing into Simon's lap, nearly knocking him over.

"Well, if you can make it, I'd love to see you there." The man standing on the other side of the puppies said this to Claire. Liv hadn't noticed him until he spoke. Tall and brown and well dressed, with a diver's watch and purposely chaotic hair.

"I don't know where Zola is."

"Just down on Main, by the yoga studio and Rocket Bakery."

"Right," Claire said.

"Fantastic jazz, and great food."

"Friday night at Zola."

"Friday at 9."

Claire nodded, and rested her hand on Simon's back. "We'll see. Thanks for stopping. It's been a long time."

"I'm sorry about Denise."

Claire nodded again.

"I hope to see you around," he said. "Bye, Simon."

"Bye, puppies," Simon said quietly.

Liv stalked to the car.

Unaffected by the swollen hostility, Simon fell asleep in the car on the drive home.

"Do you want me to drop you somewhere?" Claire asked.

"Yeah, downtown."

"How does it work if you don't have your truck, or do you just go to her place? No, wait, I know, the bathroom door locks."

"Fuck off."

"These are your errands, right, these girls? All week you bite my head off because you're out screwing at random, and somehow that's my fault. You fucking child."

"Let me out. Stop the car and let me out."

"I'd like to throw you from the car."

"Let me out."

Claire pulled over and Liv jumped out, slamming the door behind her. Staring forward, murderous, Claire stamped the accelerator. Later, it felt like the car drove itself to Bailey's.

Bailey came to the door in pajama bottoms and a pale yellow tank top, her hair in a ponytail. She stepped back to let Claire through, reached her hand to her hair, and closed the door behind them. After Claire carried the sleeping child to the couch, she crossed to Bailey and pressed her from the living room, down the hall, and into the bedroom, their bodies not quite touching, Bailey's expression worried. A strain between them as Claire closed Bailey's bedroom door, grabbed hold, and kissed her. Their clothes left on, stretched awkwardly, neither spoke, until Bailey panted Claire's name.

On the windowsill, scented candles and incense cones. Chef pants tossed onto a chair in the corner, back issues of food and wine magazines piled on one end table, and ten pounds of hardcover cookbooks piled on the other. The walls painted a cool shade of green like daquiri ice.

"What happened?" Bailey asked, on her side, with her head propped in her hand. "Did she screw somebody?"

"We're all so smart."

"So I'm revenge, is that right? I'm the dagger in the back. Et tu, bitch."

"I hate girls."

"Wait, I know this song."

"I was only sad before."

"You're pretty sad now. It's just sex, Claire. Nobody took vows or holy orders or anything. Do you care so much? You've seen the girls. They aren't a threat in any real way."

"Are you encouraging me?"

91

"I don't really have a fitting speech for this situation. I haven't even shaved my legs."

Claire laughed. Bailey's hair had pulled from her ponytail, and fell now around her face. Without makeup, she looked younger, her eyes lighter. Rocked up on her elbow, Claire kissed her gently. Claire meant to say something about this being unfair and how she was sorry, but knew she wasn't sorry, and so didn't say anything. She had wanted, and she had taken what she wanted. Just like always.

Bailey stood up and fixed her hair. "Come on, I've been baking scones. Blueberry lemon, you'll love them."

Liv pulled the old cabinets from the walls, above the counter and below, so that the kitchen looked like a shell, just the idea of a kitchen. In the end, the counter would be replaced as well, but the cabinets were first. Two days before, Claire had emptied the cupboards, stored the contents in the pantry, in boxes on the kitchen table, above the refrigerator. Liv had hitched a ride back to Claire's. Almost the moment she slammed the car door, she'd turned for home, ashamed of herself.

Heavy, ugly, and awkward, the old cabinets came down in pieces. She'd piled them in the wheelbarrow and hauled loads to her truck. She'd finish before they came back, and could start installing the new cabinets in the morning. The drill's battery had died, and the backup had lost its charge, so she re-charged one while she unscrewed the panels by hand. Glad of the struggle, glad of the weight of the wood, glad to be alone and sorry, the ache almost a pleasure.

"Does Simon like scones?" Bailey asked, smearing butter on the opened halves.

"Probably. I'm not sure he's ever had them."

Astonished, Bailey stared at Claire a moment before shaking her head. "Poor neglected kid."

"Want me to make coffee?"

"Help yourself. I think you know where everything is."

Claire pulled the grinder down and proceeded to overwhelm the buttery lemon scent with brewed coffee. They sat on stools in the kitchen, Claire's mouth alive with tastes and possibilities. The scones made her hopeful, a kid in a garden where the flowers bloom all at once. "Bailey. You have a gift."

"Don't gush. You can have another if you want."

"Are these your own recipes?"

"Sometimes. I experiment. Nothing ever really tastes the same from batch to batch."

"You should have your own bakery. You must."

"Yeah, I know. It'll happen just by wishing. That's how financing works, right? Oh, Simon, you're awake."

He came into the room with his face creased from the pillow on the couch and his hair random. He climbed into his mother's lap and nestled against her. "Butter," he said.

They gave him half a scone and a scoop of butter. Bailey poured a glass of milk and set it beside him. He woke slowly, dipping his finger into the butter, becoming more alert bite by bite.

"Do you camp?" Claire asked.

"I love camping."

"I was thinking of going this weekend. What's your schedule?"

"I'm off work by noon on Friday. My weekend is clear."

"What do you think, we could go to Missoula, camp up at Lolo?"

"And Liv?"

"I'm asking you."

Bailey looked at Simon, then back at Claire. "Let's be clear here. I like you, Claire. I do. Enough, in all probability, to make trouble for all of us, but I'm not courting trouble. This afternoon won't happen again. Liv and I aren't what we were, but I'm not out to punish her. I don't want any part of that, well, just this tiny part, but not to make a habit of it."

"It isn't like that—"

"Uh huh. I'm just saying. Ask Liv if she wants to go camping. We can make a weekend of it, the four of us."

All evening, Claire stalled. At Bailey's, at the market after Bailey's, on the drive home, she asked Simon multiple times if he wanted to go to

93

the park. Each time he refused, asked to watch a movie, eat popcorn, play with his trains. A dark and empty house, she dreaded it. Dreaded her mood and Liv's.

Her aunt had never sustained a romantic relationship while Claire lived in the house. There had been men, electrons of them, circling around, but Denise had never let any of them settle. She'd found relationships exhausting, felt they compromised her focus, hindered her work.

Claire felt this too, and on some level, believed it. So she was unprepared for the house, lit and noisy, or for the kitchen, half-dressed with aspirations, or the girl, sweating and determined. She stood in the doorway; Simon sprinted past to his trains and returned with Donald and Douglas. Liv, on her knees, continued assembling the new cabinets, drilling hardware, hanging doors. The pieces were striking and elegant, stained lightly to accentuate the cherry wood.

As she put the groceries in the refrigerator, or the appropriate storage box, Claire went back over the day in case she had missed something. She had not expected this. She had not expected the fight or Bailey or the kitchen. In the end, she put a movie on for Simon and ran a bath for herself.

In the night, she ventured back, and turned on the kitchen light. The west side of the kitchen sat unfinished like glaring eye sockets, but the east side was complete except for the new counters. Claire touched the smooth, gorgeous grain, her hands drawn across the wood as though it were a fabric. They might have been bodies, skin, as she glided her hands across their surfaces. It felt erotic—topless, in her bare feet—to stroke Liv's handiwork. Self-conscious, she switched the light off, stood in the dark before the cabinets like a temple virgin: hesitant, restive, thrilled.

Denise would have liked Liv, Claire was certain. Would have considered her unpredictability proof of her intelligence, her worth. The boring, reliable ones were bred for simple girls, satisfied with less. If a relationship was effortless, you weren't doing it right.

Claire walked downstairs, convinced less each step that she knew what Denise thought. Denise might have considered Liv shifty, irresponsible. After all, Denise had stayed—all her life she had stayed in Spokane—by the river, with her samples and her work and little else until Claire had descended. Even Simon she had fought, warred against the simple idea of him. Change a worrying variable for Denise, one outside the control of the scientific researcher and, therefore, dangerous.

In the basement, moonlight, and the past on tiptoes. Claire, unafraid, heretical, opened the closet door in her aunt's study, pulled down boxes, and began to go through Denise's papers. Alternate chapters of previous field guides, transcripts from lectures given at universities and conferences, field notes dating back to the 1970s. Piles at her feet as she worked methodically through the closet, before turning to the desk drawers and filing cabinets.

The paper trail of a life, Claire tore through every item, and felt remorseless for the first time. Stripped away like the cabinets in the kitchen, just papers, memorabilia and nothing more. Not a soul, not even a body, just documents.

Claire wanted some place to rest, some haven for this furious love. She wanted to feel less, and with more control.

She ran upstairs and outside. Her path through the grass slick with dew, it might have been 3 a.m., and Claire stumbled in the long wheatgrass, grasping at roots to pull herself back up. Down again several steps later, and she couldn't make herself get up. She didn't want this anymore. Not another step on this path, volatile and destructive. She didn't want anymore.

"I don't want you," she said. "I don't want you."

Claire stood, shivering, ten yards from the camper. "I don't want you. I don't want you." Shivering, unable to go on, or turn back.

Nineteen

Finish work

Liv finished the cabinets the day after they left, Claire and Simon, to camp in Montana. Claire had never asked, only packed their things and said she'd be gone. Less complicated, Liv thought, than their staying. She'd begin on the bathrooms while they were gone, the shut-off water inconveniencing no one.

She tore out the bathtub, found the subfloor remarkably sound, and when Bailey came by on Saturday, recruited her to help drag the behemoth outdoors to be left in the grass until the truck could be emptied of old cabinets. Bailey stayed the afternoon, chattering from a chair she'd pulled into the doorway, while Liv worked to disconnect the plumbing, and pull the sink and toilet. Grateful now for the distraction of another human, Liv offered to buy dinner and drinks.

"Did she go camping?"

"She did."

"You didn't want to go?"

"Wasn't asked."

Bailey glanced over at her, then away. Her kindness about Claire almost painful to Liv, like thinking about Claire at all. And Simon, she wouldn't let herself, no, she could not think of Simon. Not his joy playing with two puppies, or his table of trains, or his brochures about trains, or his videos about trains. Not the posters and books and sheets and clothes and toy chest of trains, or the hum of the child around her, or his attempts at conversation. In a matter of weeks, the job would be finished. Touch up still to do, perhaps, but she could recommend someone for Claire.

In the back bar at Hills' Restaurant—styled in pastels like the waiting room of a doctor's office—they ordered steaks, rare, of course, with a pitcher of beer, and a mushroom starter. Bailey, who had run into one of their old classmates, told stories of his gremlin-like daughter, and the smug way he'd kept referring to his wife as his light.

"As in he's heavy and she's light," Liv asked, "or light in the darkness kind of thing?"

"Is one less horrible than the other?"

"No," Liv said. "I'm just trying to understand the nature of the horrible, you know?"

"I couldn't say for sure. I took it as religious light, but that might be my prejudices showing."

"That's a lot of weird."

"That's pretty much how my week has been: a caravan of weird. Oh, and my housemate got knocked up. She's talking about marrying the guy. Kids today are so crazy."

"She's like thirty. I think she's older than we are."

"What are you saying to me?"

"Nothing. Not a thing."

"We're young, Liv. We're young and full of possibilities. We haven't begun to live the best years of our lives. All this homesteading kind of shit is for the fearful. You and I are the last wave of rebellion."

"Um, dude, you're in management, and you own your own home, and you're living in Spokane. The rebellion didn't stop to blow its nose in this town."

The bartender brought their plates, returned to fill their water glasses. Bailey bit into her steak and hummed with pleasure. "What will you do after you finish this job?" She asked. "Go east again?"

"Fuck that. I hate the east."

"What happened out there?"

"A whole lot of nothing."

"Did you meet someone?"

Liv shrugged, looked at her fork, stabbed at another bite of steak. "Same as here."

"You found a girl like Claire out east?"

97

Startled, Liv shook her head. "There aren't women like her—" but the sentiment died in her mouth. She ate her steak, and refused to go on.

Bailey waited her out, let half the steak go, asked quietly: "Why are you so afraid?"

And then, without looking up from her plate, Liv told her. Said more about Claire than she had ever allowed herself to think, let alone articulate: "I've never met anyone like Claire. She's so good. She's so good about everything. She's the kind of person who didn't take candy from those bins in grocery stores when she was a kid. The kind of kid who never shoplifted, or stepped on ants, or swore at her parents. All I do is fuck up with her. I feel like more of a fuck up than I've ever felt. And I see that every time I'm with her. We had a race once, on bikes, and she kicked my ass. I couldn't even beat her at a physical competition. I'm just no match for her, you know. I'm never going to be what she deserves."

"Isn't it enough to be what she wants?"

"But I'm not," Liv said, so low it was almost soundless. In the blush-colored booth, she felt small and innocuous.

"Have you talked, either of you, actually talked to each other about this?"

But Liv was done now; her sharing moment passed. Stretched back in the booth, she finished her beer and exhaled as though the rest of it were just so much air.

"Let's go for a drive," Bailey said.

They cruised through the South Hill, ended up on Cliff Drive, parked along a residential road, and got out of the car. Teenagers lounged against boulders and flicked bottle caps at one another. Bailey and Liv walked out to the edge of the cliff and looked down on the city. Sprawled and sparkling, Spokane looked legitimate, almost regal from this vantage. Like a city, some might say. A light wind teased through the pines behind them.

"I swore to god I'd get out of this town and never look back," Liv said, her cigarette smoldering as she inhaled.

"We both did."

"Still fucking here."

"No," Bailey said. "We're back."

Liv laughed. "Isn't that worse? We couldn't keep away."

"No. Never leaving, that's worse."

Liv shook her head, thought of that cold stone house in the dark: austere and expectant. "Your housemate—the chick I sat next to at the party—Sophia, right? She's keeping the baby?"

"If they get married, that's her plan."

"She won't keep it if she's on her own?"

"Would you? Fucking horrible. Look at Claire, and Simon's a good kid. They're exhausting. All those needs all the time, and you can't leave them on their own for years. Sophia works at Starbucks, for god sake. She can't afford a kid on her own. She can't even afford organic meat."

"Claire's only been on her own since January."

"Yeah, the aunt, I keep forgetting about her. Claire's had a tough year. I think her aunt was more a mother than her mother. And that's the thing, isn't it: you can start out with a partner or spouse or whatever, and still end up on your own with a kid. No guarantee about any of it. Don't think I'll mention that to Sophia, though. She's all weeping tantrums just now."

A patch of clouds blotted out the moon, and the city shimmered harder. Along the road behind them, on the hood of a car, two girls laughed spastically.

"Let's walk around," Liv said. "The night's perfect."

"Spokane in the summertime."

Bailey came by the next morning with pastries and coffee. Offered to help run the cabinets to the Waste to Energy Plant, and take the sink, tub, and toilet to the Building Supply. Neither had slept well, the morning bright and hot just after 4 a.m. Liv had kept the camper's door open, yet even so—restless, and impossibly stifled—she'd ended up dragging her bedroll to the deck and sleeping there.

While they ate berry scones and chocolate-filled croissants in the kitchen (all the foodstuffs unpacked from Claire's boxes and stowed properly), Bailey admired the cabinets. They were both simpler and more beautiful, and lent the house a refined sensibility.

"It's almost like a display house or something," Bailey said, "too posh for living. Once the counters are in, I'll be afraid to cook in here."

"I've called a subcontractor to handle the tile. I'll have him do the bathroom too. I hate tile installs."

"Oh god, cutting all the tile for my bathroom last year just blew. And no matter how careful you are, the rows never seem to line up. I take the fastest showers now so I won't have to stare at the tile too long."

They went to the dump and Building Supply together, the loads too heavy for either to manage alone. They had the new tub in before lunch.

"Tile first or after?" Bailey asked, looking at the new sink and toilet they'd hefted into the hallway.

"Are you kidding me? After. He can do the hard fucking work getting the placement just right."

She had the toilet and pedestal sink installed, and the water back on, in the afternoon. Bailey had fallen asleep outdoors on the recliner, her cap pulled over her face to block the sun. For the first time in years, in her leisure, sitting up on the railing smoking, Liv contemplated Bailey. The long, smooth stretch of her, easier to handle while asleep, and more appealing than previously, though Liv couldn't name why. Clothed in dark canvas shorts and a ragged t-shirt, Bailey's body more angular, less awkward, Liv found herself using the word beautiful. Somehow, without Liv even noticing, Bailey had become beautiful.

Liv rubbed at her neck and dreamed of a swim through frigid water. Some peace had gone from this place. Working on the house now felt like a job, any job, and she had an urge to pack up the camper and leave while Claire was away.

On the recliner, Bailey stirred and took off her cap. "What's going on? You finished already?"

"The bathroom's ready to tile. Hungry?"

Bailey stretched, nodded toward Liv's cigarettes. "Share the wealth?"

Liv tossed her the pack and her lighter. "I could eat," Bailey said. "What are you thinking?"

"Indian—that place up north."

"Oh, that sounds perfect. God, I slept for hours. Marvelous. I think I fell into Simon's afternoon nap. What about you? Did you get any rest?"

Liv shook her head, yawned.

"You, my friend, are looking bedraggled."

"That's funny," Liv said. "I've just been thinking you're looking better than ever."

Bailey rolled her eyes. "Jesus," she said. "You're killing me."

After Indian, they played miniature golf. Bailey, a wicked and obvious cheater, kept up a running monologue of the finest plays, recapped the moment after they happened. For the second round, they joined a couple of teenaged boys and trash-talked their way into a serious ass-beating.

"I think maybe you're too old to swing that thing." One of the boys said to Liv, in the most quoted line of the night.

Ultimately, Liv and Bailey ended up at the Mercury Café, shooting pool. This time, Bailey was approached as often as Liv was, and Liv, nursing her beer, enjoyed Bailey's dismay.

"It's because I'm wearing your clothes," Bailey said. "Must be. I've seen most of these chicks in here before, and not one has ever bothered to finish her first look, let alone take a second."

"It's your humility. You've got the tops swarming."

Bailey had showered at Claire's, and thrown on shorts and a tank top of Liv's. The clothes, tighter and more androgynous, did not account for all the traffic to the pool table. Liv scratched and swore, and watched Bailey head for the dance floor with a chick that had to be forty.

"I'll play for her if you like," the girl said. Short, with pink-streaked blond hair, and large breasts, she was tanned right down to her ankle socks.

"Have at it."

101

The girl sank every stripe, her posture a pleasure to witness, low and angled, and before she dropped the 8-ball, she butted against Liv, then eased forward and nailed the shot.

"That could have gone better for me," Liv said.

"It will."

Liv straddled a stool, her back firmly braced against the table, and finished her beer. Around them, the tables had emptied. At the other end of the room, gathered around a single table, several boys drank shots.

"Come on," the girl said, smaller now without her cue stick, harmless.

I can't, Liv thought.

At the moment the girl reached out her hand, Bailey, red-faced and glistening, came back from the dance floor alone. She hesitated, ten feet from where the girl stood like a supplicant before Liv. And Liv, looking at Bailey, missed the meathead chick's entrance. Decided later, she must have come in the goddamn side door and walked right past the table of boys.

"What the fuck," the meathead chick said to the girl, "are you doing?"

"Playing pool," the girl said. "What's it look like?"

The meathead, brutish and muscled, with a shaved head, blue jeans, and a tight black t-shirt, surveyed the situation: three solids on the pool table, the cue sticks pinned to the wall, Liv on the stool holding her empty beer glass.

"The fuck you are," she said. She glared at Liv. "The fuck you are."

Bailey had started over, but Liv shook her head. Beside the pool table, the meathead tensed, crouched, her gaze darting between Liv and Bailey and the girl. Liv slid off the stool sideways, but the meathead caught Liv's shoulder with her left fist, and Liv, turned slightly by the punch and the table behind her, launched the beer glass into the side of the chick's head. The glass cracked, the base still in Liv's hand. Liv dropped it, bounced on the balls of her feet, threw herself forward, and knocked the meathead into another table. Kicked her hard in the belly, as she slumped to the ground.

Before the girl, who'd grabbed a cue stick, could nail Liv with it,

102

Bailey had thrown two punches that sent the girl sprawling. Legs apart, elbows tucked, Liv stood a moment, reckoning: the tab settled earlier with cash, but the bartender knew them, as did some of the patrons, including the girl, in all probability. All night, they'd drawn attention. Too late, she thought. No help for it. And Bailey, yanking Liv's arm, dragged her through the room, past the boys who'd looked up but kept sitting, and out that same goddamn side door.

In the truck, driving across the Monroe Street Bridge, Bailey had the giggles. "Jesus," she said, breathless, flexing her fingers. "That girl's head was hard. Are you OK? I can't believe you hit that woman with your glass. She was freaking huge. Was she bleeding? I couldn't tell."

Adrenaline had left Liv feeling nauseous, trembling. She did have blood on her hand, but it might have been her own. Her mind pinged around: had the meathead been conscious? Would someone call the police? And Claire, what would she say?

"I've never punched anyone before," Bailey said. "I mean, someone I wasn't related to. Her head was really fucking hard." She started giggling again. Liv slowed down, thought about pulling the truck over, throwing up. Focused instead on the road ahead of them, and Bailey's voice. In her hand, the weight of the glass, thrusting forward into the meathead, the sound of the impact and glass breaking, and Liv's own body rushing forward. Her breath in bursts, her body bouncing—back once, forward once, and charge.

"Seriously, that chick you hit was huge. Scary and huge, and she really didn't like you hitting on her girlfriend."

"I didn't hit on her girlfriend."

"Then imagine how pissed she might have been."

"Bailey, I didn't hit on her fucking girlfriend."

"Oh, I know. You're reformed. Love has changed you. God, I don't feel good. Really, I want to retch. Seriously. Liv, you should pull over." Bailey opened the passenger door before Liv could stop, and retched bile on her shoes and the running board. "Fuck. Oh god. That was awful and wild and scary. I was so scared. I thought that chick would murder you."

"Bailey," Liv said. "Bailey, stop talking." She killed the engine.

Bailey started crying. "She really could have killed you. She was fucking giant. You broke a glass on her head. Horrible."

"Bailey, be quiet."

Bailey moaned, wiped at her face.

"I didn't hit on that girl. She hit on me. It's important, Bailey. It's important. Focus. Listen to me. I didn't hit on that girl. She propositioned me."

Bailey, mucus in her hair, mascara smeared on her face, stared at Liv. "You think it'll make any difference? You think when you explain how this one time you were the mark—you, just sitting there, minding your own business, weren't the aggressive one—everything'll be fine." Bailey started giggling, then stopped just as abruptly. "You broke a glass on that woman's head and kicked her in the fucking gut. You think you can change anything about that now? You think somehow this hasn't been coming all fucking summer? You think because this girl wasn't bent over the sink in the bathroom, or tied up in your truck, then everything's square? What the fuck's the matter with you? This is fucking serious. Jesus." Sniveling, rubbing hard at her eyes with the heel of her hand, Bailey rocked forward and sobbed in earnest.

Liv watched her and then shouted suddenly, startling both of them: "You think I deserved a beating? Is that what you're telling me?"

Tears down her face, her nose swollen and wet, Bailey shook her head. "I'm saying you earned it. You're lucky there weren't four of them with boots. Lucky you weren't dragged outside. I told you weeks ago: this is a small town, and you've been pissing people off."

Liv turned the engine over and rammed the accelerator down. They squealed through a yellow light, then a red. The streets dark and empty, the night humid and oppressive as though before a storm, and the truck racing Liv's own heart.

Several blocks from Bailey's house, the truck slowed, Liv's mind had conjured Simon, and the panic and fear and anger that had been driving Liv, as much as the truck, subdued; she could feel it quiet inside her. Mothers didn't get into bar fights, not mothers like Claire anyway. Not mothers of boys like Simon. Her mouth opened, and she leaned over the steering wheel, and no sound came.

Twenty

Of girls and gifts

Claire drove into Spokane late on Thursday evening. She'd been gone for two weeks. In his car seat, Simon slept with his head cocked, Henry in his fist. They'd driven to Canada that first day, two weeks previously, and spent a week in Nelson before driving to Glacier National Park to camp. Simon had been the ideal companion, perfect at traveling, and camping, and silence. She had decided, on a hike through Glacier, that she was over Liv. In the forest, Claire had spotted numerous varieties of lactarius and boletes and chanterelles, and had been embarrassed by her own excitement, the thrill of spotting them almost instantly spoiled by her aunt's absence, and by the end of her work in the field. Mushrooms had become meaningless unless they were in a dish to be eaten.

On the drive home, Simon had sung along to tapes, and listened to stories from A.A. Milne and Sesame Street, and finally fallen asleep outside Coeur d'Alene. The National's *Boxer* playing on low, Claire reminded herself that she was over Liv. Remembered how serene these weeks without her had been. No drama. And the house, after hotels and campgrounds, would be a respite. Its loneliness familiar, of course, but her own, tempered as it was by her abstentions.

While in Nelson, her editor had e-mailed her three pages of notes. Congratulated her on the expert way she had captured her aunt's tone. He was pleased, clearly, with the work, and his notes had been grammatical issues rather than technical ones, and easily dealt with. After the copy edit, the project would officially be completed, and then Claire might do anything. Anything at all.

Bailey would be amazed, by the anything that seemed to be taking shape in Claire's mind. A bakery: intimate, open until early afternoon six days a week, minimally staffed, and experimental with its delicacies. Claire would be the silent partner, responsible for financials; Bailey would handle management and daily operations. And prior to her decision on Glacier, Claire had given Liv the job of design and up-keep. She had seen all three of them in the business, working from their strengths, marvelously successful.

These final miles before home, she conjured both of them: Bailey and Liv. Bailey increasingly hard to figure, when she had seemed transparent at first: romantic, whimsical, stuck on Liv. It had been the night of the party; Claire saw now how the shift had occurred: Bailey's remarkable food, the pathways opened in Claire's mind by the smells and flavors. And Liv, that night she, too, had been different, firmer, stronger. The sex hadn't changed Claire's relationship with Bailey, but the food had. The food had earned Claire's admiration, and inspired, for the first time since her aunt's death, the possibility—the option—of another direction.

She drove through downtown Spokane, and felt her back muscles ease even as the tension in her jaw and belly increased. They turned at the fir trees, and slowed on the gravel road. Liv's truck parked beside her camper. Light from inside the house spilled onto the grass, and Claire parked, exhausted suddenly, the thought of carrying Simon indoors almost painful.

"Welcome home," Liv said, at the window of the car.

Claire sat still, took in Liv's damp hair, the white t-shirt clinging to her breasts, the smile brilliant against her dark face. She could not name the thing that drew her from the car, only that it was powerful, rending her will—fortified so particularly over a fortnight. Entwined in Liv's arms, she rested her head a moment and remembered no more.

Simon woke himself laughing. He'd dreamed of Liv, the two of them riding on a llama through the snow. Coming back to himself, and his room, he hopped up and ran to his table, the tracks intricately designed to maximize curves and bridges and tunnels. Found there a large box wrapped in paper with an orange bow.

"Oh, a present," he whispered. He looked about him, stepped closer, touched the present, glanced at the door to his mother's room, and then hauled the present back to his bed. He touched the paper, and the bow, and turned the box. It was heavy, and he tore the paper, dropping the package onto his bed. Carefully, he pulled the remaining paper off, working loose each fold and the bow until he exposed the box beneath: Thomas' Engine Shed and turntable. "Oh," he said. And then, "I like this present." Since the box was taped, it wouldn't come open and he hopped up again and sprinted into his mother's room. He slowed when he saw Liv, and then threw himself onto the bed.

"Help, this present. Help Simon open this, please. I like it. Open this present now." He jumped off the bed and ran into his room, then rushed back with the box, nearly toppling both of them.

Grinning, Liv scooped them both—boy and box—onto the bed. "So you like this present, Simon?"

"Oh, yes. I like it."

She tore the tape away, and let him open the box. He squealed and clapped his hands. On the other side of the bed, his mother stirred.

"I think," Liv said, "with a big shed like this, you might need more trains."

"Oh god," his mother groaned.

"Do you think," Liv went on, "that you need more trains? Maybe Neville, or Duncan, or Spencer?"

He jumped from the bed, exuberance radiating through him.

"Go check your closet," Liv said.

He hurled into his room, and flung the closet door opened: inside each of his shoes was a new engine. Dropping to his knees, he pulled one out as though it were a gold piece.

From the room next door, Liv called, "Do you like them, Simon?"

"Oh yes," he whispered, mid-extraction. "I like it. I like this present."

Liv helped him incorporate the shed into the tracks on his table. Over and over he showed her his new trains, telling her their names, recounting their adventures. He stood close to her, their arms or shoulders touching like grounds. As she reconfigured the track, she reached out to him—his presence a balm, a joy—and tousled his hair.

"I missed you," she said. "I missed your wild little self."

Once the track was laid, he circled around the table, trying out different engines and combinations of trains. Giving her assignments, trading out their freight cars.

From the doorway behind them, Claire laughed. "Because he didn't have enough?"

"Clearly."

"I'll make breakfast while you two build."

Liv debated leaving him then, to see Claire's face once Claire saw the kitchen, but knew she'd only be trading one joy for another, and so stayed, with the first, and purest.

When they heard Claire scream, Simon's head snapped up and he listened. She screamed again, and Liv asked if he wanted to go and see too. He grabbed four trains, their tenders unwieldy, and hurried from the room ahead of Liv.

The tile was extraordinary: green and yellow and orange and red all at once and also in fractions like sea stones. Beneath the cabinets in the bright morning light, it seemed to shimmer. As Claire approached it, felt its surface, the refraction calmed, and she could see the artisanal beauty of the work and the pieces.

She had walked through the room several times, her hands on every texture, before she realized that Liv had painted as well. In the time they'd been away, Liv had finished the kitchen. Claire felt them behind her, and turned.

"Don't you like it?" Liv asked after a moment.

Claire shook her head. She had not imagined this kind of beauty were possible in a mere room. If she opened her mouth, she could not trust herself to speak without sounding like Simon. *I like it, this present. Oh yes.*

"Come and see the bathroom."

Claire didn't think she could. Seeing the bathroom would require moving, and more exposure, and already she felt that her heart was unruly. Could you love someone for making you such a room? Was love as simple as that?

Liv came forward, took her hand, and led her to the bathroom. The pedestal sink, the reddish yellow marble, the large Jacuzzi bath. Liv had painted, and trimmed the wainscoting.

"I've only been gone two weeks," Claire said at last.

"Was that all it was?"

Simon climbed into the empty tub and ran his engines up the sides.

Twenty-one

Something else

Liv hadn't told Claire about the bar fight. In the end, nothing had come of it; no one had pursued them, nothing had run in the newspaper, it appeared more and more likely that the incident had gone unreported. She and Bailey had decided to avoid the Mercury, and that was the extent of their prudence.

Quiet days, sleepy and intimate: Liv and Claire took Simon on a bicycle ride along the Centennial Trail on Saturday, and to the beach at Coeur d'Alene on Sunday. Liv spent the morning mowing while Claire pruned the shrubbery around the house. They were dark, freckled, and sore. Beneath the cherry tree, Simon waded and splashed in his inflatable pool. Under discussion: a stone walkway from the deck to the riverbank, a project for the two of them.

Late Monday afternoon, Bailey stopped by with Copper River Salmon and new potatoes, fresh baked bread, shrimp and avocado salad. Bailey grilled the salmon, all four of them eating frozen fruit bars. The women groused about the bees and the stark, insinuating heat. On his back in the little pool, Simon blew bubbles with his plastic pipe.

"So, I heard something interesting today," Bailey said. Liv and Claire waited. Seated on the railing of the deck, Bailey batted her spatula back and forth as though it were a paddle. "That little café on Grand is for sale, turnkey. They're asking $145,000."

"What's turnkey mean?" Claire asked.

"Everything stays—the equipment and fixtures. They walk out, I walk in—or whoever. I've been in the kitchen, though, and they have

110

a lot of rickety old shit. Their dishwasher is just crap. The place would need an upgrade, but it's a great location."

"Why are they selling?" Claire asked.

"Divorce, apparently."

"You're considering buying this place?" Liv asked.

"Dreaming more like. I know $145,000 just gets me in the door, doesn't account for start-up, or upgrades, or employees, or anything. But if I had $165,000, say, I could do it. I could have my own bakery, in a great spot, with a built-in clientele. My house as collateral, maybe get a business loan; it's not so much money, is it?"

"But the risk would be yours," Liv said, "instead of someone else's. Financially, that would be wicked stressful, wouldn't it, worrying about the vendors and bills and payroll and accounting and price of goods, and bringing the business home with you everyday."

"Liv, wouldn't your life be less stressful if you didn't contract independently?"

"I have a low overhead, and no employees, and no rent to pay, and construction is a different animal altogether. Someone always needs work done. I've never had a lean time. And it's just me. If work dried up here for some reason, I'd pick up and go somewhere else. You wouldn't have that kind of freedom."

Bailey returned to the grill, plated the salmon, called them all to the table.

"Did you make this bread?" Claire asked. Two bites and she'd found herself a child, beneath a table, an apron pressed to her face, a dusting of flour in her hair. A fragrance she couldn't name, and in the background, a radio tuned to country.

"This morning. Rosemary's my favorite." Bailey's voice was flat. Her cap pulled low over her eyes, but her mood clear enough. She buttered Simon's bread; she'd grilled a hamburger for him, and applied a leering face of ketchup. His wet hair stood up in the middle, like a fauxhawk.

Guilty about her lecture, the discouragement she'd occasioned, Liv told Bailey about the rest of the plans for the house: built-in cabinets for Simon's room, and an update of the master bath. Bailey nodded, rolled a potato around her plate with a fork. In the end, Liv stood,

111

and announced she had a date with Simon: a movie at the Garland, just the two of them, and a vat of popcorn.

"Is it so ridiculous?" Bailey asked Claire after they had gone. "Me with my own café?"

"No," Claire said. "It isn't."

"But risky. She's right there."

"She's right about everything she said, but that doesn't mean you're wrong. Anyway, there's something she never reckoned."

"What's that?"

"A partner with capital."

Bailey sat a moment, digesting. Looked up, disbelieving. "You must be mad. That may be the worst idea I've ever heard."

"Why's that?"

"The abridged version? You and I have never worked together. Our visions might conflict; I don't know how you are about money or business or food or employees or anything."

Claire, dismissive, interrupted: "That's easily sorted. We'll know in three months whether or not it'll work—me as your silent partner. If it doesn't, it'll be a loan from me to your café—we'll have a lawyer write everything up for us—and you can buy me out at a rate of interest one point better than a bank would lend you."

Bailey stared at her plate. Something took residence in her face that Claire couldn't interpret. When she spoke again, the words came out strangled, as though she uttered them against her will: "I don't understand you on even the most basic level. A couple of weeks ago, we had sex and now you're Holly fucking Homemaker again. I don't get you. I don't understand you at all. Liv thinks you're too good, and I think it's something else altogether." Bailey stopped, chagrined, her expression changed again. She extended her hand and wiped it backward and forward as though erasing her sentences. "Sorry. Really, I'm sorry. You have no idea how badly I want this—but not this badly. I've got reflux just thinking about it. Never mind that Liv's against it, and all the unknowns—including whether or not I'm skilled enough to handle the operational side of things—you and I are very grey. It's confusing. Business is hard enough without dragging all this grey into it."

112

"I never realized you were a moralist."

"Claire, I already said I was sorry. I'm sorry I hurt your feelings and blurted this shit out without taking the time to think it over, to organize my position into bullet points with Vulcan logic. I'm grateful beyond description. Seriously, I'm grateful it even occurred to you. You're unbelievably generous."

Claire's laugh—bitter, sarcastic—punctuated Bailey's speech. She felt like spitting. On the heels of such an offer, Bailey had insulted her.

"You are so smooth, Bailey," Claire said, her voice harsh. "It's a mystery to me, how you've stayed single all this time."

"Take it easy, Claire."

"So I'm *something else altogether*? What would that be, Bailey? What is it about me that you find so reprehensible?"

"Oh, god. I have fucked this whole thing up." Bailey yanked at her hair, sucked in her breath, and exhaled, stalling.

Tears rimmed Claire's eyes. *Something else altogether.* Only a viper would say such a thing, an asp. The one thing more painful was Liv thinking Claire too good. The thief, the cheater, the liar too good for Liv, and meanwhile, Bailey refused Claire's money, and her partnership. Could not even be civil about her rejection. Stung. Bailey had stung her. And then, the final humiliation, Claire burst into sobs and sprinted for the house, but Bailey caught her, held on despite Claire's struggle.

"Stop it," Claire hissed. "Let me go."

"I'm so sorry. Please. Please don't." Claire scratched at the flesh of Bailey's back and arms, kicked her shins, reared back, and finally threw herself onto the deck, wailing openly.

"Stop," Bailey said, crouching. "Please stop. Claire, I'm so sorry. I'm an ass. If I'd set you on fire, this could have been worse, but that's about it. I suck. Please stop crying. We should totally work together. Obviously we'd be great business partners—you and me—you offer me the bakery I've always wanted, and I kick your character around and make you cry. Oh god." Bailey knelt on the ground beside Claire, and rubbed her back while she cried.

After she crawled into bed, Liv asked, "Did Bailey stay late?"

"Not too late."

"I hurt her feelings, about the café. It's not even a bad idea really. The more I think about it, the more I think she should do it. Bailey's gifted. The risk would be hers, and I reacted like it would be mine. I almost called her tonight to apologize. Maybe I'll drop by tomorrow."

Claire had a headache from crying, and shame probably. A shame headache behind her right eye, that throbbed through her skull. Maybe she was pre-menopausal. Her mood vacillated more wildly now than during her pregnancy. She felt like crying again. On her back, in the dark bedroom, Liv's arm and leg thrown across her body, Claire wanted to be comforted, and she wanted to be alone. Both notions warred inside her: to bury herself against Liv and weep, and to throw Liv from the room.

"Why so quiet?" Liv asked. "What's going on?"

"I'm in love with you." Claire said, tearing again. "Because of the kitchen tile. Bailey said you think I'm too good. And that she doesn't think I'm good at all. She doesn't want to be partners. She said I'm Holly Homemaker. And grey. And she doesn't get me at all. It's all reflux." There was more, but it was unintelligible.

This had to be menopause, or a tumor, or grief. She cried so hard that she shook. Stupid baby, she thought, pulling at Liv's t-shirt. Stupid, stupid baby.

"Who the fuck's Holly Homemaker?" Liv asked.

Claire hiccupped, wiped her nose, not entirely sure herself.

"You and Bailey had a fight?"

"Yes."

"You wanted to be partners?"

"Yes."

"In the café?"

"Yes."

"But Bailey said no?"

"Yes, because I'm not good. And I give her reflux because I'm grey, and she can't figure me out at all. She said she didn't know how I'd be about food, like I'm a freak or something. I really thought this could work: a bakery as a career. I thought I could be a silent partner. I had the whole thing figured out at Glacier. Tonight, when she told us about the restaurant, I thought it was too perfect. I'd had this idea for a partnership, and then Bailey announces this café's for sale. It was ideal, until she went all *you're reflux* on me."

"Maybe she just needs some time to think it through."

"Yeah, the offer is null."

Liv drew her fingertips across Claire's chest, kissed her wet face. Their breathing regulated. Claire closed her eyes, her urge to cry exhausted.

"You can't be in love with me because of the kitchen tile," Liv whispered. "I had a subcontractor put that in."

"Shut up," Claire sighed. She curled into Liv, pinched her Achilles tendon with her toes, inhaled the lemony smell of her skin, and dropped into sleep.

Outside the café, beside her car, Bailey stood in her white chef's uniform, and waved as Liv pulled into the parking lot.

"Thanks for meeting me. The agent said she'd give us half an hour to look around; she's got an appointment at four. A staffer's still in the kitchen, stocking the walk-in."

Inside, Liv stood by the cash register, looking the place over: a long, narrow room with high ceilings and bad paint; on the far side of the room, a beautiful wooden bench built into the wall, eliminating the need for a second chair at the two-top tables; on the side of the table opposite the bench, a single wooden chair. Beyond the counter on which the cash register stood, a display case ran the length of this side of the room, to the doorway of the kitchen. A simple setup, maximizing space and functionality; the display cases in excellent condition, as were the table and chairs.

"The cash register is kind of awkward," Bailey said, "at the head of the display cases like that, but it does create a nice flow to the display area. Come around this side." On the backside of the display cases: six feet of workspace, and two well-kept espresso machines.

"The cases are in beautiful shape, and the furniture," Liv said.

"Come see the kitchen."

The dishwasher and the standing refrigerator needed replacing, but the ovens and walk-in were faultless. Liv checked the electrical and the plumbing and approved both. They walked back through the dining area, and outdoors again.

"New paint, a couple of new appliances, some art on the walls," Liv said, examining the exterior of the building—red brick with two shades of yellow for the trim.

"New pots and pans, dishes, utensils," Bailey added. "But the bathroom's pristine, and the layout. This is such a brilliant location. This could be perfect. Just small stuff really."

"I agree."

"Do you? Do you agree?"

"Yeah."

"So the speech about risk and stress?"

"I meant it; but this feels right to me. This feels like the place for you. And you're ready for this step. I know you are."

Bailey smiled, chewed on her lower lip. "Did she tell you about yesterday?"

Liv nodded.

"I totally fucked that up. I don't know why even. One minute you're telling me, Don't do it, and the next Claire's offering me the money to do it, and then I start insulting her—totally dismissing her proposal. I actually said it might be the worst idea I'd ever heard."

"Talk to her."

"She cried for like hours. If I'd kicked Simon, that might have been worse."

"Talk to her. Bring her out here. Draw up a proposal, the two of you."

"Liv, it was so bad. I can't explain even. I pissed all over her. She offers me the chance to have this bakery—she practically hands it to me—and I start attacking her character. I don't know how to fix that."

116

"Talk to her. Today. Come back with me now."

Bailey cocked her head back, stared into the sky. "Fuck me," she muttered. They walked to the truck, climbed in.

In Simon's room, Claire had thrown the windows wide, two fans pulsing, as she finished painting a dolphin. They'd stenciled sea creatures on the walls: a shark, a sea horse, octopus and fish, a sea star by his bed. The entire room, sunken like treasure, and framing the windows: jellyfish.

Behind her, Simon played with his engines, told a ceaseless story of adventure to himself and his engines. Afterward, she'd promised him a trip to Comstock to swim in the heated pool. When the house could no longer be scraped and painted, what would she do to occupy her day? Take up hobbies, like her mother, knitting and Pilates? Specialize in brunch after thirty-mile bike rides?

"I don't know what to do, Simon."

He went on playing. She stood, with her paint roller at her side, and looked around the room. Perhaps it felt a little smaller, but more intimate as well, closer and warmer.

"Do you like it?" she asked him. "Simon?" He couldn't hear her. She envied his focus, his exclusion of the world around him. A skill he had, not only with his toys, but all his activities. Denise called it dreamy. Simon was a dreamy child. Claire's own mother had a different name for it: willful.

In the basement sink, Claire washed the roller, and paintbrush. From the kitchen, she heard Liv's voice. She warmed to it—Liv's voice moored her—physical, immediate, her nipples hard instantaneously.

When she walked into the kitchen, Bailey and Liv were unwrapping their burritos, and Simon was eating chips with salsa.

"You hungry?" Liv asked.

Claire took the proffered burrito, sat between Liv and Simon. Thai carnitas with black beans in a spinach tortilla, her favorite.

"How'd the painting go?" Liv asked.

"Fine."

They ate, examining the burritos as though they were rare artifacts.

"We have chocolate chip cookies," Bailey ventured eventually.

117

"Oh," Simon said, raising up on his knees and reaching for one.

"And I have an agenda," Bailey said, as she handed out the cookies. At least she had the decency not to look at Liv, rather she focused on Claire as she hurried on with her speech, her tone plaintive, her excitement admirably restrained.

"I've walked through the café this afternoon, and I'm convinced it'd be a sound investment. Touch-up work's all it needs. Minor really. And the café already has an established clientele, and they're in a great location. And I've got a business plan—I wrote it last night—so you'll know what I'm envisioning and that I'm serious. I'm serious, and I'd like to propose that you take a look at my business plan, and if you're interested, we could look at the property. I'd like your opinion about it—your ideas. I'd like your input." A moment of panic, and then Bailey closed her eyes, marshaled herself, and pressed on. "It was unforgivable, my behavior yesterday. I'm ashamed of it. I hope you won't hold it against me. If you'd just read the business proposal, if you'd only do that, I'd be satisfied. But I get it—I totally understand—if you don't want anything to do with this."

"What would you name it?" Claire asked.

"I was thinking *Baked*. Unless you think that's too subversive."

"Actually I like it."

"The Baked Bistro?" Liv asked.

"Yeah, yeah, I dig it." Bailey said, straining forward in her chair.

"What about *Fresh Baked*?" Claire asked. "Is that more respectable? The Fresh Baked Bistro."

They lobbed it around the table for a while. The energy between the three of them palpable, their cookies forgotten, and eaten surreptitiously by Simon, while the women examined Bailey's business plan, gave suggestions, offered amendments, and finally called the agent, asked to see the café right away, that very evening.

Formalities, really: the legal papers, the money, the sale of the café, and the lease of the building space. The pleasure of money, Claire knew, was how it simplified obstacles, made getting whatever one wanted effortless, a matter of a few phone calls. When they'd toured the café, she'd trusted Liv's opinions, believed Bailey's enthusiasm, felt the project's inevitability like a zygote inside her.

They'd agreed on paint, a local artist's work they wanted to display on the walls, dishes and utensils, font and paper for the menu—listing an assortment of crepes available to be served at breakfast or lunch. Liv had purchased the new appliances on their business card, Bailey had established accounts with the vendors, and hiring had involved Bailey handpicking four people from other bakeries around town.

To Claire, standing in the kitchen at the café—ticking off deliveries from vendors on her clipboard—felt like recovery, like the end to a mournful period of uncertainty. Bailey had given Claire a draft of the menu, and Claire had made it dynamic, the flavors enticing, the items practically bursting from print to palate. Her time with her aunt, the mycology field guides, had trained her for this. She was a seeker, Claire, a woman who made curious things more curious, more appealing. Of course, her mother was right, Claire was willful. She would have what she wanted.

Part Two

New-year's girls

Twenty-two

That's all sorted

By October, Liv had exhausted all but the most basic jobs around Claire's stone house, and accepted a job building a master suite in the unfinished attic of a stylish Cape Cod on the South Hill. Her client, Julia Drake, a humanities professor, knew precisely what she wanted, and after she'd spelled out her wishes in copious detail, she left Liv to get on with it. Every afternoon, she appeared at the top of the stairs, and asked Liv to join her for a light meal.

As the project was in the attic, and therefore an inconvenience to no one, Liv was able to keep her tools out and avoid the time-suck of the daily cleanup and put away. Liv enjoyed this project, the parameters Julia Drake set, and the license she bestowed, and her vision for the suite as well. Drake had majored in art history, and had an exquisite sensibility.

More than the project, though, Liv appreciated the opportunity provided by Julia Drake. A chance, five long days a week, to avoid interminable discussions about flour varieties, organic spices, payroll taxes, idiotic customers, growth potential, sketchy vendors, marketing platforms, and endless tinkering with tastes and presentations. Between Claire and Bailey, meals were not mere food anymore. Everything was a dish, to be contemplated and discussed like an Eliot poem.

At least once a day, typically during the lunch rush, Liv would field a call from Café Baked (as she'd come to think of it) and some speed-talker would report a meltdown of some apparatus and demand some assistance. Sometimes Liv could help, and sometimes she gave Claire's cell number and wished the caller good fortune. Bailey and Claire had contracted Liv, and provisioned a substantial hourly fee, to be on-call for any maintenance issue. Maintenance issue, Liv thought, had been left purposefully vague.

All at once, Liv had lost the pleasure of leisure and conversation, with either Bailey or Claire, and unless she expanded her social pool rapidly, the monoculture of bakery café bakery would ensure a grueling dry spell. She did not, at present, feel comfortable even grabbing a beer after work, as she worried she might slip into old habits on her own. A companion, she knew, kept her honest, and as she grew more bored, the bars became a more concentrated temptation.

When she had explained to Claire that she missed the freedom they'd had during the summer, Claire suggested that Liv take Simon to see a movie. Frequently, in the evening, while Claire and Bailey poured over recipes and invoices, discussed advertising campaigns and effective websites, Liv and Simon played trains, read stories, colored, or explored. Liv loved him, of course, and savored her time with him. But she could not, at present, recreate in many of the ways that she craved.

On Thursday morning, Liv told Julia Drake that she had to pick up materials at Miller's Hardware and offered to bring back coffee. Drake had mastered the lean. She leaned whenever she talked, in doorways, against the banister, on the kitchen counter, and Liv could visualize her in the classroom, leaned against the blackboard, or the back of her desk. Brunette, perpetually clad in button-down oxfords and khaki pants, mid-forties, glasses folded in her hand and thrust like a pointer more often than worn.

"Where?" she asked, leaned against the kitchen counter, newspaper unfurled. "Café Baked?"

"You're not supposed to call it that," Liv said. "That's my private nickname."

"I mean it like you do, as an endearment."

"Is that how I mean it?"

Drake smiled. "Yes. That's how you mean it."

"I'll stop there if you like, or elsewhere if you prefer."

"You're too accommodating." Drake considered, her glasses prodding her lip. "I'm fine with Café Baked. I'd like a scone, too, and a lemon bar. Let me get you money."

"Don't bother. I take it in trade."

Drake laughed, slid her glasses back on. "I'm sure you do."

Liv entered the café through the kitchen. Bailey, on her own, had five crepes going, ingredients prepped for dozens more. Every other station cleared, Bailey kept hers pristine, wiping its surface incessantly, like a mechanical tick. In the corner, the dishwasher purred. On the racks, pots and pans piled one inside the other, like Russian dolls.

"Hey you," Bailey said. "Have they called you about the garbage disposal? Damn thing's clogged again."

Liv cleared the disposal, while Bailey chattered away.

"Fucking insane all morning. Peter went home with some kind of drippy contagion. I don't know why I hire men. They are frail, every last goddamned one of them. And that bitch with the notions came in with her personal trainer. Actually, I'm glad I was here for that conversation."

"Which one is she?"

"The bitch with the notions? Are you from the Midwest; how don't you know this? The bitch with the notions is the one who wants us to provide comment cards, and business cards, and tells us every day who we should advertise with, and how we could improve our menu, and which suppliers we should never use et-fucking-cetera. She knows more than Nietzsche. She's got a fucking solution for everything."

"Right. Yeah, I've heard about her."

"So today she brings in her personal trainer to get his approval of the menu, and he tells us we're a little heavy on the carbs. I hate that woman. Maybe we need a new garbage disposal."

"This one's old. Just run it with plenty of water, and slowly, and it should be fine."

"You keep saying that, and it keeps clogging."

"Pleasure as always, Bailey."

"Sorry," Bailey said, adding garnish, before picking up all five plates. "Try the pumpkin bar. You'll love it."

Out front, every table filled, and the counters Liv had built on either side of the entryway as well, their tall stools invariably populated by small children kicking their legs as though treading water. Maybe twenty-five seated customers, in addition to the line waiting to order. Sophia, Bailey's housemate, quite noticeably pregnant now (Claire said she was carrying the baby high) took Liv's order and asked how her day was, and if she had any time to look at the garbage disposal.

"Maybe we should get a new one already," she added.

"It's just old," Liv said, taking her order in a little box.

"My point exactly."

"Double Americano," Liv said, handing Drake her loot. They ate at the kitchen table, from plates she'd purchased in Florence. The kitchen austere: with lean, tall cabinets, an island, rose-colored wallpaper, and high-end appliances.

"Garbage disposal or dishwasher?" Drake asked.

"Disposal."

"Maybe I should get a machine and we can make espresso here."

"Tempting," Liv said, "but think of the gossip we'd miss."

"Eventually they'll settle down, get their groove."

"It's too bad you get cell reception here. I could let it all go to voice-mail."

"They'd just call the house."

Liv smiled, shook her head. And then, the pumpkin in her mouth so affecting that she felt her breath catch, Liv remembered an afternoon wandering through a little town in Vermont, the girl beside her radiant with love—radiant—like a fucking planet the girl glowed. Cinnamon, apple, cloves, the girl's fingertips, the bite of her mouth, their hands raw from cold, and working outdoors, and Liv could feel it—the afternoon, the girl's intensity.

When she looked up at Drake, for a moment she saw the girl at the market, her striped scarf, her knit cap, the jar of syrup in her hands, and Liv smiled. The ache of that day fresh on her skin, like a piercing.

"What are you grinning at?" Drake asked.

"I'm taking a Bailey tour," Liv said. In answer to Drake's raised eyebrows, she went on. "The pumpkin … took me to an afternoon in Vermont."

"The taste, you mean? What did you call it—a Bailey tour? I love that."

"Her food does that. Her baking, especially, it's transportive."

"You're right," Drake said. "It is transportive. And the afternoon in Vermont?"

Liv blushed, looked away.

"It's okay," Drake murmured.

"You know that time when you think you might die of it—that it'll kill you—how much you feel, that your skin won't be able to contain it." Liv smiled as though her experience were a tired joke, another puppy love story. She could not say the Vermont afternoon had been an entire age—a lifetime, a reign—transformative and obliterating. She could not say how it had marked her: a thick scar in the shape of a star on her upper arm.

"You're editing," Drake said.

"It's not much of a story."

Drake said nothing, and they finished in silence. In the attic, the bandsaw whirring, Liv tried to push that Vermont afternoon from her mind, found instead the scent of wet hay, mud on their boots, a track to a barn, an old thresher. The girl had smelled musky; her nipples had a bitter taste, and discharged when she came. Taller than Liv, pale and bony, with the strange bruised look of vegetarianism beneath her eyes, she'd spoken with an Appalachian accent, a rustic music.

Simon butted a chair against the kitchen counter, and climbed up. In the mornings now, he made his own cereal, poured the milk slowly, always less than his mother poured, no longer drowning the poor Cheerios. Soon Liv would come down, and he would make her cereal too, while she made coffee. She liked bananas, torn into chunks, in her muesli.

Something was wrong. Simon knew this. But in the mornings, eating cereal with Liv, both of them at the table in their pajamas, Simon didn't worry. After she finished her coffee, Liv would ask him if he wanted anything else, and he always said yes, and she'd make him cinnamon toast, and drink another cup of coffee.

They did it every morning as though each time it might turn out differently. They ate breakfast, performed their routine, with sincerity. Simon could rely on breakfast, just like he could rely on Liv.

Bailey sat on a stool in the kitchen, her clogs on the floor, and flexed her feet. In the corner, Claire entered receipts on her laptop. The café hadn't been opened two months and the numbers were phenomenal. Ten days after they'd opened, a local magazine, a weekly paper, and the daily for the Inland Northwest had reviewed them. The reviewers gushed about the food.

Janet Nadeau, the food critic for the daily, had come back for lunch on successive days, and written a comparative review that likened the pleasure of eating Bailey's crepes to exotic travel. *Dining in Spokane has just been transformed.* The Fresh Baked Bistro *will set you on a journey through taste and memory that will seem improbable, until that second bite convinces you. You will delight in the use of basil and spinach and cheese. You will marvel at the berries and Greek yogurt, and the incomparable brioche. You will feel that you have never eaten with so much attention, your senses heightened, every bite bolder and more satisfying.*

And business showed no signs of slowing. Since then, a Seattle paper, and a regional magazine had interviewed them, and taken photographs of food presentations, and Bailey at her station. Hectic, maddening, the pace they'd set couldn't be run indefinitely, but for now, Claire and Bailey could manage the sixteen-hour days, the riot of customers, as the endeavor's urgency and newness sustained them through their exhaustion. In the evenings, it gave Claire a rush, booking their numbers—cost of goods sold, equity accounts, expense categories, receivables, payables—the strange language of business. She did the book-keeping for the café, and had, that morning, secured a CPA to handle quarterly taxes, and all the year-end formalities for them.

"How do you know this guy again?" Bailey asked. She'd taken to asking questions multiple times like a child. Claire tried not to let the interruption, or the repetition, irritate her.

128

"He was my aunt's CPA. I ran into him this summer. He's a nice guy."

"And a good CPA?"

"She always got money back on her returns."

"A restaurant is a little different, though, isn't it?" Bailey exhaled, stared at her socks. "Look, Claire, we're partners, right? I really want to be in on meetings like this. I want to meet this guy, and weigh in about whether or not I can work with him."

Claire stared at her computer screen. How was this already so complicated? Did every little decision require a committee meeting? "Are you handling the bookkeeping, or am I?"

"We're partners, Claire. We share the responsibilities. I don't know this guy, and I want to know anyone who has anything to do with the money. I don't want some ass stealing from us. I don't know anything about him, or his business, or his reputation."

"Fine, I'll arrange a meeting for the three of us."

"This week?"

"This week."

"Good," Bailey said. "That's all sorted." She slid her clogs back on and stretched. "How's Simon doing? Is he liking the place any better?"

Simon in daycare, three days a week for six hours, and it felt like lifetimes. "He didn't cry this morning."

"That's progress, right?"

"Sure," Claire said. Playing with other kids, trips to the playground, structured activities, these things had to be better for the kid than spending all day cooped up in an industrial kitchen.

"We're all adjusting," Bailey said. "I'm done for the day. I'll see you tomorrow."

"See you tomorrow."

"Hey to Liv and Simon."

Claire rubbed her neck, stared at the ceiling, let it all go. As she booked the deposit, she double-checked the line item amounts, and felt a thrill as the entry total matched the bank deposit amount. Checks and balances, tidy and analytical, all the names for money, the trails of success itemized before her.

Twenty-three

Drake pulls a latte

Drake, wearing striped pajama pants and a t-shirt, climbed the stairs to the attic at ten in the morning. Bags of insulation piled on the floor around her, Liv had been stapling insulation to the rafters, and dreaming about an achingly cold beer.

"Tell me you haven't had coffee," Drake said.

"Not for hours."

"Would you drink a latte—with soy, naturally?"

"I'd love a latte."

"Good, take a break."

Liv wanted to strip, and did, tore off her overshirt, left her boots on the stairs with her gloves, and scrubbed her face, hair, and hands in the bathroom sink before venturing into the kitchen.

On the kitchen counter sat a shiny silver Rancilio Silvia espresso machine. As Liv entered, Drake steamed the soymilk.

"I've practiced all weekend—I had brunches Saturday and Sunday for my guinea-pig students—and so far, each cup is better than the last."

The foam, a light, creamy froth, on which Drake used a straw to draw a leaf, before handing Liv her cup, looked perfect. Apprehensive, yes, about that first sip, Liv held the cup to her nose and breathed in. She sipped her drink, the taste exactly right—the soy distinct and rich, the coffee strong and easily consumed.

"It's good. I'm impressed."

Leaned against the counter with her own drink, Drake grinned. "Thanks. As soon as I said I should buy one, I decided I would. Now I feel like a Northwester."

"Isn't that a wind?"

"Yes," Drake said, "a strong one."

"So you're being clever."

"Evidently not."

"No, you are," Liv said. "You're clever. You're one of those girls who walked around reading nonfiction in grade school while the rest of us played kick ball."

"Actually, I'm rather good at kick ball."

"Are you? So what were you like then, as a kid?"

"I was the one reading a book about mythology in the queue to kick the ball."

Liv nodded. Outside, the wind shook the leaves and the branches and rustled against the house. She visualized this woman on a field with a book, her hair in a ponytail, her body scrawny and overlong. Later she'd have braces and glasses and if Liv had known her then, she'd never have expected the woman before her: confident, classical, seductive.

"I don't teach this evening," Drake said. "How would you feel about getting a drink?"

"I'd like that," Liv said. "I need to call my partner, make sure we don't have anything going on."

"Of course."

In the attic, Liv felt the coffee in her mouth, that distinctive bitterness. She approached the insulation now, reinvigorated.

Claire took Simon to Mobius, the scientific play center for kids. Their exhibit this month involved soil erosion: large bins of dirt with trowels and spray hoses; winding 3-D waterways navigated by pinballs to illustrate water flow through a city. And secondary exhibits about red-blood cells—a dome with red balls the kids could jump in— and a series on wind tunnels and magnets. Simon played in the plastic kitchen with the mismatched pots, cooking corn and zucchini. He drummed for a while on stage, and then settled in with a boat on the water-current table.

Afterward, they'd have lunch and see a movie, and probably buy a train at the toy store. Claire couldn't remember the last time they'd been out like this, just the two of them, having an adventure. Simon had grown again, his face more angular, his eyes larger, more haunting. He was beautiful. Long-lashed, delicately featured, pale, blond, tall, a striking child—empirically; she'd have thought so even if she weren't his mother.

"I'm hungry," he told her, his shirt damp at the sleeves from the water.

"Hamburger and fries?"

They left, walking side by side, and Claire put her hands in her pockets to avoid reaching out for him. It was a connection she ached for now; bound to him as she had been all these years. Still a silent, reflective child, and clearly deferential. Claire yearned for the toddler, missed being his jungle gym, the way he had buried against her, the comfort he had found in her body. It was a gradual breaking away—years of it—the tether coming haltingly undone.

Drake drove a sleek red Saab. Too fast, and too hard, barreling through turns and stop signs and side streets, butting up against the car in front of her as though she intended to crush it and keep going.

Before they'd left the house, she'd offered to spare Liv a drive home, and have her shower there. So Liv showered at Drake's, in one of the guest bathrooms: scented soaps and plush towels in a sage-and-citrus theme. Liv changed into jeans and a blue crew-necked shirt. She didn't have another pair of shoes in the truck, and had to wear her boots. Hair damp, and long enough that it had begun to curl, she returned to the kitchen, where Drake sat at the table, grading papers, also in jeans with cowboy boots and a sheer, button-down collared shirt.

Claire had said she and Simon were spending the day together and drinks with Liv's friend were fine. It still felt untoward, despite Claire's permission, to be going out with this fine, circumspect woman, all hipstered out and cowboy booted, without a chaperone.

"You keep driving like this and we're going to die in the street like gangsters."

Drake glanced at her, and then pressed the accelerator a touch harder, before a prompt downshift and the subtlest pause for a stop sign. Liv wanted to close her eyes, but it would be worse not to see it coming, the end, the tree or the other car or the child in the crosswalk. Fleetwood Mac's *Rhiannon* on the stereo, and then Drake darted the car into a loading zone and killed the engine.

"You so fucking owe me a drink," Liv said.

Seven on Friday night when they walked into Zola, the jazz band covering Ella Fitzgerald, the crowd pushing forty, moneyed and buzzed, Liv followed Drake upstairs to the open loft.

"The food here is superb," Drake said. Their server arrived promptly, clearly the youngest person in the bar, took their orders for drinks, handed them menus, and then asked them to repeat their orders.

The bar: spacious and modern with exposed brick; the upper loft designed around gondola seats, license plates nailed backward to the walls, helmets of every description—hockey, skating, fire fighter—on stands in the alcoves; wooden floors, a large great room and several anterooms, and the bar, open on three sides, opposite the short, intimate stage.

"This place is amazing," Liv said, examining the metal bars of the gondola seat that tucked into the plumbing fixtures above them.

"The whole building really. The owner—of the bar and the building—is a designer. He knows what he's doing."

The server brought their drinks and took their starter orders: mini ahi burgers and shrimp spring rolls, crab cakes and Caesar salads.

"What are you drinking?" Liv asked.

"A greyhound," Drake said, offering Liv her glass.

"What's a greyhound?" Liv took a tentative sip.

"Vodka and grapefruit juice."

"That's a heavy pour."

"Yeah, the drinks here are superb as well."

The band segued into Cole Porter. Through the metal bars of the gondola seat, Liv had an uninterrupted view of the band. Three men, middle aged, watching the pianist for cues.

"I'm glad you could come out tonight," Drake said. "I've had the longest week and it's a relief to be drinking."

"For me as well. Why the longest week?"

"I'm not sure it's anything specific. Students are students—some work hard and others don't. My colleagues are the same way. It's the familiarity of it all that makes me tired."

"Then do something unexpected."

"I am."

Liv smiled, turned the ice in her drink with her straw. I am too, she thought. Out at last, a drink, a woman, a new bar. She felt jittery, hungry, the night between them limitless.

"How is your mother?" Drake asked.

"She's OK. Not angry anymore—and that's something—but she's confused a lot. She makes mistakes, just dopey really, but unlike her. She keeps calling me when she means to call my sister, or telling me the same story four times in a single conversation. My dad's just grateful she isn't yelling."

"My mother had ovarian cancer," Drake said. "The only good thing was, she wasn't sick for long."

"I'm sorry. When was this?"

"Eight years ago. I was 36, and still, to this day, think of myself as an orphan."

"It's comforting to know it never gets easier."

The server brought their starters. The mini ahi burgers were delicious, and vanished in moments. Liv sipped at her second drink, found it stronger than the first. Drake's hair was shorn in back, and longish—swept into her face—in front. She'd highlighted the brown with red; recently, Liv thought, and the style suited her.

"I miss being part of a group," Liv said, watching the band. "I've been thinking about joining an association of some kind. I'd like to play league soccer, or Ultimate Frisbee, or take up martial arts. I feel like I never meet anyone anymore. I move in the same small circles day in week out."

"It must get lonely working by yourself all day."

"I've never minded before," Liv said. "Honestly, I enjoy being alone.

And I work faster by myself than with anyone else. Then this summer I had a little boy with me—quiet and busy—he stayed out of my way, but just having him nearby, even silent, made me feel less—"

"Alone?"

Liv had been going to say miserable, and that surprised her. She nodded at Drake's interjection.

"What if the feeling is intellectual rather than physical?" Drake asked.

"How do you mean?"

Drake considered Liv a moment, sipped at her drink, then said, "What if it isn't just the physical presence of someone else that you miss, but the intellectual interaction of peers? Maybe what you miss is that kind of stimulation. Maybe kicking something isn't going to help."

Liv thought of the stimulation she had sought for months and almost laughed. She'd never considered asking those girls anything meaningful. Meaningfulness and those girls were strangers.

"Kicking things always helps," Liv said.

"Contrarian." Drake said. "I do know what you mean. If I don't go for a run, my skin gets too tight. I feel like I'm suffocating. I start snapping at people; I get hostile without provocation. Now my colleagues have worked with me long enough that one of them will say, *Have a run. We'll talk about this tomorrow.* And they're right: a run fixes practically everything for me. But for you, I don't believe it. You're physical all day. I know exertion is different, but I think it's the solitariness. I think that's what's so difficult in your case."

"Well, now that you've worked out my problems, what do you propose as a fix?"

"Take a class. Go study German or Early American History—"

"—Or Art History," Liv laughed. "You're sending me back to school? That's your cure?"

"Yes, that's my cure: education."

"My god, you're a recruiter, and people worry about lesbians."

Drake laughed, a coarse throaty sound. "You know, I'm really not kidding."

"I do," Liv said. "I get that. There was a time, you know, I intended to get a doctorate and teach English Lit. I went to school for a while back east."

"I didn't know that," Drake said, watching Liv closely. "And then?"

"It all kind of crumbled. I didn't last a year."

"What crumbled?"

"Everything. School, me, everything."

"Liv, you need to work on your storytelling."

Liv grinned, and then said, "I met a girl my first month there. I was twenty-five and thought I knew everything. Sometimes I miss that—that cockiness, that conviction. I met this girl and she could have done anything, I would have allowed anything. I was mesmerized by this girl—she fucking shook me. You know? I felt sick all the time. I couldn't study, cut my classes, followed along behind this girl like her shadow.

"It went on like that for ages. Fall semester my grades were abysmal, and it didn't matter. I didn't care. And then, over Christmas break, I climbed up to her apartment, walked up five flights, she let me in and her eyes were red and her nose, and she said she couldn't see me anymore. She said she'd met a guy and she was pregnant and she couldn't see me anymore.

"I didn't even argue. I just stood there, not arguing, and then I went away. Down the stairs and outside and walked through the entire fucking city until I came to a bridge and then I tore off my shirt and cut a star into my arm. I cut until I couldn't see my arm or the knife for all the blood."

Liv laughed cheerlessly, unable to look at Drake. "I dropped out before spring break. I stayed out east for a while, picked up work with a crew, but I couldn't focus. I kept having accidents. I got a glove caught in a jigsaw, and shot myself with a nail gun—right in the boot—and fell off a scaffold. Last fall, I came back here."

"And the girl?"

"I never saw her again. I left her apartment that day, and that was the last time."

"What about the woman you're with now—Claire—what about Claire?"

"Hey, if you want to know something, just ask."

"Am I prying?"

"You know you are." Liv thought of Claire, and her own grief surprised her. She and Simon at the kitchen table, silent, waiting; Claire had wandered away from them. "Claire's preoccupied."

"With the café? That's not hard to imagine."

With the café, yes, that too. "What about you? Are you seeing anyone?"

Drake stretched her legs beneath the table, shook her head. "No one."

"When was the last time?"

"Oh, I had this coming. I see that now."

"No avoidance," Liv chided.

"Never in life. The last time was eight months ago—strictly short term, needs based, nothing more. I miss it, sometimes, the mess of being with someone else. It's not good for me to have things my own way all the time. Just encourages me to be difficult."

"Do you need encouragement to be difficult?"

"Would you like another drink?" Drake asked. "Liquor might help you be forthright."

"The last time I was out, I was in a bar fight."

"Are you serious?"

"Quite serious. I hit a woman in the head with a beer glass."

"Maybe soccer league is the thing for you after all."

"She hit me first."

"Of course she did. I'm not judging."

Liv nodded at this. It was true; Drake didn't judge. "Did you always want to teach?"

"No, no, I wanted to be a painter. I worked for years—and I mean worked—in my studio for hours everyday. I thought desire could make it happen. But I never produced anything that wasn't mediocre. It broke my heart not to have any talent. I have a great appreciation for art, and an absolute inability to produce it."

"Appreciation is nothing to sniff at."

"Who's sniffing?" Drake asked. "You are an unusual woman."

"I want more of those mini ahi burgers."

House music—acoustic and soulful—and the bar lights moody, Liv tapped her cigarette pack on the tabletop as the phone rang. Bailey didn't answer the first few times Liv called, but finally picked up. It was just midnight.

"Hello?" Groggy, disbelieving. "It's midnight."

"I know. It's still early. You should come out."

"Liv?" And then, "Come out where?"

"Zola. The food is superb. And the drinks; she pours like a sailor."

"My god, you're drunk."

"Bailey, I'm going to need a ride. Drake too. Even sober, someone else should drive for her."

Liv started laughing, and closed her phone abruptly.

"What did she say?" Drake asked.

Liv looked at her phone, and kept laughing. "She's on her way."

Bailey hadn't bothered with her contacts, but came upstairs tucked into her coat, her jeans expensive and worn to good effect, her glasses librarian. She paused, several feet from the table, well in view of Liv and Drake and shook her head like a disappointed parent.

"Ladies, you will now buy me a drink. One drink. And while I have my drink, you will both have coffee and two glasses of water. Then we will all go home."

"Drake, this is Bailey. Bailey, Julia Drake. I'm finishing her attic."

"A pleasure," Bailey said to Drake. "Are you celebrating something, or is this dire drinking?"

"Dire *and* celebratory," Drake said. "We're working on contradictions."

"I can't remember," Bailey said, helping herself to the rest of Liv's drink, "the last time I was out."

"The bar fight, wasn't it?" Liv asked.

Bailey stared at Liv, horrified.

"She hit Liv first," Drake said.

"Well, that's true," Bailey allowed. "And she was a big meathead mother fucker. It could have gone either way."

"Oh, I like her," Drake said.

"Told you. Drake is a professor of Art History, Bailey. She thinks education will save me."

"Not save." Drake said, flagging the server. "Fix."

"She thinks," Liv amended, "that education will fix me."

"You're broken?" Bailey asked.

"Bailey, we're all broken."

"I wish," Bailey said, "that I'd been in on this conversation four hours ago."

"I like you in glasses," Liv told Bailey. "I never see you in glasses."

"Two coffees and four waters," Bailey told their server. "And I'd like a cape cod."

"Do you work tomorrow, Bailey?" Drake asked.

"Yes, I'm working lunch. No doubt the garbage disposal will clog any number of times, and I'll have to make a few phone calls to our contractor. Liv, you're starting to look like a hippie. I can't remember the last time your hair was long enough to curl."

"I'll probably shave it this weekend."

"Off?" Drake asked.

"All off."

"Don't worry," Bailey said. "She looks beautiful with a shaved head. Her eyes are larger, if you can imagine that."

Drake looked back and forth at the two of them. And Bailey said, "Where's Claire tonight? At home with Simon? I keep telling my housemate that's what she can expect. Nights at home with the baby, nobody sleeping, and nobody having sex."

"What does she say?"

"Nothing. She just puts my hand on her belly. And, to be honest, it's a remarkable argument. When she's on her back, her whole fucking abdomen shifts back and forth like he's trying to break out. He gets pissed, apparently, because her spine's hard. I've never seen anything like it—his arms and legs and head pushing up through her skin. It's creepy and amazing and kind of hypnotic."

"So the boyfriend is going to marry her?"

"I don't know what he's doing, but she's having the baby."

Their drinks arrived, and Bailey's eyebrows arched a sip in. "I do love this drink."

They dropped Drake first; waited as she walked up the steps, waved, let herself in.

"What's her story?" Bailey asked.

"Drake?" Liv wanted to smoke, but Bailey had quit, and wouldn't abide cigarettes any longer. She tapped at the door. "Dude, I have no fucking idea."

"Those boots were killer."

"Yes, they were."

"Are you going to fuck her? If you are, will you breakup with Claire first? I don't want any more fucking drama from you two. Done with the drama." Bailey braked suddenly for a yellow, tossed both of them against their belts.

"I'm not going to fuck her. What's the matter with you?"

"Right. Tonight was just a social outing with the woman you work for. Haven't you done this already? Don't you ever get tired of this story?"

"Bailey, you're yelling at me. Why are you yelling at me?"

"Because you're going to fuck that woman, and the fallout is going to be a big nasty mess. And I don't want another mess. Claire is a little ragged even without something like this."

Along Government Way, a raccoon slunk into the underbrush. Liv checked her pack of cigarettes in her coat pocket, exhaled, said, "Claire is a little ragged. That is true."

Bailey glanced at Liv. "What's going on? What's happened?"

"I don't know. Something. I'm sure something happened, but I have no idea. She just stopped talking. There's the café, and nothing. Nothing else exists."

"I think that's true for me too. I'm consumed with the café. We bought the place, and everything else disappeared. It can't go on forever, though. We'll find a balance—get a rhythm—when we figure out what the fuck we're doing. We'll normalize. We have to."

"Oh good. I'll just wait here, shall I?"

"What's the matter, Liv? Are you feeling neglected? Is that what tonight was? Another woman to focus her attention on you—fix you. You go through women like tampons. You're killing me with this shit."

"You're yelling at me again. Stop yelling at me. I haven't done anything. I didn't even flirt with her." She reached over and turned the heater off.

"Yeah, clearly she was having a miserable time." Bailey turned it on again, lowered the setting.

"Why are you mad? I can't be friends with a woman, is that what you're telling me?"

"Friends? Like you and I are friends?"

"Yes. Like that."

"Perfect. No potential for messy drama there."

"You're acting like a jealous girlfriend, Bailey."

"You're acting like an arch brat, Liv."

"Jesus, I'm so tired of women I could scream."

Claire murmured when Liv climbed into bed, stretched her arm out, pulled Liv into her, curled around her, and promptly fell back asleep. Liv stared at the ceiling fan, craved a cigarette, and imagined a belly shifting, a head protruding through skin. She could almost feel the shift beneath her palm.

She never got tired of this story. Running up five flights of stairs on Christmas Eve, desire as clear as her pulse, a chocolate bar in her coat pocket, and she's knocking on the door, rubbing her hands together, anxious for them to be warm.

There was a part of the story that she always edited, even in her own recollection. The moment where she offered to take care of them, the girl and her child, and the moment after that, the last moment, where the girl had looked at her with pity, and shaken her head.

Twenty-four

Accountancy

Bailey and Claire waited in the foyer at the CPA's office. Butterscotch candy in the dish by the receptionist, *Outside* and *Backpacker* magazine on the coffee table that fronted the yellow couch, scenic photographs on the walls, a plain, well-lit room.

They'd worn skirts, makeup, and appealing blouses. Inexplicably formal, as though they'd both come to interview for a job. Claire felt ridiculous waiting like this, and wished she'd had Patrick come by the café, where at least they could be working.

"You're nervous," Bailey remarked. "Me too. Like I'm about to take an exam."

"I'm hungry."

"Maybe we should all go to lunch, have a cocktail."

"Since when are you wearing glasses?"

"I'm out of contact solution."

"You look good in them." Smarter, Claire meant.

An energetic, sculpted man bounded into the room and hugged Claire. His hair deliberately unkempt, his cologne subtle and spicy, his suit impeccable, he extended his right hand to Bailey, while his left stayed wrapped around Claire's shoulders, "And you must be Bailey."

Bailey shook his hand, nodded.

"Great. Let's grab some lunch. Thai cool with you two? We're expensing it, of course: client meeting." He shuttled them out the door, sunglasses on, his suit jacket and no coat, his shoes Italian leather, gorgeous.

142

Patrick talked the three blocks to Thai on First—a boating trip in August—and after they'd chosen a booth, and been handed menus, and water glasses—a climbing trip to Colorado—and then he ordered a round of beer and iced coffee, and told them about biking to Portland.

After they ordered food, he paused to look at them. "This is exciting. I'm excited to be working with the two of you." He raised his glass. "To the café's continued success." They raised their glasses as well, Bailey's head tipped forward to smother her smile.

Claire put her hand on Patrick's sleeve before he could say another word. "Patrick, we only have forty minutes."

"Right. Right." Patrick looked at Bailey, and said, "I've read the reviews of the café. I've looked at the preliminary financials, and I've heard the buzz around town. You're doing extremely well, and I can help you do better. I can look at your business from a numbers per-spective—dispassionate, with a focus on long-term profitability. I can help you use your profit to bolster the business. I'll watch your expenses and draws and contributions—I'll keep as much of your money working for you as is legal. I'll handle your taxes, and your investments. Claire is doing a bang-up job on the bookkeeping. You really just need me for quarterlies and year-end, and as a purely financial perspective."

Their plates arrived: a tureen of sour soup; spinach chicken with a peanut sauce; spring rolls; red curry with vegetables; a large pot of rice. Claire ate, while Patrick fielded Bailey's questions. Patrick was a goof-ball. He talked too much and too excitedly. As a child, he'd never learned to hide his ardor. It was disarming and enticing and annoying, and it was working on Bailey. Claire felt herself beyond enticement anymore. The café was supposed to make everything better. That had been the plan. Not a distraction—the work, the investment—but a livelihood, a life. What had happened to her life?

She felt cheated now. She felt cheated of the life she was supposed to have. The field guides, and her aunt, and the writing, and the peace of their house with Simon. Something wild, something foreign welled inside her. It felt like bitterness. And fear. In the mornings, coming into the kitchen, Simon and Liv at the table with their cereal bowls, Claire knew herself to be an interruption—a Russian sentence in a Portuguese story. She'd stepped outside her life, and could only orbit now like a moon.

"Thanks," Bailey said, in the car on the drive back to the café, "for setting that up. I feel so encouraged about the whole situation. Patrick's fantastic. He's like a little kid—all ideas and energy. He talks more than I do. And you just trust him. You're with him like five minutes, and you just know he's going to take care of everything. It's fantastic, really."

"Good. I'm glad you approve."

"I do. I approve. He's fixated on you. You're aware of that, right?"

"Yes, I'm aware of that. It's not a problem."

"Of course not. He knows about Liv?"

"He knows."

"Well," Bailey said. Her feet on the dash, her skirt high on her thighs, her legs bare. "This chick told me recently that knowledge can fix anything."

Claire read to Simon for an hour. He kept hopping up to grab another book, or asking for the same one to be read again. And then he wanted more kisses, and more kisses before he finally let her turn off the light, and shut the door. He'd clung to her, his arm wrapped around her hand. He hadn't done that in months, and she felt worn down now, depleted. She ran a bath, sat on the edge of the tub, her hand dipping occasionally into the water. Could she be tepid? Is that what had happened? She'd become tepid.

She stripped and climbed into the bath. The water a breath away from painful, red patches spread up her skin. She rolled onto her side, and saw Liv in the doorway.

"Hey," Liv said.

"Hey."

She stayed in the doorway. Claire wanted to call out—she wanted back into her life, even if it required a collision.

"How was your day?" Liv asked.

"Bailey and Patrick met, and it went well. Good numbers today, especially lunch."

"I'm sorry I missed story time."

"We had a marathon session. How's the attic?"

"Coming along. The electrical is finally done."

Liv stepped forward, crossed her arms, and tugged her shirt over her head. Claire held her breath, loved this moment of exposure, the drawn torso. Liv yanked off the rest of her clothes, and climbed into the bath. Claire had shifted onto her back, and welcomed the weight of Liv's body, the tremor of the water, the inflexibility of the tub behind her. Crushed.

"Liv," she said. The word jagged in her mouth, torn from someplace. "Liv." And it burned—the water, the girl, the stress of re-entry—it burned and Claire wanted to fight, to tense against this vulnerability. Tears slipped down her face and into the bath, her foot kicked against the faucet, she strained against Liv and into her. Her orgasm hurt her, and left her laughing.

"Carry me to bed," Claire said. "Tuck me in. I want to sleep like a child."

And she did. She slept while Liv watched her. She slept when Liv climbed from bed. She slept while Liv paced and smoked, huddled into her jacket beneath the quarter moon.

Twenty-five

Daycare and other bureaucracies

Claire phoned Liv on her march back to the car, and several times while driving to the café, and from the parking lot. And as she walked into the kitchen, she gave up on the notion of a conversation, and left a message, her voice tight with fury.

At the oven, Bailey looked at Simon, his hand in his mother's, his face turned up to watch her as she closed the phone, clenched it in her fist, and growled. A terrible, rumbling growl, from which Simon looked away. He focused on Bailey, his eyes dilated.

"Come over here," Bailey said. "Tell me what's happened."

Claire stood a moment, her body moving slightly as though it were considering. She stooped down to pick Simon up, then walked over to Bailey's station.

"When I got to daycare, there was a note in his cubby that they needed to talk to me right away about Simon's socialization."

"He's a puppy now?"

"He's got a new teacher; she's been there three weeks and she's decided that Simon's autistic. She wanted me to take him to a specialist to figure out where he is on the spectrum."

"What?"

"She said he only speaks in a whisper, and refuses to play with the other kids, and never wants to do crafts. She said he's only interested in trains, and never uses more than three words at any given time."

"This is the same kid that's been reading for months?"

"The very same."

"And this teacher has some sort of accreditation to make this diagnosis?"

"She has a special ed background. That's how they said it. A special ed background. I don't even know what the fuck that means."

"Claire, you know Simon's not autistic. He's exceptional. He's amazing. He just hates those other kids, and this woman bores him. He's unhappy at daycare. That's the extent of this."

"Why won't Liv answer her phone?"

Bailey walked over and took Simon from Claire. "Go outside, and take a walk. Simon will be fine here with me. Go take a walk, and don't come back until you're calm. I don't care how long that takes. Simon and I will be here baking. Simon, will you help me bake?"

"Oh yes," he said. And he hurried to the cupboard for his apron.

Claire walked south on Grand, the wind a furious press, the cars a torrent until Manito Park, where they crawled at 20 miles per hour for the three blocks of the park. Dog walkers and runners, a fat kid waiting for the bus. She tried Liv's cell again. Why didn't she notice that he hated daycare so much he'd completely closed down? How had she left her kid in a climate like that?

She walked up the hill, past the beautiful homes and the dental offices and the looming maple trees. She walked past the piled leaves, the air smelled of wood fires.

Autistic. She'd countered with reticent and shy, and they'd looked at her like she was deluded. Poor, stupid woman doesn't even know her kid is sick. Outrageous, and the conference felt like an attack, an attack on her parenting, and Simon's nature. Her phone's disco ring startled her.

"Liv, those assholes at daycare think Simon's retarded." She told the story, disjointed pieces of her distress mixed into the narrative, making the recital more tangential than anything else. Liv didn't ask questions like Bailey, simply listened until Claire exhausted herself.

"So we're done with those fucks," Liv said.

"Yes, we are."

"How did Simon react?"

"When I came out of the office, he walked over to his cubby and grabbed his hat and coat."

Liv laughed. "He's a marvel, that boy."

"I hate myself for making him go there."

"You can't protect him from assholes, honey. They're everywhere."

Simon licked the frosting from the knife. "Hooray," he told the cupcakes. "Happy birthday everyone."

Across the table, Bailey laughed.

"Mama's cross," he said.

"Mama's cross at daycare." He dipped the knife into the bowl and licked off more frosting. "Mama's not cross at you. You want a cupcake?"

"Yes." She handed one to him. "Thank you, Bailey."

"You're welcome, Simon."

"I like this cupcake. It tastes real good."

"Thanks, kiddo. You want to learn how to bake a cupcake like this?"

He stood, nodding, ready. And said, "I'll bake them for you."

"Perfect," Bailey said. "I needed a helper."

Simon loved his blue apron, cracking eggs into bowls, and working at his station on his wooden stepladder. He loved the scent of the baking, and Bailey's laugh, and the buzz of customers in the café, and the girls who rushed in for plates and kissed him and rushed out again. Sophia, the one who brought him chocolate milk, was his favorite, blond like Bailey but short and heavy with a white apron.

Once Claire returned, Bailey made lunch for the three of them. They ate on stools, Simon with a second glass of chocolate milk, grinning with happiness.

"You'll bring him here with you," Bailey said. "We'll setup some trains in the office, and you've already stockpiled play dough and crayons and stickers and books. He's grown up around you working, and he's just fine with it. He's respectful of all of us when we're working—he was of Liv in the summer, too. We'll all be happier if he's here with us."

Claire, her eyes brimming, nodded.

ભ ભ ભ

Drake listened to the story; Liv's variation had a distinctly muted rage. "Autism," she said, "is the new ADD. Any kid that doesn't fit a teacher's notion of average is labeled autistic. I hate to tell you this, but you two are probably in for a long struggle with this kind of shit. You may have these battles with the system for years. Simon is an advanced kid. Our school system works to make all kids the same. We don't want originality and creativity and liberated thinking. We want cookie-cutter kids."

"Last week you told me education would fix me."

"Higher education. Higher education will fix you. The rest of it is a gamble."

"Jesus, Drake. Doesn't that terrify you? Aren't you angry?"

"My dear, I have speeches about this. I can go on for days. Just let me grab my flow charts."

Liv laughed. "I need a drink first."

"You and me both. Come on, my treat."

"All right, but I'm driving."

At the Lion's Lair, death metal vibrated from the walls where skateboards—painted with skulls and contorted naked girls—hung. The bartender had a tongue ring, a baseball cap, and full-sleeve vivid tattoos on each arm.

"You in this bar makes no sense to me," Liv said.

"I love this place. The music's too loud, but the drinks are stiff and the crowd is artistic and studied."

Liv watched the trio at the bar, attired like Bolsheviks, each listening to an iPod.

The bartender came over to their table, turned a chair backward, and sat down. "Julia, I'm in a contest next week—tastiest original drink—want to try out some of my ideas?"

"Of course."

"I'll make one for your friend too."

He came back with drinks that glowed pink like dainty toxins.

"Yes," Drake said after she'd tasted it. "I dig it."

He looked at Liv.

149

"Yeah," she said, "Sweet." Like syrup mixed with turpentine.

"Right on. I've got two more."

"I get it now—the appeal of this place," Liv said, once he'd gone. "If your drinks aren't radioactive, they aren't really trying."

They'd had five rounds by the time Drake leaned so far forward that Liv felt she'd practically crawled onto the table. "I want to ask you something. And I don't want it to be awkward. Just bear with my questions, will you? I'm actually headed somewhere."

"OK."

"You and Bailey are friends?"

"That's right."

"Do you know if she's seeing anyone?"

"She's single."

"And available?"

"Yes. Single and available."

"Do you think she'd be interested—do you think possibly, that she might …"

"She thinks you're hot. She told me the other night. Are you saying you'd like to go out with her?"

"Yes."

"Do you want me to arrange something?"

"Yes."

"Consider it done."

"Is this weird—my asking you?"

"Not at all."

"Good. I'll leave it to your discretion."

"Do you want me to call her now?" Liv asked. "Have her meet us here?"

"My god, no. I have to prepare for things like this. Spontaneous dating, no thank you."

"Right."

"Did you two date?"

"Nope. We've been friends since college. She asked me what your deal was."

"What did you say?"

150

"That I didn't know."

"I'm open."

"And affirming?" Liv grinned.

"Completely affirming."

"That's important. Affirmation is important."

Liv finished her drink, and considered that she hadn't eaten lunch, and it was time for dinner. "Death metal blows."

"Yes," Drake said. "Yes, it does."

In the café, Bailey held her knife up as though it were the string of a balloon. "What are you telling me? You're saying that she wants to date me?"

"Yes. That's what I'm saying." The kitchen had a battered, overly scrubbed quality to it. Each station pristine, Liv in her steel-toed boots and Cartharts always felt like a workman here, whether or not she'd come to repair the equipment.

"Julia Drake. That woman from the bar—the one with the attic—she wants to date me."

"That's right."

Bailey turned back to her station, chopped several bell peppers, her knife blade knocking rapid-fire against the counter. "She's fucking hot."

"I agree."

"And she's like twenty years older than I am."

"Eighteen."

"Eighteen is better."

Liv shifted, unable to look at anything other than Bailey's knife. It occurred to her now that Claire might have been a better emissary for Drake. "We could double if you want, or just the two of you. Whatever."

"Did she want to double?"

"I told her I'd arrange a date. She didn't specify anything except that she wanted to go out with you."

Bailey grinned. The kitchen door opened and Simon rushed in, threw his hat and coat on the chair, and ran to the cupboard for his apron.

151

"Hi, Simon," Bailey said.

"Hi, Bailey." He dragged his stepladder from the corner, and pushed it out to the stations. Bailey soaped his hands at the sink, and handed him a towel. At his station, she laid out dough and a rolling pin.

Claire came in with her laptop bag, and a box of register tape. "I didn't know you were coming to the café," she said to Liv.

"I'm arranging a marriage."

"What?"

"Drake asked me to hook her up with Bailey."

Claire glanced at Bailey. "That's unexpected."

Liv shrugged, ready to be done. "What do you say, Bailey, dinner and a movie?"

"Dinner at Luna on Saturday night."

"Just the two of you?"

"Yeah."

"Cool. I'll let her know."

Liv kissed Simon and Claire, and took an apricot scone for her trouble.

"A date with a hot professor," Bailey said to Simon. "Here's me hoping to be liberally educated."

Twenty-six

Doubles

Liv had the last of the wallboard up in the main room before the plumber finished prepping the attic's soon-to-be-bathroom. After the plumber, the only subcontractor left would be the tile guy. She'd use the same guy who'd tiled the bathroom and kitchen at Claire's—he'd been efficient, reliable, and remarkably skilled. The attic felt more confined now with the wallboard up, and like a Quaker meeting hall: sparse, stripped, silent. Her knees hurt, and she stretched toward the ceiling, tried some lunges, before finally abandoning stretches for a cigarette.

Drake met her at the base of the stairs. "I was just coming up for you. Coffee?"

"Oh yes, please."

When Liv returned—hands and cheeks wind burned—she found her mug on the kitchen table. She shuffled out of her jacket and scarf, and stretched forward toward her boots.

"Are you limping?" Drake asked.

"I hate wallboard."

"I've just sneaked up there. It looks amazing, like the skeleton of a room."

"It's tearing along, that's certain. I'll need to run to Home Depot this afternoon for materials."

"How's the plumber doing? I can't really estimate."

"He's a focused guy." And a dick. He'd told Liv that she looked like a boy, that it was a shame because she could be pretty. "If I saw you on the street with a guy," he'd said, "I'd think you were a fag."

"What kind of answer is that?" Drake asked.

153

"He's doing the work."

"You don't like him," Drake said, amused. She wore a bandana this morning; her bangs pulled back, her face pale, eyes sunken.

"He's OK."

"You should have been a diplomat. The disapproval barely registers."

"Not barely enough."

Drake laughed, and pulled her knees up to her chest.

"Am I allowed," Liv asked, "to ask about the date?"

"Yes, you may. It was fun. She looked exhausted by nine, but it was fun."

"Bakery people drop early."

"Hmm. Next time we'll try brunch."

At Benny's Pizzaria, the servers were antiheroes, prone to ignoring the clientele, and scoffing. Tucked into a baked wheat calzone with spinach, roasted garlic, goat cheese and peppers, Liv drank a beer, rubbed at her knees, felt old. Claire had checked back in. She'd yanked Simon from daycare, and suddenly reappeared in their lives, passionate and garrulous. Now she made breakfast—bacon and eggs, or pancakes with berries, cream cheese crepes, or hot oatmeal cereal—every morning. And played with them both in the evenings: board games, coloring books, puzzles, an easel with paints, and, of course, trains.

These past months, Liv's singular desire—for Claire to engage— had finally transpired, and now Liv found herself wandering off, her mind distracted, her conversation stifled. And she could not blame Claire. Liv knew her own disaffection was not revenge, nothing so petty and calculated. Not boredom either, but something more insidious, something more troubling: Liv was frightened. Frightened to enmesh herself with this woman. Frightened to care for this woman more than she already did. Frightened that any more depth of feeling would result in an even harsher abandonment the next time that Claire left them.

Abandoned. Liv had thought that word a dozen times in the last weeks. Each time it appeared in her head, she was ashamed of herself. A little child left in the dark, is that how she imagined herself? When had she become so fucking sad?

Bitter, the wind blew like a wound to the bones. In her truck, she pumped the accelerator several times before attempting to turn the engine over. Lighting a cigarette, she pulled down a side street and headed toward the bluff. It was nearly four in the afternoon, the light dim, the air smelled of snow.

Bailey answered the door, phone to her ear, and waved Liv inside. "No," she said. "I do understand what you're saying. Yeah. Absolutely. No, I hear you. Yeah. I know exactly what you mean." She scowled at Liv, shook her head. "Really, Mom, I do get what you're saying. Really. Right. I know it's outrageous. Yes. I agree with you. Whatever you decide is fine with me. Just let me know. Right. Mom, I have to go. Sure. You just let me know. OK. Bye bye."

She threw the phone at the couch. "Oh my fucking god. I don't even know if she's messing with me. It's like she has Alzheimer's. I'm having the same conversation with her all week like fucking leftovers."

"About?"

"Oh god, it's so tedious it doesn't even bear repeating. And I should know. I've witnessed every reprise. What's going on with you? Why aren't you at work?"

"I want to go for a walk. You feel like a walk?"

Bailey stared at her. "You want to go for a walk right now?"

"Yeah."

"Outside?"

"On the bluff. We can hike the High Drive trails."

"It's almost dark," Bailey said. "And it's frigid. And windy."

"All of this is true."

"God, don't make me feel bad. OK, let me grab my headlamp, and my hiking boots, and my glove warmers, and a thermos of hot chocolate. Yes, brilliant, Liv, you make hot chocolate while I get ready."

Twenty minutes later—Bailey's headlamp blinding Liv if they walked abreast—they picked up the High Drive trailhead two blocks from Bailey's house. A man and woman ran past with two Rhodesian Ridgebacks.

"Why aren't we running? You're so timid, Liv."

"Old. Today I'm old."

155

"Don't worry, tomorrow you'll be twenty-eight again. Are those raccoons?" Liv followed the cast of Bailey's lamp and saw two pairs of eyes by a pine tree. One pair a couple of feet off the ground, the other four feet higher. Bailey, pulling Liv's jacket, dragged her several paces along the trail. "They freak me out with their little hands."

Liv laughed. She could hear their footsteps, their breathing, the wind in the foliage, a train whistle in the distance.

"So, Julia Drake," Bailey said. "The word voluptuous was made for that woman."

"She told me you two had a good time."

"I almost nodded off during dinner, but that wasn't her fault. Look, I'm sorry about that drive after Zola. I'm sorry I said that wicked shit to you. I don't have any excuse, really. I misinterpreted everything."

"Bailey, I—" Liv stopped at the edge of the bluff, and stared down into Vinegar Flats. In the darkness, Latah Creek flickered as it meandered through the gully below the train track. She could see the industrial greenhouses, imagined the hum of them. *I don't know how to do this.* She was a lousy storyteller. The girl on a bridge poised with a knife, while in a fifth-floor apartment, another girl cried, ice at the edges of the windowpanes. Each girl afterward a sip of the same drink, just a sip. Could you be present and permanent all at once? "I want to be better at this."

Bailey turned off her headlamp. She stood beside Liv in the darkness, facing the valley. "Better at what?"

"I don't want to be vulnerable anymore."

"It doesn't work that way."

"I just want to know how it ends."

"Then what?"

"Then," Liv said, "I'll stop worrying about it."

"Maybe you're having withdrawals."

"Don't be an ass, Bailey. This isn't about those girls, it's about Claire."

"Because Claire is different?"

"Yes."

"How?"

156

Because I love her. "She just is."

"Tell me."

I would build her cities. "Because she's hard, complicated—and Simon. I have to work. She's not a head on a platter, you know?"

"She's not a gift?"

"I'm not talking about gifts." Liv strained her neck backward and glared at the sky. It had begun to snow. Silently, the flakes fell, fat and drifting, the night around them silent, pregnant. The head on the platter had been a sacrifice, a demonstration of power, of ruthlessness. Claire wasn't a demonstration of anything.

"I can't explain. She's a challenge. She has worth—to me—and I don't know if that's because I value her, or because she's valuable—but either way, I know it's true."

"How," Bailey asked, "will it help to know how it ends?"

"I want to know the worst thing that will ever happen to us."

"Wait and see."

Liv had more to say, but no way to communicate it. She and Claire were off by a degree, never in the same location at the same time. And patience, patience stifled her. Couldn't love be effortless too?

The snow fell around them in flurries, not sticking yet, but insulating all noise. They walked along the trail, the snow hitting rocks and ruts and wetting their faces. Ahead of her, Bailey began laughing, her face turned into the snow, her cap pulled off so that the snow caught in her hair. The sky opened onto them, rendered the world elemental and precious, and Liv and Bailey were the only witnesses, the only ones who knew.

Claire sliced Simon's grilled cheese into quarters and cut off the crust. He watched Bailey work while he ate, as though he were memorizing her technique. The lunch rush had dwindled and now Bailey plated the final order.

"Why don't the four of us have drinks on Saturday?" Bailey said.

Claire, still beside Simon, her knife tapping lightly against the counter, considered. She was curious about Drake. She couldn't name the last time she and Liv had been out together like adults. "Why not?"

"Exactly."

157

"Where?" Claire asked.

"Mizuna at eight?"

"Works for me. I'll tell Liv."

The plumber was a fuck. Without merit, tact, or skill. He kept running outside to take calls. As he came back up the attic stairs now, Liv asked, "How much longer, do you figure?"

"Another few days."

"It's done tomorrow, at bid, or I get someone else."

He chuckled. "Tough, huh?"

"It's done tomorrow."

"That could be."

She'd turned, and walked back to the floor sander. The floorboards were fir, and not too disreputable. He followed her. His hands were large blocks. Liv ignored him.

"Hey," he said.

"You can be done now too."

"I don't need your fucking permission. I'm done when I say."

"No," Liv said. "You're done now. My client's not paying for your temper tantrum."

"What'd you say?"

"Pack your tools and go."

"Who the fuck are you?"

"Her name's Liv Tannen," Drake said from the staircase. "Forgive me, I thought you'd been introduced. Liv's the builder on this project."

His face—swollen and red—trembled around his eyes.

"Mr. Rory is packing up his tools," Liv said to Drake. "His work on this project has come to an end."

Drake climbed the last stairs to the attic. "Thank you, Mr. Rory."

He wavered in the doorway, then turned and raged about the bathroom, muttering invectives. Drake stood nearby, silent, as they waited him out.

Claire wore a short black skirt, her hair had grown longer through the fall, and she tucked it behind her ears now as she curled her eyelashes. Simon stood on the toilet seat behind her, craning around her body to watch her reflection. He had gloss in his hand, and had applied it to his lips for whole minutes.

She buttoned her olive-green silk shirt. Scrunched her hair at the back, and turned to Simon. "How does Mama look?"

"Beautiful," he said. "Too cute."

"Too cute, huh?"

She pressed her face into his neck, kissed his ears, lifted him. "Sophia's coming over to play with you tonight while Liv and I are out."

"Watch some movies?"

"Yes. You can watch some movies. Sophia will make popcorn."

"I like popcorn."

"I know you do."

"What about chocolate milk?" Liv said behind them. She held a glass toward Simon. "Do you like chocolate milk?"

"Oh yes. I like chocolate milk." He took the glass from her. "Thank you, Liv."

"You're welcome, Simon." She kissed Claire's cheek. "You're gorgeous."

"So are you."

Liv wore black slacks, a woven sweater, her recently shorn hair feminized her features, softened the lines of her cheek and jaw bones, made her eyes appear brighter and larger.

In the car, her hand in Liv's, Claire said, "I've missed you. The summer seems like years ago. I've missed that kind of leisure, sitting on the deck with you, drinking wine, talking talking talking. I kind of skipped out on you, and Simon. I let the café overwhelm me. I'm sorry for that. I'm sorry I got so distracted. I won't let it happen again."

Liv leaned across and kissed her. And Claire heard her, as clearly as though she had spoken.

They met Bailey and Drake at Mizuna. They had a table in the corner, on the far side of the bar, beneath a wrapped, hanging lamp. The posh Symphony-goers had vacated the restaurant, leaving behind young

159

couples whispering to one another over scrumptiously prepared vegetarian entrées. In the corner, surrounded by wine racks, a man plucked a guitar. Her hair pulled up, Bailey wore a vintage blue dress with a choker, and looked stunning. Liv and Claire both stood a moment, staring at her, before they sat down.

"Who are you?" Liv said to Bailey.

Bailey blushed, and it made her appear younger, and even more striking. She said, "Claire Bernard, this is Julia Drake."

Drake, amused, shook hands, winked at Liv, poured wine for both of them.

"I've just been telling Bailey about the plumber wanting to murder you."

Liv shook her head.

"Is it a death wish?" Bailey asked. "Do you have a death wish?"

"He sucked. I fired him. He didn't take it well. End of story."

"Oh, Liv," Drake laughed. "You mutilate stories."

"What happened?" Claire asked, and Liv smoothed her hair before responding.

"The plumber wasn't what we wanted—his work was adequate, but plodding. He was milking the job. I told him he had to be done by Friday, and he didn't like that. He didn't like what I was telling him. He didn't like me. He had some ideas, and decided to express them. Then Drake walked up the stairs and introduced the two of us."

"He had just asked, 'Who the fuck are you?' when I walked upstairs."

"Oh, Liv," Claire said.

"What was I supposed to do, not fire him?"

Bailey laughed. "A big surly guy who doesn't like you? No, always fire those guys. Did you have to do it on your own?"

"Wow," Liv said. "Am I five? Are you parenting me, Bailey?"

"No. I don't mean to lecture. I'm worried is all."

"Well, next time I'll call for advice first."

"Before or after you hit someone with a beer glass?"

Liv tried to stand, but Claire put her hand on Liv's arm and pulled her back to her seat. "Enough," she said quietly. She looked across at Bailey, "Enough. No more disapproval."

160

They sat like naughty children, glaring at one another. Drake looked at Claire. "Is it terrible that I thought the whole thing was comical? I admired her."

"It isn't terrible," Claire said, her hand a vise on Liv's thigh. "Let's order appetizers."

They ordered three starters, another bottle of wine. Drake told the table the story of her last trip, chaperoning six students in Paris. "I had a girl lose her passport, not once, but twice. She lost it at the hotel the first time, and another guest found it two days later. The second time, she left it in a restaurant, and didn't notice until the next morning that she'd misplaced it. We had to call the restaurant, and she took a taxi over, then caught up with us at the airport. She didn't even have the decency to panic—either time."

"And you?" Claire asked. "Did you panic?"

"My god, yes. I kept thinking, I'm going to have to leave this girl alone in Paris, and she's going to walk in front of a bus, or spontaneously combust, or take a plane to Africa by accident once the embassy sorts out a temporary passport. I was genuinely terrified. I swore that was the last time I'd chaperone a trip, but this Christmas I'm going to Rome."

"Tough, your life," Liv said.

"Honestly, I'd be bored if students weren't a little crazy." Drake had an arm around Bailey, and ran her fingertips along Bailey's upper arm while she talked.

Their selection of artisan cheeses, figs and olives, bruschetta and breads, and the Greek platter arrived with a bottle of Tamarack Firehouse Red.

"Honey peppered almonds," Bailey sighed.

"This wine," Claire began, but could say no more. She bit into the goat cheese instead, her palate sparking, her face enraptured.

"What was it you said, Liv?" Drake asked. "When you ate Bailey's food, you were taking the Bailey tour?" Liv nodded. "I've thought a lot about that since you said it, and it's true. Two bites in, my senses meld together, and I'm transported to another time, another self. Music does the same thing to me. I listen to a Steve Miller song and I'm twenty-two at a house party in the tiniest little strip of a bikini, strutting around on heels as thin as ice picks. I was the hottest thing you've ever seen—Jimmy Beyer said so."

"Scents do that for me," Claire said. "That yeasty smell of breast-fed newborn. The papaya lotion my aunt used. They are transportive. That's exactly right."

"I remember," Liv said, "the first time I had a coconut. I was seven, and my grandfather split one with a hammer. He told me there'd be milk inside, and I hadn't believed him. I drank that milk and have fucking despised coconut ever since. Even the subtlest taste of it takes me right back to that carport, my grandfather in his snakeskin boots, and that nasty husk of milk."

"What?" Drake asked Bailey.

Bailey had gone still, her face a mask. "Love is like that too: a thread through your life. One you can pick up here at this table and follow backward for years. You can follow it to the bedroom of your best friend, Emma, who you made out with for an entire afternoon the spring you were nine; or to the room in the retirement center where you dusted your grandmother's teacups while she drank hot water with her knitting rested on her lap; or to the Thunderbird with the screwdriver rammed into the ignition where Doug slid your panties over your Keds and tossed them onto the floor mat."

Claire thought of the night Simon was conceived, how it had felt different, more serious. Without even making an excuse, she had pulled on her jeans, grabbed her shirt, which she slid on in the hallway outside his apartment, her bra stuffed in her purse, and left while he showered. A thread to Simon: that seedy room with a loser musician.

The afternoon she'd first met Liv, Claire had just put Simon down for a nap, and come outside to stroll through the property in the sunshine. Liv's yellow truck sat in the drive, with the door opened, and the girl bent across the seat, searching. She came upright before Claire reached her, a bottle of water tipped back to her mouth. Claire had stopped, mid stride, had gaped as though this were the rarest of creatures—a girl drinking water. Liv turned then, the water pouring down her chin and shirt, and bowed her head, wiped at her face with her sleeve, and grinned at Claire.

Or the car by the road the day her aunt died.

Or Simon in the kitchen at the café, his sleeves pulled over his elbows, rolling dough, flour on his forehead.

Or waking, that first morning, to Liv pressed against her.

In the restaurant, Claire sensed Liv's concentration, and knew Liv was watching her. Bailey's grandmother was right. Love shifts you.

"I don't know what I've been thinking," Claire said. Bailey and Drake stalled across the table. Everyone watchful. "It's funny, isn't it? I'm the one who's supposed to be keeping track of everything— accounting for us all." She wasn't drunk, or angry. She knew this. "You were just drinking water. It was simple. Easy. One minute I'm walking in the scrub and the next—" She smacked her palms together. "I don't know what I've been thinking." Claire put her fingers to her lips, and looked up at Liv. She would not cry.

"This is all code, right?" Drake said to Bailey.

"Yes," Bailey said, her voice brittle.

They drank coffee at Drake's. Seated on the plush sofas in the living room, the fire keen. Liv had walked them through the attic project, acknowledged the appreciative murmurs graciously. Strange, to guide Claire through this familiar house, as though Liv herself weren't a guest here. Liv's body buoyant, her conversation rapid and jostling like Simon's freight cars. Drake had kept her a moment in the kitchen to whisper, "She was telling you she's in love with you, right? Isn't that what she was saying?"

"The code, you mean?"

"Yeah. The code."

Liv grinned.

"Not so distracted now, is she?" Drake teased.

And so, as easy as wishing, she'd got what she wanted: Claire. She'd sat at the table, hating coconut, and then Claire had startled all of them. Liv thought then, carrying the tray of coffee to the living room,

163

that perhaps the tension in the summer and fall hadn't been entirely her own creation. She had held herself apart, she had wandered away, and she had pursued a woman who mirrored this behavior. They had stood in the corners of the same room shouting, Over here. Come over here.

"That woman who always wears a shawl," Bailey was saying, "the one who liked the oat bars—she's not due until January, and she's already huge. She and Sophia have a bet going about who'll have the shortest labor. I feel like offering foot massages every time I see these women lumbering around."

"Sophia's breasts must weigh fifteen pounds," Claire said. "I thought mine would split open while I was breastfeeding. That my skin would just burst."

"How was your pregnancy?" Drake asked. "What was your labor like?"

"My pregnancy was easy. I biked until I was thirty-seven weeks, and only gained sixteen pounds. Except for evil evil reflux, and acute absentmindedness, I had no complaints.

"I was induced a week after my due date, and that went smoothly too. Dee—my aunt—coached me, and I had an epidural; labor lasted nine hours, and was never much worse than uncomfortable. Then Simon. He had this little mullet of black hair. The most beautiful newborn I've ever seen, with long slender fingers, and perfect lips."

"You weren't afraid?" Bailey asked.

"Afraid? You're joking. The week before they induced me, I cried in the shower every day. I'd just stand in there, weeping. I thought I could fail. I'd read that labor made women the way war made men, and I thought I'd be a miserable coward who deserted."

"Labor makes women the way war makes men?" Drake mused. "What a wicked thought."

"It is, isn't it?" Claire said. "It troubled me for months. I worried I might behave dishonorably."

"Labor isn't destructive," Drake said. "War and labor aren't at all analogous."

"They both require courage," said Liv, "and sacrifice."

164

"Sacrifice?" Bailey said. "How do you figure?"

"You have to be willing to die—you have to accept that it's possible."

"Help," Bailey said, "the hyperbole's killing me."

"You're giving your body over to another organism," Liv said. "That organism takes your nutrients, saps your energy, grows until it literally cannot thrive in its environment any longer, and has to be ejected. I do think that labor requires sacrifice, Bailey. Less than it did thirty years ago, sure, but a lot can still go wrong."

"Well, this is pleasant," Claire said.

"Why don't you two arm wrestle?" Drake said, "And then we can all be friends."

"Sorry," Bailey said lightly. "Am I being aggressive?"

Inflexible and dismissive, Liv thought, and yes, aggressive as well. The beer glass comment in particular had caught Liv unawares. All evening, Bailey's behavior had been hostile, almost goading.

"You're romanticizing it, Liv." Bailey said. "You want pregnancy to be heroic—noble rather than biological. I mean, we're animals, pro-creation is a basic function of our existence."

"Not of mine."

"But that's a choice, isn't it?" Bailey said.

"No. That's a reality: an absence of contact with sperm."

"What is all this?" Claire asked, looking from one to the other.

"Bailey's dictating," Liv said.

"Liv—" Bailey and Claire began.

"You are, Bailey, you're dictating. You're telling me about my own experience as though you were qualified to explain it."

"What experience? What am I dictating? Hello, Liv, you've never actually been pregnant."

"And you're telling me that was a choice."

"Yes, you chose not to sleep with men."

"Because every sexually active straight woman chooses pregnancy? That's spurious."

"Liv, what is your argument exactly?"

"Bailey, we aren't wombats, or fucking orangutans. We're analytical and verbal, and our brains are developed enough that we're conscious of

165

parenthood—of the consequences of behavior. Humans are more than their biology. Simon is a marvel. A child with arteries and musculature and organs, but that will never explain him. You're minimizing motherhood. You're minimizing the endeavor of creation."

"The endeavor of creation," Bailey repeated, looking around the room at the others.

"You said Sophia's strongest argument was to put your hand on her belly. You're moved, Bailey, because it's moving."

Drake had leaned back in the sofa, her coffee cup rested on her thigh. The fire crackled beside them. Claire's hand rubbed the small of Liv's back, gliding back and forth like an eraser on a blackboard.

Twenty-seven

Swim lessons and other advances

Liv and Simon held hands as they hurried through the snow to the Y. The stretch of pavement beside the curb was particularly treacherous, and Simon bent his knees, leaned into Liv, and let her brace him. His down jacket, and thick navy sweatpants gave him the appearance of bulk, but he was still slight enough for Liv to lift him easily with one arm.

After the lesson, they were to meet Claire for dinner. It would be dark by then, but now the light glared off the snow so that they squinted as they hurried, spurred by the idea of a heated pool.

This was Simon's third lesson. His instructor, Stacy—a petite blond, twenty, taut, and perky—mesmerized him. Whenever she stood near him, he found it difficult to hear, and had to concentrate on each word to ensure it wouldn't get lost. Her hands were small, and nimble, and she usually held his torso while he kick kick kicked. She loved to yell emphatic things like, *Tear it up!* and *You are so awesome!* and *Way to push!*

Liv wasn't allowed in the water, but would sit on the sideline with a battered copy of *Outside*, and cheer for him. He could hear her voice, like a hum through the water. Today he was going off the diving board. Stacy had promised.

"There's my boy!" She yelled as Simon hurried poolside. "Are you ready, Simon? We're going to have a super lesson. Hop in here, buddy!"

The water, though heated, always surprised him. To submerge felt like he was being swallowed. For half an hour he cupped his palms, kicked his legs, reached with his arms, kept his head down and his eyes squeezed shut. He pulled through the water as though he had a destination.

"Yes, Simon!" Stacy hollered.

And he stroked and stroked. He stroked though her voice diminished. He stroked and heard Liv, very clearly, roaring his name. He knew their voices carried to him, that they weren't nearby. Still, when his hands touched the side, and he hoisted himself up, he was surprised to see Stacy on the opposite side of the pool.

"Simon, you did it. You swam across the whole pool. You're super amazing. You swam all by yourself."

He clutched the side of the pool, grinning. Liv was hopping up and down, and Stacy had submerged and streaked toward him like a dolphin. She lifted him from the water, and set him on the side of the pool, then pulled up beside him.

"You ready for the diving board?"

Simon nodded.

"I only let my brave, super strong swimmers jump off the diving board."

Simon looked up at her. On the other side of the pool, Liv had stood, and paced along with them now to the deep end.

His first few steps on the diving board, Stacy held his hand and walked the pavement next to him. "Liv's going to come stand by the diving board, and I'm going to get back in the water, and I'll tell you when to jump, OK? I'll be in the water, and you'll jump toward me, OK. I'll be right in the water, waiting for you."

Simon blinked rapidly. He looked at Liv, his heart somersaulting in his chest.

"Alright, Simon!" Stacy called from the water. "Take two more steps and look at me."

He took two steps. The board dipped beneath him as though it had inhaled.

"You're going to jump right to me!" She yelled. "Right to me, Simon. You can do it!"

He heard Liv behind him, and Stacy in the water, chanting, rooting, cheering. He heard his name like an anthem, and leapt off the shivering board. Water closed around him a moment later, and then her hands.

Claire had stopped by Patrick's office to give him copies of payroll reports. She would start paying quarterly taxes herself in the New Year, but for now, it was a relief to let him manage the forms and payments. She should have blown him off, and gone to Simon's swim lesson, but she'd already re-scheduled with him twice, and guilt had compelled her to come.

The reception area was deserted. Claire stepped into the hallway, lined with more photographs of isolated mountaintops, and called. Patrick appeared a moment later.

"Claire, it's a pleasure to see you. How's business?" He wore dark blue jeans, a rugby shirt, and his glasses atop his head. He touched the small of her back, and kissed her.

"Wildly busy. We've had a couple of offers to open a second location downtown."

"That's fantastic. What does Bailey think?"

"She thinks one café is plenty, and I agree with her."

"Well, it's early yet to consider expansion."

"Yes."

"You look good."

"Thanks," she said. "Here's your report."

"Great. How about a quick bite? We could grab some appetizers around the corner at Zola?"

She shook her head. "I can't. I'm eating with Liv and Simon."

"How about coffee? Lattes at Conti's?"

"No, thanks. I'm meeting them, so I only had time to drop this to you, and now I really have to go."

"Claire," he said. "You're always rushing off."

"If we weren't busy, we couldn't afford you."

Patrick stretched his arm to her hair. He pulled gently, and Claire stood, regarding him.

"This," she said, "isn't going to happen."

"Claire."

"Patrick, this isn't going to happen."

He stepped back. "Thanks for dropping this off."

"Come by the café this week. You won't believe the éclairs."

They ordered Simon a colossal burger and fries at Frank's Diner. They'd let him choose the restaurant, knowing he'd opt for the train-car diner.

"One huckleberry milkshake for the high diver," the waiter said. "With extra cherries."

"Did you really jump off the diving board?" Claire said again. "How did I miss that? I can't believe it."

"I should have had a camera," Liv said. "He was the most fearless, amazing fellow. You've never seen anything like it. He threw himself right into the air."

"Were you frightened?" Claire asked.

"Yes."

"You were frightened, and you still jumped?"

"Yes."

"Will you jump again next week so I can see you?"

"Yeah, OK."

"I can't believe I missed it."

"And he swam across the pool alone."

"What?" Claire said.

"Yeah, the whole thing."

"You're kidding."

"He was brilliant. Weren't you, Simon?"

He drank the last of his milkshake, and asked for another.

Drake steamed the soymilk, added shots, and stirred. It was ten in the morning, and Drake had called Liv down from the attic for coffee and éclairs.

"These are masterful," Drake said. "The woman's blessed."

The custard took Liv to a train station, herself in a dress and pinafore, her hair wound into braids and pinned up. She might have been four. Her mother on the bench beside her, the luggage pressed against their legs. Liv had no idea where they were. She and her mother, halving an éclair, awaiting a train.

"I asked Bailey," Drake said, "why she was so mad at you."

"Yeah? What'd she say?"

"She said she wasn't, and then she got mad at me."

Liv shrugged.

"Do you have a theory?" Drake asked.

"I don't, but clearly you do."

"I think Bailey wants a family—a child and a partner and a mortgage and a pension. I think she's wanted that life for a long time, and somehow, you walked right into everything she wanted, and—from her perspective—it seemed effortless. Maybe even something you took on reluctantly. I think she's mad that you have it, and mad that you don't value it, like she does."

Liv sipped her coffee. "Value" might just be unfortunate diction. "Are you hypothesizing?"

"Entirely."

"I think all of that is true. I don't feel like I've earned Simon or Claire, or the life I share with them."

Drake looked her over, said, "You're mad."

Liv finished her latte.

"Why are you mad?" Drake asked.

"This has nothing the fuck to do with Bailey. She doesn't get to be mad about this. She doesn't get to judge me anymore."

Liv stood up and walked outside with her cigarette. She wanted to kick the brickwork, tear up the dormant trees in the front yard. She wanted a dirty fight, blood on her knuckles, a swollen lip. She wanted to call her mother.

"I'm reading," her mother said, and Liv could picture it. The stiff blue chair beside the arched front window, the light frail, the book propped on her knee. "A novel about a basketball team in Montana. It's pleasant."

"Do you remember a train trip we took when I was four or five?"

"A train trip?" Her mother's voice sounded distracted.

"We were eating éclairs."

171

"No," her mother sighed, and Liv heard her readjust the phone. "Why would we take a train anywhere?"

"I don't know."

"It doesn't sound like us."

No. It didn't.

"How do you feel?" Liv asked.

"Worn out. How are you, Olivia?"

"I'm well."

"And Christmas? What have you decided? Do we get to meet them?"

Liv kicked at the lowest cement step. "We're so busy here. I've got several jobs going. And Claire's got the café."

"You're going to be working on Christmas? Really? You can't take two days? A flight over and back?"

"Look, I just—"

"Thanks so much for calling," her mother said. "Take care now."

"Mom—" the call ended.

Liv closed her phone, slid it back into her coat pocket. She lit another cigarette; stared at the grey sky, grey snow, the grimy cars rolling past.

The stone house seemed to strain against the very air, the wind battered against the windows, howled at the door. Liv and Simon set the table; it was six-thirty. Simon helped himself to some butter, and slathered his baguette. All three of them wore fleece vests. Claire had broiled fish, served green beans and couscous. Liv had brought home a bottle of wine, and Simon's favorite Odwalla juice.

"What did you do today, Simon?" Liv asked.

"I baked cookies," Simon said, licking butter off the baguette so that he could apply another coat.

"What kind of cookies?"

"Oh, every kind."

"What about you?" Claire said. "How was your day?"

Liv tapped her green bean against her plate. "I talked to my mother."

"How is she?"

172

"Abrupt. Distant. And I can't remember how it used to be, talking to her. I can't remember something better than this."

Claire tore her bread into chunks, studying each piece in her hand. Liv's voice had broken on the word better.

"Drake bought éclairs for breakfast, and when I bit into mine I remembered waiting at a train station with my mother. I called to ask her if she could remember where we were going, and she said she couldn't, and that it didn't sound like us. I feel like an alien with my own mother."

Simon set his bread down on his plate, and looked up at Liv. She'd bowed her head, and gripped her fork in her left hand. Her body seemed to tremble.

"Never mind, Liv," he said.

She laid her fork down, and rubbed at her hair. All those girls, one after another, and she'd never felt vulnerable; they'd provided a kind of stability: the inevitability of each of them. She knew that one would follow another. But now, in this house, with this woman, and this child, what could she rely on? Where were the assurances? All she knew anymore was vulnerability.

The previous afternoon, they had taken Simon to his pediatrician to discuss the socialization concerns of his old daycare. The doctor had laughed when they'd told him. Autism. The word spoken with defiance by both of them, as though they dared the doctor to agree. He hadn't agreed, rather he'd proclaimed Simon ahead of the developmental trends, and thriving. Regardless, Liv had left the office troubled, the concerns of parenting boundless, the feedback so various as to be completely discordant.

She'd wanted to call her mother then. To tell her that she understood—that she finally understood how much of it was guesswork, how much of it was worry. She wanted her mother to know them, Claire and Simon, but that meant more vulnerability still.

Simon, staring at her, waited until she started eating again, and then he picked up his baguette.

"I came to this house," Claire said, "to vanish. I really thought I could disappear in Spokane with my crazy mushroom-hunting aunt.

I figured I'd live here for a year, save money, move someplace cool like Austin or San Francisco. I'd been here a couple of weeks, and my aunt made dinner, and gin and tonics, and we ate and talked, and suddenly, I realized it was two in the morning. We'd sat up half the night, drinking and picking at our plates, and talking. It was like that for the rest of her life."

Claire's leg shook beneath the table. "It was never a struggle with her. She loved me. It never felt like she held love from me, or flipped it off and on. She talked to me, and taught me, and nurtured me. I didn't even know I was being nurtured, really, but I was. And when she died, when she died, all of that was gone. Overnight almost.

"I didn't know how painful it would be. Not just her death, everything: our conversations, and her work, this friendship, this mothering. My whole experience with her was an adventure."

Liv nodded, Yes, the nurturing adventure. Good fun, until your mom called you a predator.

Sprawled on the sofa, they drank hot chocolate in front of the fire. Simon brought his books in, and they all three took turns reading. Liv read *Winnie the Pooh* while Simon brushed his teeth. Claire tucked him in.

"Would you drink wine?" she asked Liv.

"If you'll have a glass."

"My mother wrote this letter to my aunt when I came here." Claire handed the letter to Liv, after she'd given her a glass of wine.

Liv read: "We admire what you have taken on. We are grateful. Claire will always hold herself apart. She is steadfast without loyalty, and loving without demonstration of feeling. She is, always, patient and controlled. You may find her difficult. We believe that she is difficult. We hope that you will understand her better than we. We hope she will thrive there with you."

Liv read the letter through again, looked up without comment.

"I found it when I went through her things."

Liv shook her head. "I'm sorry."

"Me too. It's not a letter I can imagine writing about Simon."

"It's not a letter you would write about Simon."

174

"I hope not. Dee was always generous with love. I don't think that's true of many people. I'm not sure it's true of me."

"Why would you say that?"

"Liv." Claire took the letter back, folded it, ran her fingers along the creases. "I wrote all of my aunt's field guides. She did the research, but I wrote the books that made her famous. Simon's dad is in a boy band. He's a bassist, and I slept with him. He never knew I was pregnant. I have no idea why I told you I was artificially inseminated. Shame, I think."

She crumpled the letter, threw it into the fire, and then went on: "When I was twenty, I stole $117,000 from this guy I used to nanny for in Seattle. I found the money in a broken cupboard in the laundry room, and didn't even hesitate. He assumed his wife swiped it when she took the kids and left him. Dee invested the money for me, and we made a fucking killing."

Liv cocked her head. Imagined crime-spree Claire, the ghostwriting action figure. "Anything else?"

"I slept with Bailey, in the summer. That day you got out of the car."

Ah, that one stung a bit. Liv took a sip of wine, held it, swallowed.

"Say something," Claire said.

"I'm not mad."

"How?"

"How what?" Liv asked.

"How aren't you mad? I'm a thief and a liar. How is it you aren't mad?"

"I've done things I'm ashamed of. Things I wish I hadn't."

"I don't believe you. I don't. Of course you're mad."

"I'm not mad."

"Stop saying that." Claire stood up. She drank her wine in a gulp, and pulled at her hair. She'd done it. She'd fessed to everything—and now, exposed, vulnerable, frightened—she wanted to take it all back. She wanted her secrets, and her crimes; she wanted to get away with it all.

"I'm in love with you," Liv said.

Claire heard, and her eyes stung. She felt Liv behind her.

"You've changed everything," Liv said.

175

Claire had turned, and backed away now, as though Liv were pointing a gun at her.

"We suck at this, you and I," Liv said. "We suck at love. In the end, I'll make you cry. In the end, the whole fucking thing will be grim and painful, and you'll hate me. I love you anyway. I can't help it."

Liv neither moved nor blinked, though the firelight threw shadows around them. Claire's eyes closed, and her head felt heavy and dreamy. In the end, she thought, we'll both die. All of this will end, like Dee, running along the roadside, and then a body in the snow. She leaned forward until Liv's arms wrapped around her, and she willed them both to live.

Twenty-eight

Oh and fuck you too

The letter came from Liv's mother several days later. It began with a description of the weather forecast, already begrudging the projected spell of rain, and then gave a recap of Liv's father's projects, and their nearness to completion. A bright letter, and the first Liv had received since her mother's diagnosis. And the third paragraph: *"We took a train to Montreal, you and I. You were nearly four. We were leaving to spend the summer with my mother. I had thought, at the time, that you and I might stay in Montreal. Your father came, at summer's end, and we returned with him. My mother told me that you were the most solitary child she had ever met. It was true. You played outdoors by yourself all day. They kept goats, and you fed them. Those goats followed you everywhere; you'd laugh when they nibbled at your clothes. I'd forgotten about the éclair."*

Liv thought she remembered the goats, milking them, the coarse toughness of their bodies, but it might all be invention now. The news that her mother had contemplated leaving her father did not surprise Liv, though the telling did. This was a revelatory time. All these months, she had thought Claire virtuous. What a relief then, to find she wasn't.

Liv finished her letter, and her cigarette, and returned indoors. In the kitchen, Simon sang his version of nursery rhymes along with the CD. "Merry, merry, merry, merry. Life is a big dream."

"Come color with me, please," he said.

"What are we coloring?"

"Trains."

"Ah," she said, and sat down beside him. "Then I'll need my purple crayon."

Claire emptied the dishwasher, then filled it for another load, and set it growling. They'd been slammed all morning and afternoon. She and Bailey were at the point where they could figure, within eighty dollars, their numbers for the day.

"Maybe we should get someone else for the front," Bailey said.

Claire had been advocating this for weeks. "That girl Sophia recommended would be perfect."

"The little one with the eyebrow ring? Yeah, I like her."

"Great, I'll give her a call."

Simon had fallen asleep on the loveseat in the office, wound in the fleece blanket Bailey had bought him. Bailey plated four orders, expedited to the tables, and returned to clean her station. Afterward, with no new tickets, she sat on a wooden stool and swigged from her water bottle.

"How's Julia these days?" Claire asked, banding, by date, a pile of receipts.

Bailey blushed.

"That good?" Claire said.

"It was so bad the first few times, really, really bad. I almost gave up."

"What?" Claire came round the metal table to Bailey's station. "It was bad?"

"I know, that was my reaction, too. She's intelligent, sexy, rich, funny, interested, I mean, how was this not working. But it so wasn't working. It was like being with a virgin. I wanted to stop her, and say, 'Here, let me talk you through this.'"

Claire laughed. "What did you do?"

"I decided to dump her. We had plans to go out; she picked me up in her Saab, and I couldn't even look at her. I kept applying makeup, and noticing things outside the window, and talking into my purse. It was awkward. And then she stopped the car, and turned to me, and told me to lift my skirt. I looked up at her, startled, like she was on meth or something, and then I looked outside, and she'd parked at that cul de sac down by Polly Judd Park."

Since Bailey had lowered her voice, they huddled together like schoolgirls on a playground. "So I lifted my skirt, and she reached over me and dropped my seat back. It all felt illicit and dirty and really fucking hot. Whatever hadn't been working suddenly did."

Claire straightened up. "You're telling me she fucked you in a car like a sixteen-year-old boy, and that did it for you?"

"That's what I'm telling you."

"Well, that's hard to reconcile, but this is your dirty fantasy."

Bailey capped her water bottle, and asked, "How's your dirty fantasy?"

"That's private." They both laughed. Claire returned to her receipts. Bailey stretched her back.

"Is she mad at me?" she asked.

"Ask her and see," said Claire. "Do you want to come over Saturday evening for dinner at the house? With Julia, of course. We'll have crab."

"Dinner sounds good. I'll text Julia." Moments later, her phone chimed. "We'll bring wine."

"Perfect."

After borrowing Liv's truck—she wouldn't need it, she'd said; only finish work left—Claire spent the day running errands for the café, returns mostly, goods for credit, and a trip to the Valley for a filing cabinet offered online as free to anyone who'd haul it away. That evening, she and Simon swung by Drake's to pick up Liv. Simon galloped up the stairs, ahead of Claire, and rang the bell.

"Hello, Julie-ah," he yelled when she opened the door.

"Hello, Simon." She made way so that he could run up to the attic to see Liv. "Hello, Claire. You'll want to see the attic as well."

Claire followed behind them through the kitchen and hallway. Already she could hear Simon greet Liv. The stairs were carpeted—sand-colored with reddish flecks—and they'd thrown plastic runners down to protect the carpet. Liv stood in the center of the attic, holding Simon, beaming. Overhead the fan oscillated, the walls were painted a pumpkin orange, the accents were sand, and red.

"Oh, Julia," Claire said, struck by the vibrant tone, the colors like an oriental carpet. "You must be so pleased."

"Come and see the bath."

Drake opened the door to terracotta tile in large squares on the floor, and smaller squares on the sink counter, and the shower stall. The ceiling was pumpkin orange in here as well. The fixtures gleamed. Despite the absence of furniture and the expansive space, the attic didn't feel cold, but radiant.

"It's lovely," Claire said. "Liv, your work is beautiful."

"That's just the tile talking."

"The tile's beautiful as well. Julia, what do you think?"

"I think it's gorgeous, and tragic. I don't know how I'll function, entire days without Liv's company."

"I know," Claire said, "exactly what you mean."

"Well, at least we'll have dinner on Saturday," Drake said. "And in the spring, you'll build the garage I dream about every lousy day I scrape ice off the car."

Simon helped Liv carry the last of her gear downstairs. At the kitchen door, Drake shook her hand.

"Thank you," she said. "I've enjoyed every minute. The attic is even better than I imagined."

"I'll see you Saturday."

Drake waved to them from the porch, her arms wrapped about her, her feet in green felted clogs.

"Well," Claire said, squeezed between them on the bench seat. "That's exciting."

"It is," Liv agreed. They pulled onto Maple, and coasted down the hill.

"What will you do next, that kitchen remodel?"

"I have a couple of quick jobs to do before Christmas; I've promised Hoffman I'll handle his kitchen remodel in January."

"You'll go see your folks for Christmas?"

"I will," Liv said. "And I'd like you and Simon to come too, if you're willing."

Startled, Claire almost knocked the truck out of gear. "Do you mean it? All of us at your parents' for Christmas?"

"I do."

"And they won't mind?"

"Not a bit. They'll adore Simon."

"Who's worried?"

"And you," Liv said. "They'll adore you as well."

Claire grinned. "What do you think, Simon? Shall we go home with Liv for Christmas?"

"Oh yes," he said. "Presents!"

Claire had a little belly. Nothing grotesque, but one that made her neglect cropped shirts. At another time, she might have worried, forced herself to take a long morning run in the frigid dark; these days, she found a belly comforting, a milestone for her middle thirties, for the development of her character. And Liv slept with her palm just there.

Naked, before the full-length mirror, she admired this new body—less firm, less tense—marked as it was by Simon, and now, by Liv. Rings on a tree, she thought, the scars on her shin, and knee, and hand; the rounding of her shoulders; the ache in her wrist. Stories her body kept. Privately, she'd become sentimental enough to rub her belly, like a Buddha, and dream of another child.

Liv followed the thin, harried man up two flights of stairs and into the first apartment. He'd raked his hand through his hair so many times that she'd begun to worry for his roots.

"I came in here to paint and lay new carpet, and look at this shit." He grabbed one of the cupboard doors and the door came off in his hand. "They're all like this: shoddy shit. The guy I bought this place from was a fucking cockroach. But I'm not a cockroach. People deserve better than this dysfunctional crap." He raked his hair again. Turned to glare at Liv. "Tell me, you can put some good cabinets in this apartment, and the two others on this floor. Good but affordable. You with me?"

"I'm with you," Liv said.

"You want this job? I got twelve apartment buildings now. I feel like you're doing right by me, I'll do right by you with more work. Steve told me you're skilled."

Steve the tile guy, that accounted for this guy having her cell number. Liv eased right away. Referrals were exactly what she'd hoped to cultivate.

"I'll take care of this for you," she said.

He unwound, for a moment, and shook her hand.

In the kitchen at Fresh Baked, Liv flipped the switch for the garbage disposal and nothing happened. Nothing had been happening all morning. She swore, and pulled out her phone.

"Steve, yeah, it's Liv. Hey man, do you know a good plumber? Yeah, you got a number?" She walked to Claire's desk and wrote it down. "No, that's perfect, and thanks for the apartment job. That's good of you, man. Yeah, so long."

She hung up and looked at Bailey. "You're getting a new disposal. This thing's a piece."

"Thank you, god," Bailey said.

Liv called the plumber, mentioned Steve, and had the promise of a lunch install. This town, sometimes she loved it.

"You want me to hang out and handle this?" she asked Bailey.

"Yes, please. I'll make you lunch."

"Fair enough."

In the office, Liv ate at the desk, feet up, watching the front staff glide in and out of the kitchen. She'd had a couple of lattes, and an apple fritter, and now a sausage crepe. Hives were like this, frenetic and productive. She enjoyed being on the cusp of it, an observer essentially, another drone.

"Try this," Bailey said, holding a cookie to her.

Liv bit into ginger and cream cheese and a hint of lemon. Followed a path through a field, to a dugout, a girl on a bench, waiting. Grasshoppers launched in the outfield. Liv started down the steps, the girl sat up as though to meet her. And Liv knew she tasted of ginger candy. Knew before she kissed her, that it would be searing.

"What do you think?" Bailey asked.

Liv came back to the humming kitchen, Bailey's voice. She reached out, asked, "Can I have another?"

Bailey handed her the plate of cookies, and returned to her station.

Simon used both hands and the heaviest wooden spoon to stir the chocolate and butterscotch chips with the coconut and pecans in the bowl. His mother stood beside him, her hand on his back, and encouraged him. He had been the only one to touch the ingredients for seven-layer bars; he would make dessert by himself.

"OK, now we're going to layer everything from the bowl onto the baking pan, just like we did with the graham crackers and butter and sweetened condensed milk. Let me hold the bowl, and you can scoop everything out."

He let her take the bowl, his arms stretched beside hers, as though he might be forced to snatch it back if she tried, instead, to pour the contents from the bowl.

"It smells yummy," he said.

"Oh, it does. You've done a beautiful job."

He rested his hand on her forearm, and then dug the mixture out, spreading it, as she advised, as evenly as possible over the previous layers. His first dessert, and he had made it for his mother and Liv, and Bailey and Drake, for their dinner party. A baker, officially, like Bailey. He'd have a chef's coat with his name in swirls above the pocket too.

"The oven's hot, honey, so I'll put the pan in."

He stood back, sighed deeply, watched his dessert slide into the oven.

"The light on, please," he said, pointing to the stove.

Claire turned the oven light on, and they peered in, warmed by the stove, by this accomplishment.

Liv made a shredded potato casserole, and a sweet potato soup to have with the crab. Claire was responsible for the crab, the seasonings for the table, and glazing the carrots.

It had snowed all day, thick and admirably suited to packing snowballs. Simon and Liv and Claire had had a war in the side yard to celebrate the snowman they'd spent an hour rolling, stacking, and dressing. Simon, adept at feigning injury to draw his victim close, and then whitewashing snow down the back of her shirt, had them all soggy, and hysterical.

In his hurry to let them in, when he heard Bailey and Drake stomping their boots on the deck, Simon slammed headlong into the door. Claire picked up the crying child, and ushered them in.

"Oh, Simon," Bailey said, taking the boy from his mother, after she'd handed her coat, hat and gloves to Liv. "We've brought you something to cheer you right up. You'll love it. Do you want your present?"

"Yes," he sobbed.

Drake set a handled Sesame Street bag that might well have been heavier than Simon on the kitchen table. His crying forgotten, he dropped from Bailey's arms, and stood before the bag, admiring it far too long for Bailey's taste.

"Chop-chop, open the present."

"Chop-chop-chop," he laughed. There were three boxes in the bag: the Collapsing Sodor Suspension Bridge; the docks set, complete with Cranky the Crane; and the Load and Sort Recycling Center. They'd spent something like $400.

"What have you done?" Claire said, looking over his shoulder. "Are you kidding me?"

"I'm leaving soon," Drake said. "So I had to give my present before Christmas."

"And the rest of it?" Claire asked.

"I refuse to make excuses," Bailey said. "I meant to spoil him. Do you want to set them up, Simon? Preferably in the great room by the fire, my toes are numb."

"Yes," he said, hefting the bag, "it's winter. It's cold."

She smirked at Claire. "The great room OK, matron?"

"I'm going to buy your first child a drum kit—cymbals and everything."

Drake handed Claire two bottles of wine. "Presents for the rest of us."

"Drake," Liv said, "those boots are mythic."

The boots were black leather and reached to the hem of her fitted black skirt. She wore an emerald green sweater, and a silver choker.

Arms crossed, she leaned against the kitchen counter, and winked at Liv. "This is a fabulous kitchen. Put me to work."

"Simon and Bailey need engineering assistance," Liv said.

"Then I'd better take your place at the stove."

"Go play," Liv instructed.

After Drake followed Bailey and Simon, Claire rounded on Liv. "You don't have anything to say about the gifts of the Magi? You approve, I suppose. What's next, a car and driver?"

"He's already got a couple of those," Liv said. "Now a motorized scooter, that'd be a novelty." She'd opened the wine bottles to facilitate breathing, and took a minute now to rub Claire's shoulders, before returning to the stove.

"I like your last argument, with the massaging," Claire said. "You should develop it a little."

"Hold that thought."

Bailey and Drake studied the back of the box, to figure out exactly how the pieces fitted together. On the floor, skirts hiked up, they poured over the diagrams. Simon had memorized these sets from the catalogs months ago. While they conferred, he built the dock set, incorporating the suspension bridge and the recycling center into the track. Singing to himself, as he puzzled these bright, new pieces.

He'd run to his room and brought back Edward, Toby, and several freight cars before they'd quite finished their debate.

"Look at you, Simon," Liv said from the threshold. "All set for a tragedy on that collapsing bridge."

He kept his head down, scooted around the track, narrating for the engines.

"I told you the bridge would fit," Drake said, sliding her glasses back on and kneeling for a closer inspection.

"Show off," Bailey said to Simon.

Claire called them all to dinner, and though Simon protested, declaring that he wasn't hungry, he was brought summarily to the table with tears on his cheeks, S.C.Ruffey stowed in one pocket, and the recycling truck in another.

CR CR CR

"To opportunity," Drake said, raising her glass.

"Cheers!" Simon hollered, startling her with his vigor, and his raised glass of milk. Drake toasted him, and the others followed.

"I love presents," he told them. "I don't want to eat. I want to play."

Bailey glanced at Claire. "Simon, do you want butter for your crab?"

"Yes," he exclaimed.

"When do you leave for Rome?" Liv asked Drake, spooning soup from the tureen into each of their bowls.

"The redeye in ten days."

"Are you excited?"

"Absolutely. Do you have requests?"

"Yes," Bailey said. "I want to come too."

"Could the café spare you?" Drake asked, looking pointedly at Claire.

"No," Claire said.

"Then I want a photo of that lion's mouth that Gregory Peck stuck his hand into."

"I loved *Roman Holiday*," Claire said. "We should all go to Rome."

"Next year," Liv said.

"Next year," Drake said, "I'm going to Vienna and Prague on summer tours."

"My god," Bailey said, wiping Simon's hands with her napkin, "the way you live."

"I want to play trains," Simon told them. "I don't want to eat."

"Simon," Claire said.

He pushed his plate away, and scowled at her.

"Simon made the dessert," Liv said.

"What are we having, Simon?" Drake asked.

He growled to the tablecloth, "Seven-layer bars."

"I know they'll be delicious," Drake said, "since you're Bailey's apprentice."

He looked interested.

"Do you know what an apprentice is?" she asked.

186

He shook his head.

"You're my assistant," Bailey said. "You're my go-to guy."

"Go-to guy," he whispered.

"I'm going to eat every bite of my dinner," she said, "so that I can enjoy your dessert."

He watched them for a while, and then, tentatively, soaked some of the crabmeat his mother had given him in butter, and devoured it. Before long, he was asking for more, and they helped him dig meat from the body, and pinched him with the warlike claws.

"This soup," Claire said to Liv, "is delicious. Clearly, you should be cooking more."

"It's all really tasty," Drake said. "I've missed you, Liv, at the house. It's more house than it ever was, and that much emptier."

"I miss you too. And your espresso machine."

"Harsh," Drake laughed. "Have you started your next project?"

"Monday."

"What will you do, Liv?" Bailey asked.

"Kitchen cabinets for some apartments downtown, and then I'm finishing a basement for a pregnant couple on the hill."

"All done," Simon said. He knelt on his chair now, and had finished his own crab, and taken the rest of Bailey's as well.

"Have some potatoes," Claire said.

"I don't want potatoes. I want to play trains."

"Two bites," she said.

He crammed two forkfuls into his mouth, slipped under the table, and away.

"I get it," Bailey said, "lavish presents after dinner."

"That's what you've learned?" Claire teased.

"I'm a quick study, Claire."

"Oh," Drake said, "that reminds me. I'm throwing a New Year's Eve party, and I'd like Fresh Baked to cater it. What do you two think?"

"Won't you be in Italy for New Year's?" Liv asked.

"No, we're back on the 30th," Drake said. She looked at Claire and Bailey. "What do you think?"

"We'd planned to close the café for New Year's Eve, and Day," Claire said. "How about it, Bailey, are you interested?"

"We'd use your kitchen?" Bailey asked Drake.

"Whatever's easiest. And we'd put everything out on the dining room table, so we wouldn't need anyone to serve."

"I like it," Bailey said. "I'm all for it."

Bailey and Liv cleared the table, and made coffee to have with dessert, while Claire showed Drake through the house. Drake, a professional appreciator, was a pleasure to guide.

"You've chosen startling colors," Drake said, using her glasses as a pointer to emphasize the tour's particular pleasures. "Remarkable."

She stood in the bathroom Liv had remodeled, and ran her hand over the tile reverently. "Doesn't he do the most marvelous work? Sometimes I stand in the attic bathroom and it's like looking at a fresco, I'm just mesmerized by the detail, and the depth. He's the most nondescript guy on the planet, but he can do this."

"I fell in love with Liv because of the kitchen tile."

"Do you know, I get that, I really do."

When Bailey knelt beside Simon, her loose hair brushed against his back and shoulder. "I want to be Gordon," she said. "Where's Gordon?"

Simon hopped up, and sprinted to his room for Gordon and the coaches. "Here you go." He set them on the track for her.

"Thanks."

"You're welcome, Bailey."

They looped round and round the track, occasionally dangling one of the freight cars from the crane, or running a train off the collapsed bridge.

"This track is cool," Bailey said.

"It's a real good track," he agreed.

"Dessert?" Liv asked, hefting a tray of bars and plates to the coffee table.

Drake and Claire followed with mugs of coffee. Seated, they waited for Simon to select his bar. "Hmm, I like this one."

They each chose, and then bit into the bars. Delight, a contagion, they applauded him, causing the small boy to blush, and stare at the carpet.

"You," Bailey said, "are the best of all boys."

After a second bar, he lay on the ground, with his cheek on the carpet, and ran Edward back and forth along a stretch of track.

"Are you sleeping?" Bailey whispered.

"Time to take a nap," he said.

"Will you let me tuck you in?"

"OK."

She lifted him—the recycling cars gripped in his fists, his head tucked into her shoulder—and carried him to his room.

"Her go-to guy," Claire laughed. "Liv, you and Simon can do all the cooking from now on." She poured wine for them, and sat back to savor the myriad flavors.

"I needed a night like this," Drake said, brushing her finger around the rim of her wineglass. "I feel like I've been adopted, like I've been taken into your family."

"You're telling them?" Bailey asked, returning to the room, and promptly curling around Drake on the sofa.

"I have had, this semester, the most brilliant student I've ever taught. She has the kind of mind that stuns you. She'll say something during a lecture, and I'm literally incapable of response because I'm so moved by the way she's articulated an idea, or a theory. She expresses things that I've never had more than the vaguest sense of, or perhaps never considered at all, and her observations are profound. She's just phenomenally bright, this girl."

Drake swallowed wine, her hand squeezing down Bailey's arm as though she were testing for a break. "But she's mean too. Vicious. She takes pleasure in cruelty, to the other students, to me. The kind of kid who crushed kittens."

Claire shivered, drew closer to Liv as though Drake's description were a draft in the room.

"This morning, I had a phone call from my department head. This girl had attacked her roommate, and her roommate's boyfriend while they were sleeping, with scissors. She was in custody.

"I've met a lot of gifted people—as a student, as a teacher, as an appreciator—but I've never met someone I'd name a genius, until I met this girl. And now she's done this horrible thing—and I'm not shocked, I can see how she would come to do a horrible thing—I'm just sick with it. Sick with disappointment. Sick at heart."

"And the roommate, and boyfriend?" Liv asked.

"The boyfriend's wounds were superficial, but the girl's under observation. She had deep punctures in her chest and throat."

"Deranged, do you think?" Claire asked. "I mean, do you believe in derangement as a defense for what she's done?"

"No," Drake said. "She's sadistic. I think she's a sociopath. She was always calculated in her cruelty."

"That's tragic, Drake," Liv said. "For all of them."

"Yes, it is tragic, and, I can't help thinking, worse as well. Worse than some AP headline. She had so much promise. She might have been one of the great minds."

"A customer," Bailey said, "recently told me that we'd never have another great mind because we'd medicated all the genius out of people."

"Was this girl on meds?" Liv asked.

"I have no idea," Drake said, "but I would guess not. She had no subtlety. If she were medicated, I think she'd have announced it to the class."

"Finish the story," Bailey said.

"My god," Claire said. "There's more?"

"My department head called me this morning, and this afternoon, the girl's mother phoned me. She began by telling me how we had failed her daughter—we, meaning the university, her professors, her friends, fate—and went on to say that she understood why her daughter had done what she'd done. How it was justified.

"I felt ill, speaking to this woman. I felt diseased." Drake's voice trembled, and she paused, before carrying on. "For some inexplicable reason, I argued with her. Tried to reason with her. Can you imagine? Then, I said, 'I hope prison inspires your daughter, since college couldn't.

Oh, and fuck you too.' And I hung up on her." Drake stopped again, leaned backwards, seemed to collapse into Bailey.

"Why would I say that?" She looked at Liv. "Why?"

"Why would I carve a star into my arm with a knife?" Liv said. "You were distraught."

Claire and Bailey flinched. Quietly then, Bailey said, "You carved that into your arm with a knife?"

"Yes."

"I thought," Bailey said, "it was a brand. I don't know why this seems worse."

"Because with a knife," Claire said, "it wasn't over all at once."

Liv exhaled, and said to Drake, "You've decided something."

"I think I'm done."

"Teaching?"

"I think so."

"What?" Bailey said. Claire felt it too, that Liv and Drake had a subtext not readily apparent. She'd found herself imagining Liv with a knife plunged into her arm, and in the conversation now, lagged behind.

"You didn't fail this girl," Liv said.

"I know what you mean," Drake said. "And, to some extent, I believe you. But there was failure here. Not all mine, and not all the university's, and not all her parents, or even hers. I don't know how to say that I have a responsibility for these kids. Like that girl with the passport, it would have been unthinkable to leave her in Paris unchaperoned. I would have done it because I had a responsibility to the rest of the group too, but it would have cost me something to board that plane without her."

"No," Liv said.

"No?" Drake sat up.

"No."

"I don't understand you," Drake said.

"The incidents aren't analogous. The girl with the passport didn't do anything criminal. She didn't injure anyone. I understand that you feel guilty. But you're talking about apples and rocks. And grief. You

191

have lost something, and that's huge. But it isn't everything. To quit teaching because of this girl is to devalue what you do."

Drake shook her head. "I'm not explaining right."

"I don't think that's the problem," Liv said.

Drake's voice hardened perceptibly, when she said, "What, in your estimation, is the problem?"

Claire's hand tightened on Liv's arm, a warning, and a defensive gesture.

"The problem," Liv said, "is a Christ complex."

"Is it?" Drake said.

"You're going to martyr yourself to an ideal you've created—the notion that this girl might have been great."

Drake gave a painful, mirthless laugh, and pressed against Bailey. "Oh, Liv, you're so fucking perceptive."

Bailey moved slightly on the sofa, so that she could look at Drake.

"You too?" Drake said, and laughed again.

"Dinner was lovely," Bailey said, standing.

"We can't go yet," Drake said. "Not when there's still so much to analyze. So much insight to glean." She smiled at Liv and Claire and Bailey. "Maybe I'm with the great minds now, in this very room."

"She went after kids with scissors, Julia," Claire said. "If it seems reasonable to give up teaching, then give up teaching."

Drake opened her mouth, but Claire went on, "I don't think you want to say anything more just now." For some reason, maybe the authority of Claire's mother-voice, Drake sat back on the sofa, and closed her eyes.

"Those really were good seven-layer bars," Bailey said, clearing the empty wine glasses from the coffee table.

"I know," Claire said. "He is your apprentice."

Liv had a cigarette in her hand, and rose beside Claire. Brighter, the fire climbed and dipped. Outside, the snow fell heavily, cloaking the landscape.

"Who drove?" Liv asked.

"I did," Bailey said.

"Have you looked outside?"

Bailey came to the window. "It's like eight inches."

Liv murmured, "Should you stay, do you think?"

Bailey glanced over her shoulder at Drake. "I don't know."

Drake had lain back on the sofa, her arms crossed on her chest.

"Let me grab blankets," Liv said. "Or you could sleep in the spare room?"

"Here's fine," Bailey said. "I'll help you."

They passed Claire coming from the bathroom.

"They're going to stay," Liv said.

Claire nodded, patted Bailey's back. "I'll get some pillows."

At the cupboard, Liv handed Bailey several large blankets, and grabbed two comforters.

"I don't know what to say," Bailey said.

"She's had a rough time," Liv said. "It happens. And I went after her, a little."

"Still," Bailey said. In the dark of the hallway, she held Liv, the blankets and comforters like another person between them.

Twenty-nine

Simon's kitchen of civilized people

Simon woke to a buzz in the air, electric, and knew it was snowing. At the window, he saw white in every direction. The fir and pine branches crushed beneath it. Next door in his mother's room, they slept. He grabbed his slippers, and his fleece pullover, and ventured down the hall.

In the living room, he stood next to his new track, reveling in the fact of it, the sleek newness. He had dreamed of Cranky lifting recycling cars. He had dreamed of Bailey bossing Gordon. Before he knelt down, he noticed a pair of bare feet sticking over the arm of the couch. Slowly, he backed toward the kitchen.

At first, he didn't recognize the woman at the table, drinking from a coffee mug, her hand in her hair, her head tipped forward. She shuddered, and looked up at him.

"Oh, Simon," Drake said. "Good morning."

"Morning," he said, and went to the fridge for milk.

"Last night it snowed and snowed," she said. "So we stayed here."

He climbed the step stool, and grabbed cereal and a bowl. Behind him, she went on talking, as though he needed explanations. All he wanted was to play with the new track, to go round and round in that comforting way, the noise of the magnets, and the wheels on the wood.

"Three glasses of wine," Drake was saying. "Not so much really. Just enough for me to wake at 4 a.m. discomfited."

She drained her coffee, and stood for another cup. She'd wrapped a blanket around her shoulders, and another around her body like a towel. Her voice, like the river, seemed to snag at the edges.

194

"I was belligerent," she said, "and deliberately hurtful. And if you'd seen the look on their faces, well, you'd know, wouldn't you?"

He poured milk into his bowl, climbed down from his chair, and returned the milk to the fridge. From the drawer, he grabbed a spoon, and climbed back onto the chair, poised to enjoy his breakfast.

"It's like I was raised by wolves or something. Is this what comes of being so often alone?"

The cereal crunched in his mouth in a gush of milk. Like bones, he thought, like little skulls. He might have been devouring his enemies.

"You know the funniest thing," Drake said. "It never even occurred to me to quit teaching. Not until the moment I said it last night. And then I had to run with it. I'd fumbled, and I couldn't say it. I couldn't say I was graceless." She reached across the table. "But I can tell you, Simon. I can tell you, she surprised me. Liv's like a comet. Her intensity is that bold."

Footsteps behind him, and then an arm snaked around Simon's torso, a python squeeze, as Bailey nuzzled his face and set him giggling. "I wish I had a fleece pullover," she said. She held him a moment, and then poured herself a cup of coffee.

Simon had jumped off the chair, and run into the mudroom. He returned with two fleece coats, and two knitted caps. Each woman took her share, and thanked him gratuitously.

"How'd you sleep?" Bailey asked Drake.

"Really well until 4."

"The snow maybe."

"And the wine."

"I'll make breakfast," Bailey offered. Simon perked at this. "If Simon will help me."

"I'll help," Simon said, and stood beside his chair, keen to begin.

"Finish your cereal," Bailey said. "I have to pee."

She returned with sweatpants for herself and Drake—on Bailey they were nearly Capri's they were so short—and wool socks, and Henley shirts. Simon thought they could wear those outfits camping, or robbing banks. Drake went and stoked the fire. They commented several times that the kitchen needed a wood stove.

Soon the oven warmed the room. Bailey let Simon season the potatoes before she spread them onto the baking sheet. "We'll have waffles, I think. Sausage and bacon, and potatoes, and some kind of marmalade—tell me this house has a stockpile of marmalade. Where's the jelly, Simon?"

"Down here," he said, and pointed to the basement door.

"Lovely," Bailey purred, and sent Drake to reconnoiter.

Liv woke to Claire's brown eyes. After blinking a moment, Liv smiled, and curling her knees up, pressed them into Claire's belly.

"Why are you awake?" she asked, noticing again, Claire's remarkable warmth, like a furnace, the burn of it.

"I don't know," Claire said, yawning.

"Is everyone up?"

"Probably. Bailey certainly is. I've heard her rummaging in the cupboards."

"She's probably freezing. Girls wearing skirts in a snowstorm."

Claire pressed two fingers against Liv's star scar, felt Liv stiffen. "Does it hurt?"

"No. It feels weird, is all, the skin tingles."

"You did this with a knife?"

"Yes."

"Over a girl?"

"Yes."

"All at once?" Claire asked.

Liv hesitated, raised her head.

"Did you cut your arm all at once?"

"Yes." Liv, fully awake, dropped her legs, their bodies entwined. The bedroom was cold, improbably tidy (in preparation for their dinner guests), and too light for sleeping.

"Are you ashamed of it—the scar—now?"

"Ashamed of people's reaction more than anything."

"We do suck at this," Claire laughed.

"Yes."

"I thought you might sleep with Julia," Claire said, her palm on

196

Liv's jaw, each scrutinizing the other. Their faces shiny with sleep. "I worried about it."

"Nothing there. I like her fine, except her arrogance—those little flickers she can't quite smother—burns me just here." She pointed at her throat.

"Here?" Claire kissed her neck.

"No."

"Here?"

"Lower," Liv said.

The house smelled of sausage and bacon. Simon held the egg timer in his hands, and appeared to be vibrating in his chair. Drake toasted bread, beside the renewed pot of coffee. And Bailey turned from the stove with another plate of waffles, and had to clear space on the kitchen table. Liv and Claire came in together, like guests, neither wearing hats.

"All done," Simon shouted, and ran to the stove.

Bailey opened the oven door, and forked a potato. "Tender," she said, nodding. "Good call, Simon. Everyone to the table."

Drake passed marmalade, eggs, the coffee pot. They ate as though for the last time, and to avoid speaking. Simon hummed and licked whipped cream from his waffle.

A snow day, Claire thought. Light blazed through the windows; from the table, they could hear the fire in the great room. Liv, distraught, with a knife, carving constellations; this body broken for you, take you all of it. They were poles, Claire and Liv. Claire more likely to puncture someone with scissors than take a knife to her own arm. Around the table the plates emptied, and they ate without looking at one another, except for Simon, who watched face by face, puzzling them like another set of tracks.

Thirty

On parents

Liv used birch for the cabinets in the apartment building. The harried landlord, Kyle, met her on the second floor to let her into the apartment. Since her last visit, he'd taken down the old cabinets, painted the entire apartment, and laid new carpet.

"I like birch," he said, when she showed him the wood. "Thought I'd save you some time dismantling the old shit."

"I appreciate that. This job should go quickly."

"Just come across the hall if you need anything. I'm painting in 2F today."

She'd precut and stained the wood in Claire's garage, having taken measurements when he'd walked her through the place, so today was just an assembly job. A tarp to protect the carpet, another for the counter, she had the job finished by two o'clock.

Kyle came across with her to inspect them. He opened the doors to each cabinet, moved them back and forth on their hinges, admiring them.

"A simple thing," he said. "You know, good work is simple and functional. That's all people need. I like this. This is good work."

"I'm ready for the next one," Liv said.

He grinned at her. "How long'd it take for prep?"

"A good day."

"Steve's never pointed me wrong," he said. "Never once."

She finished the second set before seven, and Kyle took her out for dinner. They ate pork soft tacos, and ordered a pitcher of Manny's Pale Ale at The Elk. Still in their gear, reeking of paint and stain, they devoured their food, threw their voices above the din of the large, bustling room.

"Am I allowed to ask how you bought apartment buildings?" she asked.

"Settlement money. I used to work at Costco. One of the palettes fell on me. Thought I'd never walk again. Big, big fucking money."

"You don't mind the hassle—maintenance, and tenants, and all those rentals?"

"Nah, it keeps me busy. What the fuck else would I do? I got a good plumber. I never touch plumbing. I just paint and do the grunt stuff. I like it; five years now." He sipped at his beer. "What about you? You like independent?"

"I do. Good luck with clients so far. No shirkers or assholes." Their table was below the portrait of the white hart that Simon called a reindeer. When their waiter—a serene guy in a baseball cap and leather cuffs—passed, they ordered another pitcher.

"And you like Spokane?" Kyle asked. "Not too provincial for you?"

"It's not so bad."

"I used to hate this fucking place. Wanted to burn it down. Felt like a chump living in this no-place town. Then I had kids. You got kids?"

"A boy."

"How old?" he asked. Kyle had paint in his radical hair, and on the backs of his arms.

"Three."

"Shit, just a baby. Mine live on the mountains all winter—snow-boarding—and the lake all summer waterskiing. It's a cush life for them. Made me appreciate this place, showing it to them. We camp and kayak all the time. It feels good, growing old here. I'm settled in. What about your boy? What does he like?"

"Trains."

"He like dump trucks? I got a bunch of dump trucks from when mine were little. I'll dig them out for you. Mine spent hours trucking dirt from one hole to another. They wore capes when they were his age, with cowboy boots, talked about being super heroes. Love that

199

shit." He grinned again, pulled at his hair, knocked his unlit cigarette against the tabletop.

Three staff up front, two in the kitchen, a dozen customers in line, and the tables full; Claire pulled the coffee while the girls took orders, plated pastries, and bused tables. Bailey expedited crepes to the tables. Claire had just called a triple macchiato when a berry scone smacked her in the shoulder. Bewildered, she looked at Sophia, who stood nearest her behind the counter, but Sophia's gaze was fixed across the counter at a girl.

"Fuck you!" the girl screamed. The café went still, and Claire took in the girl's blackened eyes, her pink-streaked blond hair, her fury. "Look at you in your fucking lip gloss, trying to be respectable." She pitched half a lemon bar at Claire, but missed, hitting a carafe instead with a sickening splat. "My girlfriend got nine stitches, you fucking bitch!" Claire had not moved, had not processed even the berry scone, when Bailey and Drew came running from the kitchen. The girl pointed at Bailey, and flung the rest of the lemon bar. "That's right, Amazon. I've found you fuckers, and I'll make you pay. Smashing glasses into people's heads! You sick cunts! You twisted—" Then Bailey and Drew had her, and sailed through the door with her, leaving a strangled, defiant *bitches!* in their wake.

When Claire saw Simon in the kitchen doorway, she began to move. She approached the tables and murmured apologies, offered everyone a free coffee from the bar. Sophia came round to clean up the smear of lemon bar, and Miss Jenkins suggested, in her powerful stage whisper, that perhaps they should wear raincoats behind the counter because you never knew when deranged girls were going to be slinging lemon bars at you, and you never could be too careful, and almost at once, Claire felt the strained scene from minutes before morph into a kind of rowdy misadventure they'd all enjoyed. The most unexpected performance anyone had seen in ages. Claire brought their free coffee, and Drew and Bailey returned to much applause.

It almost felt like a promotional gimmick, as though they'd staged the entire thing. On her way to the kitchen, Bailey winked at a two-top of regulars, and told them it was now safe to eat their lunch. Claire slung more free coffee, refused to let herself consider the fact that the girl had recognized Bailey—had looked right at her, and called her an Amazon—had mentioned a glass smashed into a head, had commented on her lip gloss being a disguise.

After Sophia punched out, she asked Bailey and Claire if they were going out later, maybe to smash some glasses into some people's heads. She laughed and left before either of them could respond. Claire finished counting the till, and looked at Bailey.

"When did it happen?"

Bailey told her the story.

"A bar fight," Claire said, watching Simon eat goldfish from the back of a dump truck. "My god. And now this girl's come to the restaurant."

"And the police have a report on her, and she'd be insane to come back."

"Because this morning she wasn't crazy enough? Oh, Bailey. In front of the customers and the staff. Right in the middle of the lunch rush." Claire stood, rolled her neck, and pressed her fingers into her temples. "When does it stop? I thought I only had to worry about strange girls in bathrooms."

Bailey looked drawn, haggard. Claire had noticed this previously, but hadn't commented. For herself, the same could be said. It wore them down, this business, successful, relentless, consuming. Could one screaming girl spoil the entire endeavor?

She stared about her. Initially, she'd planned to paint this tiny office something funky, like polka dots. Something to enliven the place: a cell, more than a room, with one thin, high window, two 3-drawer file cabinets, a squat wooden desk, a loveseat, and two corkboards full of notes, recipes, magazine articles, and employee schedules. But she hadn't had the drive to empty the space, even for a couple of days. She had the drive now. Field guide to your relationship: start by tidying the office.

Claire put the bank deposit into her bag with her laptop. Nobody could have predicted this, and she hadn't been exactly forthcoming about her own indiscretions, not even with Liv. Claire sat down beside Bailey on the sofa, and punched her in the thigh. "If pink-girl comes back, I hope it happens while I'm in Portland."

"Yeah, I'll see if I can arrange that," Bailey said. "When do you leave?"

"Thursday afternoon."

"You worried?"

"Of course."

"You'll be fine. Simon's the perfect ice-breaker."

"He's in bed by eight."

"They might be too."

"There's nobody like Dee," Claire said. "It makes meeting people harder. They all suffer from comparison."

"My grandmother did that for me."

"It's such a stupid thing to miss, but it's what I think of most. I miss that she was alive."

"Sophia's mom was at the house last night, yapping at her about gaining too much weight. And this thing with the crib—on and on about why isn't the crib assembled, and why hasn't Sophia bought bedding, and what kind of mother doesn't have the nursery ready and waiting, and, I swear to you, I nearly bounced her. She was just so mean about everything."

"I called my mom to tell her what the publisher said, about this being the best field guide he'd read, and she said, 'Wouldn't Denise be pleased?' like I was a traitor." Claire laughed.

"What would Denise say?"

"She'd say, 'Now we're ruined.' And pour me a shot."

They gave Simon gummi bears for the plane ride; he ate them four at a time. He'd never flown on a plane before. The attendant gave him extra pretzels.

His mother had let him pack his bag—he'd been allowed to take seven trains—and his favorite red pajamas, and his shark t-shirt, and both Curious Georges.

"Do you see the mountains?" Liv asked.

He pressed his face against the window. "Clouds," he said, wondrously. "They're right there. Look. There they are."

When he climbed back into his mother's lap, reclined against her chest, and pulled her arm across his belly, he told her again about all the presents of trains Santa had left under the tree for Simon. Because Santa knew all about this adventure, the clouds, and gummi bears, and luggage, and Santa thought Simon had maybe not brought enough trains with him, and would need more.

On the ground again, more surprises still: they didn't have snow here, and he didn't have to wear his heavy coat, and this green car rumbled as they drove across the long Steel Bridge. People on bicycles zipped past the rental car at stoplights, and the cranes were as high in the air as the plane had been. Liv's mom had promised to make a special dessert in Simon's honor, Angel food cake. He said this over as they drove, Angel food cake.

When they pulled into the drive, Liv's parents came out to greet them. Bundled in coats, hats, gloves, and scarves. The mother was small, like Liv and his own mother. The father had a beard, and a voice full of money. Simon hugged them, took Liv's mother's hand, and led her back toward the house. "Simon's special treat," he told her. "Angel food cake."

The father helped Liv and Claire carry the luggage in; he'd patted Claire's back when he'd hugged her as though she were a child. Comforting, she thought. Steady, and kind, and comforting. She followed behind his plaid wool coat, and paused in the entryway of the house, as he did, to set the luggage down. A two-story, with leaded windows, green shutters, white exterior paint, a gabled roof, an apple pie and baseball home.

He hung their coats with the rest, and pointed to the shelves where they could leave their boots. Indoors he wore a blue cardigan, slippers, a frank and untroubled oldness. Upstairs then, to separate rooms, their luggage and themselves left to be idle until supper. Supper, Claire smiled. Her parents still celebrated cocktail hour, knew only rubes used words like supper, and rube.

She left her bags by the bed, and wandered down the hallway, to the room the father had indicated would be Simon's. Liv's old room, Claire recognized. Maple bookcases, a navy bedspread, plain curtains, a desk and lamp, all rough and sturdy, like the girl herself. On the bedspread, a bedraggled teddy bear, and a hand-carved racing car lay against the pillow.

"Homespun," Claire said, when Liv stood behind her.

"Yes, ma'am." Liv took her hand, led her downstairs to the kitchen.

Simon stood on a chair at the counter, and licked the remainder of the frosting from the bowl. At the oven, Liv's mother tested the pork chops.

"You girls go sit," she said. "The table's set, and now we're ready to eat."

Claire rinsed a cloth to clean Simon's hands and face. She couldn't remember if she'd been told their names, the mom and dad, *The Tannens*. She almost laughed. Nerves, she knew. She couldn't remember the last time she'd desired approval so deeply. She'd wanted Liv's this much, and Denise's. A rare thing though, in her experience: to feel assailable.

The mother wore a knitted cap. Her face looked pouchy and yellow, though her eyes were bright with pleasure, and she moved nimbly. A formidable woman, Claire thought, one to intimidate teenagers.

They passed green beans, salad with artichoke hearts and candied walnuts, and warm brown bread round the table. On the walls hung prints of Japanese characters. Marinated in a spicy barbeque sauce, the pork chops had a sharp tang.

"Good flight?" the father asked.

Liv nodded. "Simon's first."

"That right, Simon?" he said. "How'd you like flying?"

"It's a great adventure."

"What'd he say?" the dad asked.

"He said, 'It's a great adventure.'"

"Did he?" The father inspected Simon.

Simon had macaroni and cheese with diced ham, and a side of raw carrots. He ate happily.

"Your father baked the pork chops," Liv's mother said.

"They're tender," Claire said, "with a kick."

The father inspected her. "Yes," he said, and dabbed at his mouth with his napkin.

"We'll have a tour after dinner," the mother said. "Give Simon a chance at the tree."

"What are you working on, Liv?" the father asked.

Liv told him, and then they discussed the café, and Claire's field guide, and Simon's swim lessons, and as the mother served Angel food cake with coffee for the adults, and chocolate milk for Simon (she'd scouted his preferences in a phone conversation earlier in the week) the father pointed his fork at Claire and asked, "So, do you want to hear Liv stories? And, if so, would you like the emergency room escapades, or the detention dramas?"

"Yes," Claire said. "And both."

"Enlighten me, if you've heard another version of any of these," the dad began. "Well, the first trip to the emergency room, Liv was four, and she'd come down the slide and cracked her head open on the playground cement. Second time, she was nine—"

"Seven," the mother said.

"Right, forgot that one. She was seven when she fell from the tree and broke her right elbow. Nine when she had two teeth knocked out fighting at school. Twelve when she broke her leg. We never did know how exactly, had something to do with that Lewis boy." He scowled at Liv, then winked.

"Sixteen, she got a concussion in a car wreck. Seventeen—god, we went three times that year: two broken fingers, stitches along her left elbow, and, I've forgotten the last one."

"Appendicitis," Liv said.

"Right, appendicitis."

Claire had been taken once, with a fever so high that her parents had convinced themselves she had a critical infection. She'd been given Tylenol, and sent home.

"The breaks to the fingers, and the stitches?" Claire asked.

"Fighting," the mother said.

Liv shrugged, finished her cake. The frosting had cream cheese in it. Simon had already devoured two pieces, and drunk his milk.

"Detention for fighting as well?" Claire asked.

"In high school," the father said. "For fighting and skipping. In junior high, she was suspended for building a bomb in the girls' locker room."

"It wasn't a bomb," Liv said, wearily. "Fire crackers, and silly putty, with a long fuse, so they'd blow after everybody left."

"Instead?" Claire grinned.

"The putty smothered the fuse, and the smell of burnt plastic brought the gym teacher running."

"Did the fire crackers ignite?"

"Nope."

Claire laughed.

"Tell them about your time in detention," Liv said. "They tell these stories like I'm the only kid that got in trouble in school."

"Smoking," Claire said. "A couple of times for smoking; once for cutting; several times for mouthing off in class; and most frequently for tardiness. I was always late."

"See," Liv said.

"As a parent," the father said to Claire, "has your opinion about your behavior changed?"

She put a brown sugar cube into her coffee, and stirred. "Not yet. I have a lot of affection for that girl I was, and pity too. But I'm relieved that I have a boy."

Liv's parents laughed. "Oh, my dear," said the mother, "it's just another kind of trouble."

"Another kind of worry," the father added.

"An other," Claire said, "still keeps it from being like mine."

The mother turned to Liv when Claire said this, but the father regarded her, his fingers rubbing at his beard as though it were unexpected.

Liv and Claire cleared the dishes, filled the dishwasher, while the parents entertained Simon. Delighted with them, Simon filled the house with squeals and giggles.

"What were the fights about?" Claire asked.

"Girls."

"So early?"

"From the beginning."

Claire considered this. "And your parents?"

"They've known for so long, I can't remember a time when they didn't."

In the kitchen, a motif of yellow roses, Claire touched the wallpaper, this house made her nostalgic: for the child, Liv, and something unspoiled in herself. Liv's hands, then, at her waist, and Claire closed her eyes. Listened to the murmur as Liv held her mouth against Claire's throat, intoxicated—two ungovernable girls alone in the parents' kitchen—and yes, transported.

The tree had to have grown in the living room. No one could have squeezed such a behemoth through a door or window.

"This is the biggest Christmas tree," Liv said, "that I have ever seen."

Uninterested by the lights, ornaments, or scale of the evergreen, Simon played with a set of old wooden trains on the floor by the nutcrackers.

"I've been reading to him," Liv's mother said.

"Has he read to you?" Liv asked.

The parents both looked at Simon.

"Simon, do you want to read a book?" Claire asked.

"No, no, thank you."

"Just this one about trains?" Claire asked.

He hopped up from the floor, and climbed into her lap. She turned the pages while he read. The parents, vigilant, incredulous, the mother whispering, "But he can't have known this story, Olivia. This is one of your books." As though this were a magic trick, amazing, but staged. Afterward, she brought Simon into her lap, and had him read aloud from the pile of books beside her.

Claire scrutinized the ornaments while the parents carried Simon to bed, and tucked him in. A strange house, and strangers, but he kissed her and Liv goodnight, and wandered away from them willingly.

"What are you parents' names?"

"Dennis and Susan."

"Great, now I can stop thinking of them as 'the parents.'"

"I have this sense that they like Simon."

"It's possible," Claire said.

"He's certainly at his best. I thought my mother would go into shock when he sounded out *expedition*."

"He's a faker. His story at home—*Jane's Perilous Expedition*—is an old standard. But he is in rare form, same as you. How does she seem to you?"

"It's hard to say. She looks better, more energetic, but she might just be high on Simon."

"Are they winding down?" Claire asked.

"Oh yes. And you? Do you want to go out?"

Claire shook her head, astonished that it had never occurred to her that they might escape for a few hours on their own.

"Are you sure? For a drink, or some music?"

"Shouldn't we all be on our best behavior?"

"What does that mean, no fun? I wasn't raised by Congregationalists, my folks are cool with us going out."

"No," Claire said. "Tomorrow night, maybe. I think I'm done for the night as well."

"Ready for your own bed in your own room?"

"Are they light sleepers?"

"The lightest."

"Fun."

Liv turned off the lights on the tree, and wandered through the main floor, checking that the doors were locked, and the rest of the lights off. In the darkened entryway, Claire waited for her. Standing there, she could see it, Liv at seventeen, dropping from her bedroom window to the grass below, to meet some girl in some park, to huddle among the trees, or in a car, both of their hearts unstable.

"Your boy," Susan said from the landing above Claire, "is precious."

Claire had started, and gasped. She cleared her throat, willed herself not to laugh. "Thank you."

"Has Liv explained to you about the rooms?"

"No," Claire said. "She hasn't."

"My great aunt played poker. She was incorrigible, lied just to hear herself talking. Every one of her stories ended with a close friend of hers getting shot. I admired her." Wood on the landing shifted with her weight. Claire closed her eyes a moment to listen to the house— the fan blew air from the furnace, shifted the pale curtains in the room beyond them. "She said the worst thing a host could do was deny any guest the right to a room of her own."

Claire opened her eyes, peered into the dark. She could see Susan's teeth, a glare from her eyes.

"So I always give each guest her own room, and allow her to choose." She'd started back up the stairs when she laughed. "Good night, girls."

"Asshole," Claire whispered to Liv.

"Told you I wasn't raised by Congregationalists."

"Your mom's great aunt had a lover."

"Several."

"How many girls have you brought home?"

"Dozens."

"Liar," Claire said.

"Come to bed."

"Say you're a liar."

"I am."

Liv took two steps and looked back, a negative: her shorn hair, her luminous eyes; her neck, her arm on the banister, her forehead; light reduced her to fractions.

"Wait for me," Claire said, thinking of boot prints in the grass, a girl checking her watch, anxious that it might not happen.

Thirty-one

Cancer mom and other bedtime stories

Liv followed the light downstairs. In the rocker, her mother slept with her head bowed. On the glass table at her right, potpourri and an African violet, a blue-jean quilt across her lap. Unsure whether waking her or leaving her would be crueler, Liv hesitated, and her mother woke.

"You're here," her mother said.

Liv stepped forward.

"I thought I couldn't sleep," her mother said.

"I'll help you back upstairs."

"No. Maybe the couch."

Liv grabbed the folded fleece blanket from the back of the couch, attempted to swaddle her mother before she'd even managed to lie down. Cold, and imperiously white, this had always been Liv's least favorite room. Stark and sterile, vaguely medicinal; she sensed that now more than ever, tucking the blue-jean quilt around her mother.

"Well, this is snug. You'll get the light?"

"I will," Liv said. "Do you need anything to drink?"

"I'm fine. I should sleep, I think. And if I don't, I'm already downstairs."

"You look good," Liv said, perched on the edge of the sofa. She wanted to touch her mother's face, but resisted.

"Yes, cancer's made me glamorous."

Liv reached out, rested her hand on her mother's forehead, brushed her fingers over her eyes. Touched her as though she were Simon.

"You don't have cancer anymore."

210

"Or my breasts."

After the scare, Liv thought. After the scare is worse. You think you're free, that you have survived the worst of it. Your mother's anger is harder than her cancer.

"I've never met a Simon before."

"I hadn't either."

"She could be your double."

"My stand-in for my film career?"

"Yes, precisely. She's the sort of woman—capable—a consummate woman, isn't she? Adept at everything, the sort of person the world seems to be generous with."

Liv smoothed her mother's eyebrows, followed the course of her cheekbones.

"I've always envied," her mother said, "women like that: powerful."

"Sleep," Liv whispered.

"And you with a child, Olivia. You with a child was worth staying alive for."

Her breathing deepened, her eyelids fluttered, but Liv kept tracing her mother's face. Kept thinking the word, *Indelible*.

Thirty-two

Naps with Chinese dinosaurs

Almost before anyone else sat down, the bacon had been consumed; Susan had laughed at the empty dish, patted Simon's head, and made more. Now he ate pancake shapes at the table with huckleberry syrup and slabs of butter. Liv and Dennis were taking Simon to the OMSI exhibit of China's Ancient Giants—they'd offered to take him to the zoo to ride the train, but he'd elected the dinosaur exhibit instead. They'd take the convertible, despite the month, just for the adventure of it.

Simon had imagined a car that changed—that converted—into a robot, and so, standing in the garage looking at the blue Dodge, was disappointed. Once they pulled onto the road, he freaked completely. He worried that his hat would sail away, that he'd be blown out, that someone could grab him and he'd be lost.

Claire had stayed with Susan to help bake pies, and de-bone the turkey. Susan had advocated that she was perfectly capable of handling all the prep for dinner on her own, but she had been overruled by the others, and been awarded her assistant by coup.

In the backyard, with the recycling, Claire stood admiring the fence, the tidy garden area, the lawn furniture. Dressed in a sweater, she found the Portland morning bearable, and like most visits, clear-skied. She heard the door open behind her, and said, "The weather always behaves when I visit."

"Then you should come more often," Susan said. "In the spring, Simon would see the zoo at its best."

She carried two garbage bags, and Claire relieved her of them. "Dennis loves this yard. This summer, I slept in the hammock while he weeded, and watered, and mowed. Laziest summer I've had in decades."

In the kitchen, Claire peeled and cored apples, zested lemons, chopped anything laid before her. They listened to Hank Williams. Susan told stories of her own children when they were small. Seemed, now, grateful they were grown.

"Olivia was a great contrarian: everything was its opposite. 'Close the door' meant 'open it' and 'no thanks' meant 'absolutely' and I spent years interpreting every sentence. Later, when she was in school, and bored, I wondered if she needed complication in order to thrive. You know what I mean? Simple would never be enough for Olivia. I don't know if that's a bad thing or a good thing, but I think it's true.

"She brought home her first girlfriend for Thanksgiving dinner when she was fifteen. I'd never actually considered the possibility, but in comes this chatterbox, and Olivia looking at her like she's Helen, and I thought, 'well, yes, I see that alright.'

"It was one of the most eventful dinners we ever had. The pumpkin pie exploded, and one of the dogs discovered the box of chocolates, and this chatterbox asked if she could have a glass of wine." Susan laughed. "And I was young; hardly forty. My god." She brought Claire several sweet potatoes and yams to cube. "Speaking of wine," she said. "We should have a glass. Red or white?"

"Red."

"Good girl."

Susan poured a cab, set the glass at Claire's station. Sliced a baguette, Irish cheddar, one of the skinless apples. Claire wondered if Liv's succession of girlfriends had monikers, and what her own might be. *Simon's mother*, in all likelihood, or *the one with Simon*.

Susan, wheezing, sat down beside Claire, and admonished her for working. Forced her to rest and indulge. They finished the cheddar before anything else, and Claire sliced more on the plastic cutting board with the unrelenting German knives.

It was painful to her, sitting like this with an older woman, listening to stories, drinking wine, tending the kitchen subversively, as though this were the field trip, and the others on some tedious errand.

"Were any of them serious," Claire asked, "Liv's girlfriends?"

Susan pulled another chair round to her side to rest her legs. Her little socked feet hung off the end of the seat. Above her, a crocheted canary swung on fishing line from the ceiling.

"I know she had one on the east coast that got serious, serious enough for her to leave school after they broke up. And Meg. Meg was serious. I wondered at the time—" Here she looked up at Claire, and dropped the story.

"Wondered?" Claire prodded.

"Some things are effortless—skills, athletics, friendships—for some people. Meg and Liv were like that: effortless, intuitive. I remember thinking they must've had each other wiretapped. But, like I said before, simple was never enough for Olivia."

Claire drank her wine. Wondered where Meg had fallen, high school or later.

"Tell me something," Susan said.

"Alright."

"Are you lonely, raising Simon on your own? Besides Olivia, I mean. I remember being so lonely when my children were little, so isolated. I don't mean to be maudlin, or self-indulgent, but cancer has been like that for me too. Illness is, I suppose, isolating. Have you been lonely as a mother?"

"Not while my aunt was alive. She died last January. Afterward, I got so frightened. At the funeral, I started shaking and couldn't stop. Terrified what would become of us, Simon with just me to look after him."

"You lived with your aunt?"

"Yes."

"I stayed with my mother for a summer after Olivia was born. She kept a goat farm in Canada. We were like frontier women. I hated every goddamned minute of that arduous summer. Deprivation. That's the way I remember that summer. No men, no conversation, no newspaper. We had the radio, the goats, and each other, and none of that was enough."

ભ ભ ભ

After the museum, Dennis drove them to Peanut Butter and Ellie's for lunch. Simon talked endlessly, to everyone in the café, about 'the king one' that he'd seen at the exhibit. Liv had bought him a model of the Tyrannosaurus, and Simon waved the model about, roaring at the rest of the patrons.

They ordered two peanut butter and banana sandwiches with local honey, and a peanut butter and marionberry special on French toast. Simon ate his, and half of Dennis' and drank a milkshake as well.

"Growth spurt," Dennis remarked, as Simon finished off their carrots. He growled at Liv. "The king one eats your face!"

"If your dinosaur doesn't, you probably will."

"Simon," Dennis said, "what say we go home, and I show you my trains?"

He paused, nodded, and walked straight from the restaurant, leaving his coat, his hat, and his party behind. Liv sprinted after him, found him on the sidewalk admiring a yellow bicycle with a banana seat.

"Look, Liv," he said. "Look. We'll ride it?"

"We're going to ride in the convertible."

"No. No, thank you. I want to ride this."

"You'll pedal?"

"OK."

Proprietarily, he placed his hand on the bicycle, but Dennis came out, spoiling their getaway, and Simon let go of the bicycle, followed obediently behind to climb again into the topless car.

Cinnamon. More than any other scent, cinnamon informed the kitchen. Claire grinned with wine, her sentences brighter, the air around them lightened, comical. She'd been frightened of this woman. Intimidated, as though it were her own homecoming rather than Liv's. She'd been afraid of Susan's anger. Instead, she found herself baking pies, sewing a turkey, opening a second bottle of wine.

"Mama," Simon shouted from the porch. "Mama, look."

They'd grabbed him, and Claire could hear the scuffle, the soothing pitch of Liv's voice, the child struggling as his winter layers were removed. "*Mama!* Stop it. Let go. *Mama! Help me.*"

She and Susan came out of the kitchen, their aprons greasy, and officious, as though they were lunch ladies on a cigarette break.

Liv had lifted Simon to remove his shoes, and held him straight out like Superman. He extended his dinosaur to Claire.

"Look, Mama. The king one."

"Scary," she said.

He roared, and—released, finally from Liv's stranglehold—lunged at his mother.

"The king one," he whispered as he curled into her. "I like this one." The dinosaur kissed her as she carried Simon upstairs. His blanket pulled to his chin, he was asleep before she left the room.

Liv had followed her up, and waited in the hallway.

"You've never seen anything like this kid ate today." Liv cocked her head, grinned. "Oh, you're drunk."

"Yes."

"How's Mom?"

"Drunk as well."

"Yeah? Interesting afternoon?"

"I've been hearing all about Meg, and the chatterbox, and the suck-face kisser, and the summer of goats and deprivation, and the time you and Kimmie Grant played chicken on the freeway, and the cops brought you home and your mother slapped you."

"Wow."

"You were a troubled kid."

"Do you think, maybe, you should lie down for a nap too?"

Claire considered this. "Yeah. I think so." She walked into their room, and crawled beneath the comforter, still wearing her apron.

"So, Mom," Liv said as she walked into the kitchen. "What's with the drunken indiscretions?"

"Claire wasn't indiscreet. Come sit down."

"How did you know about the suck-face kisser?"

"Bailey told me."

"Traitors," Liv said, sipping her mother's wine. "This is good."

"Have the rest of Claire's glass."

216

"They're both out."

"Your father too."

"You'd better have a nap as well."

"I don't nap."

"Uh huh," said Liv. "The turkey smells amazing."

"I've never sewed a turkey before. It was a little gruesome, holding it together."

"If you tell all your stories this trip, what will we talk about next visit?"

"Oh, Olivia, I could never exhaust all the stories about you. I forgot to tell her about the time you started the brawl at the basketball tournament, and then won the Best Sportsmanship plaque."

"Mom, you get that I like this woman, right?"

"Yes, darling, I have sussed that out."

"Great. So we're done with the mayhem stories. I'm actually not that fucked-up kid from high school anymore. I haven't been rushed to the emergency room, or hurt in a fight in—" Liv stopped, closed her eyes, exhaled. "She doesn't have to learn it all at once."

"Let's watch a movie," her mother said. "*Best Years of Our Lives*? I'll make some popcorn."

When Simon woke, his dinosaur clutched in his fist and pressed into his face, he remembered that he'd been promised a look at some trains, and had somehow been derailed into a nap.

He hopped up and went in search of Dennis. The house smelled of food. In the family room, Liv and her mother were asleep on the sofas, an old black-and-white movie playing unheeded on the television. Simon wandered into the kitchen, and watched Dennis pull a steaming metal tray from the stove.

"What you got in there?" he asked.

"This," said Dennis, picking up the child, "is a turkey. We're going to have it for dinner, as soon as everyone else wakes up."

"No, I don't like this turkey. No, thank you. I want to play trains."

"Trains, is it? Well, we might be able to find some trains for you."

Down a flight of carpeted stairs, Dennis pulled the string for an overhead light to illuminate his workshop. Biplanes, racing cars, roadsters, sailboats, engines, cabooses, trains with coaches, vehicles elaborately designed and carved and glued.

"Wow," Simon breathed. "I like these."

He squirmed down to walk the line of the worktable, his hand outstretched, though carefully withheld, from the vehicles. They were larger—wider and taller—than any of his Thomas trains. The coaches on the train were attached to one another by hitches. A solitary engine made of cherry wood sat last in the line. Soft, beautiful lines.

"I like this one," he said, then looked up at Dennis.

"Go ahead and try that one," Dennis said.

Simon picked the engine up, ran his hands over the wheels and stack, and the hitch at the back. Then he knelt and drove the train along the cement floor before the worktable. Smooth and fast and strong, a good train. With this train tucked under his arm, he returned to his examination of the remainder of the vehicles. In the end, he picked two cars, a train with coaches, a caboose, and the cherry engine. Dennis said yes to the lot, and helped Simon carry them back upstairs.

Claire woke at ten that night, and tore down the stairs, flushed with apologies. In the living room, sitting on the floor before the tree, Dennis and Simon played with trains. A bright fire burned in the hearth; Bing Crosby on the stereo.

"I've missed dinner," Claire said.

"Simon and I had bowls of Honey Nut Cheerios."

Claire glanced around, instantly blissful. "I'm not the last to wake?"

"Look, Mama," Simon said. "Trains."

"Liv and her mother fell asleep watching a movie."

Claire knelt down beside Simon to admire his train. "And the turkey and pies?"

"In the fridge. We'll have them tomorrow for Christmas. No harm to anyone."

"These are beautiful trains," Claire said. "Did Dennis make these trains?"

"Yes," Simon said. "He made these real good trains for Simon."

"Simon and I have had a little walk, and played with trains, and had

218

some hot chocolate with whipped cream—the real stuff, naturally. We've had a lovely Christmas Eve, isn't that right, Simon?"

"Oh yes."

"Thank you," Claire said to Dennis.

"The purest of pleasure, all of it. I've been spoiled all evening."

Simon stayed up another hour; fell asleep in his mother's arms. Liv was up by then, disoriented from sleep, and sat at Claire's feet, rested her head on Claire's legs. Dennis made hot chocolate for them as well, and lit his pipe contentedly, the smell of vanilla tobacco enticing.

"I can't believe I slept for so long," Liv said, again. "Crazy."

"I think I was drugged," Claire said.

"Mom put something in the wine? That would explain everything."

Her father chuckled. A log broke in a tantrum of sparks. They were dwarfed in the room between the fire and the colossal tree.

"What happened to the Carpenter's Christmas CD?" Liv asked him.

"You'll hear it the moment your mother joins us."

"Swell. I was afraid maybe it broke, or was smuggled from the house, or something."

"Not in time, no."

"I was looking forward to eating a sewed turkey," Liv said.

"Me too," Claire sighed. "We were like renegade doctors putting that poor bird back together."

"Why did you let me sleep so long?" Susan asked, shuffling into the room, a fleece blanket wound around her.

"Except for Dennis," Claire said, "the rest of us have only just woken."

"Claire thinks you drugged the wine."

"A sound theory," Susan said, sitting at the hearth. "Cereal for dinner?" This to her husband.

"We enjoyed every bite."

"Did he like his trains?" she asked, noting the many wooden vehicles on the floor.

"Oh yes," Claire said in a voice piped to mimic her son's. "These are real good trains."

"Do we all get a Christmas Eve present?" Liv asked.

"Yes," her mother said. "Yours was a long nap."

Thirty-three

Clutch

Claire couldn't remember Simon climbing into their bed, yet here he was, lying perpendicular to her and Liv, with his arms thrown wide like a savior of men. She checked her watch, and marveled that she had slept until nearly seven. Certainly they'd been drugged.

"Are you awake?" she asked Liv.

"Hmm?"

"Are you awake?"

"I need coffee."

"I need to shift this little guy."

Liv sat up and they moved him between them, his eyelids flickering, a little moan as he scrunched himself into a ball.

"I'm in love with your parents," Claire said. "And this house." Their room wallpapered in blue and white stripes, watercolors of girls in gardens in dark frames, a sewing machine by the window, piled with fabric. The air smelled of cloves.

"Mom's so much better. Last time I was here, breathing seemed to hurt her. Yesterday she was drunk, and carousing in the kitchen."

"The one with the hair," Claire said smirking.

"Jesus."

"You dated someone they refer to as *the one with the hair*. I love that."

"You don't get to be alone with my parents ever again."

"I don't think you being present is going to stop them."

"Trust that." Liv stretched across Simon, and kissed her, rested her

220

forehead against Claire's chest. "I'm glad you're here. It actually feels like Christmas."

"Pigs in a blanket?" Liv asked, incredulous.

"For Simon," Dennis said.

"But we always have monkey bread."

Her father filled her coffee mug, added milk. Behind him, her mother laughed.

"Told you," she said to Dennis. "We've made both, Olivia."

His hair in rogue waves, Simon came downstairs in pajamas, holding his mother's hand.

"Where'd my trains go?" he asked, hugging each adult in turn. "Where'd they go?"

"Check the tree," Susan whispered.

He ran into the living room, and they all followed, gathered just beyond the threshold to listen as the small boy screamed at the presents: the bicycle with training wheels; the legion of trains, and cars, and sail boats; the paint set; the stockings on the mantel crammed with gifts; the Thomas comforter and pillows; the puzzles and candy.

"Hooray," he said, hopping toward them. One by one, he pulled them into the room, placed them on the chairs nearest the tree, and brought them gifts.

Susan, in her robe, sat on the armchair in the guest room while Liv and Claire packed their luggage.

"I slept for half your visit," she said.

"We did too," Liv said. Simon needed two suitcases for all his loot. Liv had taken the bicycle apart, wrapped each piece, and stowed it in the suitcases with the rest of his hoard. "Free babysitters, and we didn't even go out, get trashed, and kick some ass."

"Goals for next visit," Susan said. She sniffed, and both Claire and Liv looked up, alarmed. "I'm fine, really. I'm just fine."

Claire reached her first, and lifted Susan from the chair, scooped her up and held her.

221

"I'm fine," Susan assured them, the sobs wrenching, sonic. "I'm fine."

Claire rubbed the mother's back, and thought of muscles, glands, veins, organs: the marvelous body and its desperate living. And she held on tighter, touched the stubble of new-growth hair, ached.

Thirty-four

A little something

Bailey held the door opened, her grin tore her face in half. Hair jutting from a clip, pajamas plaid and baggy, she looked beautiful and jubilant. When she squeezed Claire, she whispered, "I'm so glad you're home. I fucking hate Christmas."

"You should have come with us. I got drunk with Susan."

"Did she tell you Olivia stories?"

"They are so harsh. I kept wondering what my nickname would be."

"Neo, in all probability."

Struck, Claire paused, wanted to kiss her, shook the impulse off.

"Come and have a beer with me," Bailey said, moving backward into the house. "I've missed you."

"I've missed you too." Claire slung her coat across the back of the sofa, followed Bailey into the kitchen, heaved herself up on the counter. Admired, again, Bailey's immaculate workshop: the bowls and plates in frontless cabinets, the copper pots gleaming on shelves above the stove, the herbs and spices in uniform glass bottles. She took the beer gratefully, saluted. "What happened with Christmas?"

"I bitch all the time about the hours, and how exhausted I am, and how burned out, and how managing people sucks, but after three days lounging around the house I was in withdrawals. Life outside the café is pretty fucking boring."

"That's funny, I wanted peace and sleep. Liv asked me to go to a club for drinks, and I kept coming up with excuses not to." She swirled her beer in the bottle, kept her head bowed. "I liked them; I hadn't expected to, but I did."

"I know."

"I came away envying her. Except for the cancer, their life felt idyllic."

"Her who? Susan or Liv?"

"Both. How is Julia? Has she called from Italy?"

"I've talked to her every day," Bailey said. "Her life's idyllic as well. I've missed her too."

"Missing is good."

"Says the woman who spent the holiday with her girlfriend and son. I wish I'd gone to Italy. I could have flown over for a few days. I never do anything spontaneous. I've been knocking around here for three days, wishing I'd been bolder."

"I don't know. Owning your own café seems spontaneous and bold to me."

"You minimized the risk considerably."

"Speaking of that." Claire took a folded envelope from her pocket, handed it to Bailey.

"What's this?"

"A little something."

Bailey tore off an end, and pulled out the check. She sat, staring at it. "I don't understand."

"A shareholder distribution. The café is doing really well. I'm sorry you didn't have it before Christmas." Claire doesn't mention that the bank check was drawn from her personal account, not the business account. This is her gift to Bailey.

"This is for me? $20,000. Are you for real?"

"Yes."

Bailey jumped up so quickly that her stool toppled as she rushed into Claire's arms, shrieking happily. "This is amazing. I'm so happy I might vomit."

"Let go of me first."

"Claire, can we really afford this?"

"We can."

"For both of us?"

"Yes."

Bailey jumped up and down, lifting Claire with her.

Thirty-five

Manito run

Liv dug the toes of her boots into the snow to drag the sled and Simon up the hill. Around them, dozens of children raced past on sleds, inner tubes, skis, and snowboards. At the base of the hill, dogs—off lead and hyper—bounded at toppled children, and each other. The hillside gave an excellent dash, then a long gradual finish. On the other side of the park, at the duck pond, boys played ice hockey. Lightly, snowflakes fell upon them.

Simon had covered his eyes the first few runs, slid, deliberately, off the sled at the bottom, and fake-cried. Each time, as Liv pulled him back up the hillside, she'd turned to see him grinning at her. Woodstoves burned across the street in the residentials, and days like this—the air iced and draped in indigo—she loved Spokane.

At the top of the hill, she pushed him, cheered, and raced after him, reaching the plateau just as his momentum languished. As they turned, began the climb again, he said, "You want to slide with me, Liv?"

"Yes, but your sled is too small for both of us."

At the peak, Simon jumped off his sled and ran to another boy, said something and pointed back at Liv. He had to repeat whatever he'd said before the boy nodded, brought his inner tube with him as he followed Simon back to Liv.

"We're swapping," the boy told her, handing her his double inner tube, and taking Simon's sled.

"You sure?" she asked the boy.

"Yeah. Take three rides, then we'll swap again."

She agreed. Simon had already climbed in front, and instructed her to get on. They were down so quickly that she almost hadn't had time to enjoy herself before she remembered she had two rides to go. Simon hefted his side of the inner tube, grinned across at her: "Hurry. Let's go." And began to run back up.

They sledded for two hours, then stowed the sled in the truck and walked around the park, watching the hockey players; the women wheeling SUV strollers through the park with down-filled sleeping bags, like blinds, around the children; the kids building snowmen.

He kept his gloves on, and his scarf and hat. Occasionally, he'd nail her with a snowball. On the drive home, he fell asleep in his car seat, his head nodding abruptly as though sleep might give him whiplash. For a while, she drove around, stalling, enjoying the ridiculous yard displays, the electric candles in windows, the frantic lights.

Tomorrow she'd meet with Kyle to handle a couple of quick projects, and then she'd tackle the kitchen remodel for the retired Army colonel, Hoffman. Good, interesting work, all of it, and she hadn't advertised, or had any famine spells. In fact, all of her customers had paid quickly, and praised lavishly. On side streets now, the fan roaring, Simon jolting occasionally beside her, she pronounced herself all grown up: practically thirty, a partner, a parent, a reliable and steady wage-earner, a reputed builder with a growing customer base. The girls of the summer were fable now. Stories her parents would tell. As relevant as firecracker bombs, or basketball brawls. Some crazy shit she got up to when she was wild.

226

Thirty-six

With with-child

Simon stood on the toilet seat, watching his mother's reflection. He'd applied lipstick repeatedly, to his tongue as often as his lips. He loved this part, the preparation. The smells, and trial of outfits, and his mother's wet hair, the curl and style of it—she looked most beautiful damp, and in progress.

"I want to come," he said again.

"You'd be bored." She hovered, inches from the mirror, her mouth opened as she applied eyeliner.

"Please." Plaintive, the way she hated. "Please, Mama. I want to come too."

"You're going to stay with Agnes, and sleep on bunk beds."

"No. I don't want to."

His mother's brown eyes—direct, cautionary—focused on him. He grinned at her, as though there'd been some misunderstanding. It didn't matter to her that she was beautiful. She didn't seem to notice.

"Tomorrow we'll watch movies on the couch in our pajamas, and eat popcorn and ice cream."

He'd lost already. He knew, and almost didn't mind.

"These?" She held up a pair of dangling blue earrings, then a pair of silver ones. "Or these?"

"The silver," he said.

She nodded, put the silver ones on, examined herself again. "Well?"

"Your dress."

"I guess I'll wear the black one."

She returned to her room; he paced behind her, certain she'd choose something other than the black. She'd wear the dark purple.

Clothes lay strewn on chairs, the bureau, the bed, the floor. With no place to sit, he stood beside her, looked where she looked.

"The black, don't you think?" she asked.

"The purple."

She bent, touched the purple dress, glanced at him. "The purple? You're sure?"

"Yes."

She tried the dress again, and shut the closet door so that the full-length mirror aligned properly. "This one?"

"Yes."

He would remember her like this always. His mother in stockings, a deep purple dress, the earrings he'd chosen flitting about her like summer insects. Both of them occupied, yet expectant, the party and the bunk beds, and the adventure ahead.

Liv's new pinstripe slacks were impeccably tailored. She looked, even in her own estimation, fucking hot. She'd left this much too late, but hoped to please Claire so much with the product, that the lack of foresight and efficiency might be forgiven.

They'd arranged to meet at the party. Now, in her new button-down silk shirt, and polished black shoes, Liv left the store amidst a clutter of people who were downtown for First Night—a tour of galleries, shops, and restaurants, replete with bands, food, and activities for the entire family—with their distinctive First-Night buttons and their best intentions.

Liv had been recruited to help Bailey shift her entire kitchen to Drake's. An hour's work had turned into three, and somehow Liv had forgotten that she still needed to pick up her pants—they'd been held for alteration—she'd arrived just before the store closed. She held her breath now, hurrying down the sidewalk, and exhaled slowly, a tension headache on the perimeter, threatening. They should have had the party at Bailey's: all that shifting, only to be shifted again tomorrow.

She checked her watch again, began to jog.

CR CR CR

Claire envied smokers. Their unapologetic stall tactic, standing on the cusp, poised, observant, not quite ready to enter with the rest. She hadn't spotted Liv's truck, but couldn't wait out here for long. Bitter, insidious, the wind snarled at her.

Despite herself, she compared this party to the dinner party Bailey had thrown in her honor. Decades ago now, when she hadn't particularly cared for Bailey, and was terrified to find the life she had known crumbling beneath her. Another ten days, and her aunt would be dead a year. Time compressed and expanded around her like a brilliant accordion. Soon enough, Simon would be in school. There, on the sidewalk before Drake's house, she could see it, her future. Simon in a school play at ten, a soccer tournament at fourteen, theater his junior year. A Fresh Baked Café franchise would open downtown, another out north, and one in the Valley. Bailey would recruit bakers from all over, her own reputation highly lauded. Liv would incorporate, hire employees, and take on design jobs as well as building ones. Eventually they'd let Bailey buy the business, and they'd move to Portland, dabble in real estate, retire.

"Hey, beautiful. Aren't you freezing?" Her face flushed from cold and haste, Liv stood before Claire, bouncing in her dress shoes, and rubbing her hands together.

"Yes," Claire said. Only just remembering they were going to a party, that the event had yet to transpire.

Liv kissed her, quickly, unexpectedly, and reached an arm around Claire as they dashed up the steps, urgent to get indoors, to join the revelry.

Liv took their coats, and disappeared, leaving Claire to navigate the crowds. She hadn't expected this many college students. Couldn't remember the last time she'd seen such a horde. They were everywhere, in suit jackets, or button-down shirts with ties, the boys holding wine glasses solemnly, the girls in short dresses that glittered, their laughs like hatchets.

From the doorway, Claire could see a hierarchy to the arrangement, the students placed against the walls, standing, those perched on the furniture, those sitting on the floor looking up at Drake and two paunched men in sweaters. Drake saw her, called out, and waved. The students turned, applied their critical thinking skills, and began to write a character for the person they observed.

Claire waved back, edged through the fringes of the group, and into the dining room. Laid out on the dining table, delicacies on platters, several varieties of wine; on the floor in buckets of ice, beer; and a ruddy, soccer player fellow in the corner aspiring to bartend. He winked at Claire. Said, "Gin and tonic?"

"Is that your specialty?"

"Absolutely."

Eventually Simon would be one of these. "Okay," she said, walking over to him.

He poured an improbable amount of gin. Winked again when he handed it over. She took her drink into the kitchen.

"You're here," Bailey said. From the stove, she pulled two baking sheets loaded with brown-crusted croissants. "I'm experimenting with marmalade."

"I'll guinea pig."

"Let it settle," Bailey said, the pitch of her voice dropped to indicate seriousness. Claire had to be bullied into letting food cool properly.

"Have you left the kitchen?"

"This is my last batch."

"How many people are here?"

"Julia says seventy."

"Jesus." She'd taken a sip of her drink, and asked Bailey now for a larger glass. In the fridge, she found several tonic waters, opened one to mix the drink properly, sipped again.

"OK," Bailey said. "Try this."

Claire bit into the croissant. Walked into her aunt's bedroom: English muffins on a morning tray, Simon with his trains in Dee's bed, giggling over some picture book she read to him. They both looked up when she helped herself to a bit of Dee's muffin, sat on the edge of the bed, insinuated herself.

"No?" Bailey asked, her voice anxious.

Claire couldn't speak, and put her hand, instead, on Bailey's arm, for support as much as reassurance. She wanted to take another bite, but feared the moment she interrupted them, knew herself to be an outsider.

"Is she alright?" Sophia's voice brought Claire back to Drake's kitchen. Claire let go of Bailey, watched the exponentially pregnant girl cross to the sink and fill a glass with water.

Another bite, then, as she tried to place that morning. Not the last, surely. But late, Simon in the red-footed pajamas he'd got for Christmas the previous year.

"Drink this," Sophia said, handing her the water. "It'll help. Bailey, are these magic croissants? If you're lacing the food, that'd certainly explain what I just witnessed in the solarium."

Claire swallowed the water. "No, Bailey, they're glorious. Really exceptional."

Bailey shook her head. "Says the woman who blanched after a single bite."

Liv added their coats to the pile on the bed in one of the guest rooms. Back in the hallway, she wound through a group of girls blocking the staircase as they waited to use the restroom. On the top step, one of the girls flashed—that was how it seemed to Liv, that the girl flashed like light on a lake—and whispered, "Hey you."

"Happy New Year," Liv said, as she pressed past.

Downstairs, in the front rooms, Liv wandered through the professors and students—uniformed in spite of their efforts—keen for her tribe. Hailed then, a hand on her arm, she tensed instinctively, found herself in Drake's enthused embrace, which included back-thumping as though they were politicians.

"I haven't had a chance yet," Liv said, "to hear about Italy."

"My god, the best trip yet."

"I want a full report."

"Coffee this week?" Drake asked, "Or drinks?"

"Either, or both." Liv threw an arm over Drake's shoulders. "Where's the liquor?"

Drake led her to an earnest kid at the bar in the dining room.

"My friend, here," Drake said, "would like a mojito."

He juggled the limes, bantered. Liv examined the spread, plated herself spinach quiche, and a butterscotch scone. She'd finished these, and scooped herself some ice cream—strawberry with balsamic vinegar—when Drake brought her drink over.

She took a sip, struggled to get it down. "Subtle."

"He's got a mean pour that kid."

"Yeah, here's to lost fortunes."

"Cheers," Drake said, holding forth her own mojito. "How's your mother?"

"Remarkably well. It was a good visit. Have you tasted this?"

Drake served herself some ice cream, ate it with one of the finger-like cookies. She murmured and swooned.

"Oh, we're taking a trip to Napa in three weeks—Bailey and I. I have to remember to thank Claire."

"For?"

"Making the trip possible."

Liv nodded, knowing nothing of the money, she assumed Claire had simply approved Bailey's time away. She scooped more ice cream; ate a croissant that tasted of orange peel. Three young men dragged Drake away to tell a story of a decrepit church in Italy. Abandoning her mojito for a beer, Liv made her way through the crowd to the kitchen.

On the threshold, she noted, for the first time all evening, Claire. Her dress a deep purple that slid across her breasts and hips, and drew a line to her legs; her dark hair swept from her face strategically, her eyes lit, her lips stung and glossy. Liv had crossed to her without considering, kissed her as though they were alone in the room.

"Hey," Bailey reprimanded. "There's a fetus present."

Liv felt Claire kiss her neck, and looked over at Bailey. "That strawberry ice cream is ode-worthy."

"Ode-worthy." Bailey laughed, folded her apron, and stowed it in one of the many boxes Liv had hauled in that afternoon. "Charm, girl, charm."

Bailey's dress was green, sleeveless, fell at the top of her thigh, and set off her eyes and hair. She'd pulled the blond into a bun, and looked like a French assassin.

"Hi, Sophia," Liv said. The girl leaned on the counter, rubbing at her back.

"Hi," she said.

"Is he boxing?" Claire asked.

"Kick boxing."

Claire led Sophia to a chair. "Here," she said, and massaged the girl's shoulders, down to her lower back, making circles with her palms. Liv thought Sophia might cry.

"What are you naming this kid?" Liv asked her.

"I can't decide. His dad thinks he should be called Chase. That's a game, not a kid."

"What do you like?"

"I like Riley."

"Riley," Liv said. The girl was ringed like Saturn. "Yeah, I like that."

"Thank you," Sophia said. This time, her eyes did tear. "You guys are so sweet. I wish I felt more like a party. Right now, all I want is a sedative, and a Caesarian."

Bailey returned to the kitchen after a brief exploration. "That kid at the bar is murdering the cocktails."

"Yes," they agreed.

Sophia brightened, reminded them she'd bartended her way through school.

Bailey stood at the head of the table, and took the praise like a champ. Smiled at their compliments, dipped her head graciously, and encouraged them to try a quince scone, or a slice of the chiffon cake, another scoop of ice cream. Claire felt that it really should be midnight, and checked Liv's watch just in case her own had lost track. Refused to believe it wasn't even eleven.

Sophia made a wicked cocktail. Claire had another gin and tonic with extra lime. She had a terrible impulse to wander among the revelers as though they were safari animals. Play-doh student creatures transitioning toward their grownup shapes, lubricated enough at this point in the party, that they'd shed their coyness, and seized instead their vigor. The professors were drunk, seated in chairs in the living room, their knees apart, their faces flushed, their diction imprecise.

"Oh, Claire," Drake said, and kissed her on the mouth. "We're going to Napa. It's all because of you. It's just so exciting. And thanks." Drake kissed her again, and then said, "I think we might need to make some coffee."

"Would you like me to handle that?" Claire asked.

"That's true," Drake said, regarding her. "You know how to pull coffee."

Claire's espressos re-introduced to the party the jittery atmosphere that had gone after the first bout of nerves. The line of students trailed back into the dining room, and Liv and Bailey had to squeeze past them, trundling empty platters, half-filled glasses, and bottles to be re-cycled. They re-stocked the bar for Sophia, and brought news to Claire of the mayhem beyond the kitchen, as though the kids in line weren't proof enough. Most of them were painfully young, much too young to be drinking, or in college, or up this late.

"A capo. A capo chino," a boy said, his head drooping between phrases as though it were heavy. "A cappuccino with extra foam. The foam is key. An important key."

The girl behind him giggled whenever she hiccupped, and then rushed, suddenly, from the line with a grunt. Field guide to partying: volunteer to work in the kitchen.

A horn—possibly a trumpet—sounded from deep in the house, and the line finally broke as the kids ran to discover the purpose of the summons. A professor meandered away with his latte, and Claire felt Liv's arm around her waist. "Do you ever think," Liv murmured, "about having another kid?"

"Mostly I've been thinking that I've never seen so many kids in sweater vests."

"I'm serious," Liv said. "I look at Sophia and I'm—I don't know—envious. You don't think about it? You don't wonder?"

Claire had imagined this discussion in a different setting, but she had imagined this discussion. Had craved it. She turned to scrutinize Liv, to evaluate how serious these questions were, how sober.

"Drunk," Drake said sorrowfully at the door.

"Sorry?" Claire murmured, rattled by the interruption, her mind alight with calculations: the arithmetic of probability.

Drake straightened, and stepped forward, and then paused to collect herself. "I'm drunk."

"Well," Liv said, "you're in good company."

"Yes, indeed." She slid off the counter on her first attempt to sit, but made it with a second, more concerted effort. "I didn't expect we'd all be quite so debauched."

Claire handed Drake a coffee, and said, "Just so no one's hit in the head with a beer glass." Beside her, Liv stiffened.

"We're using plastic cups," Drake said, reasonably.

Bailey ushered in a platoon of kids demanding champagne.

"Champagne!" Drake said, and clapped, hopping off the counter. "That's why I came in here. Let's pour champagne." She handed round plastic flutes, while Bailey fired off the first bottle.

As though there were no disruption, no one else in the room, Claire turned in Liv's arms, and said, "I do. I wonder." She kissed Liv lightly on the lips, neither closing her eyes.

The students had smuggled silly string into the party, and attacked their professors with it at midnight. A nerds' equivalent to dumping Gatorade on the football coach after winning league playoffs. Bailey stood by the bar with Sophia, Liv, and Claire, admiring the chaos.

Sophia took a sip of champagne, and then set the glass down. "No one at this party should be driving. I'm the designated driver for the three of you."

"You hate driving in the snow," Bailey said. "Besides, I've only had sips."

"You aren't staying?" Claire asked Bailey.

Bailey moved back into the kitchen. "I'm dead on my feet, and still have all this to transport home."

"Leave it, Bailey," Liv said. "I'll help you pack it home tomorrow."

"You're certain?"

"Yes."

"Thank god. Let's go home. I'm as old as I've ever been."

Liv fetched their coats, and she and Claire braced Sophia down the steps and across the street to her Volkswagen. *Yes,* Claire thought, helping Sophia into the car. *Yes, I envy her.* Bailey followed a few minutes later. Despite the raging heater, the windshield was still foggy, the car's interior achingly cold.

"Hooray," Claire said, in the front seat. "These seats are heated."

"Then what am I doing back here?" Bailey said. "Soph, you sure you want to drive?"

Sophia had already edged into the street, her window cracked to release the vapor, her neck and face pushed forward to allow her to peer through the windshield.

"Shh, I'm concentrating," she muttered. Beside her, Claire smiled. Her back muscles relaxed as the seat warmed, and her eyes closed, pictured Simon, asleep in a bunk bed, on his side with his fists clenched, his little jaw grinding. Envied him as well.

Thirty-seven

Ever think about the big stuff?

Hoffman wanted to be called *The Colonel*. Even his wife called him *The Colonel*. He wouldn't know who she was talking to, if she called him anything else. Liv nodded. He'd led her through his latest projects: a bathroom remodel in the basement, an armoire he'd built for his new grandson, an Irish shed he'd raised in the backyard as a workshop.

His work was good, inelegant, but clean and functional. He hoped to be able to assist her with the kitchen remodel. Guaranteed not to hinder her in any way. Liv had expected this, and ordinarily, would have declined, but he'd proposed his plan while she examined the armoire. Again, as she walked through the shed, and so she found that she could not refuse him.

A new year, a new girl. Now she took on assistants, old retired guys with vainglorious nicknames. She wasn't afraid anymore. Not of her mother's illness, or Claire's orbit, or her own boredom. Not even a pink-haired girl with a mouth like a bullhorn could intimidate Liv. Not anymore. Not when Claire knew and had forgiven everything.

She had Hoffman help her haul the beams into the kitchen. They'd brace the ceiling before they demolished the wall into the dining room.

That evening, her shoulders already sore from wielding the sledgehammer, Liv swung by Kyle's apartment building. Phoned him as she used her key on the exterior door, and started up the stairs.

"Second floor, back apartment," he said, and then hung up.

She could see the watermark in the hallway. The pipes had burst in the bathroom, and ruined the woodwork, flooded the subfloor. Kyle had pulled up the carpet, and toweled the floors.

"Tell me you can finish the fucking bathroom," he said. "I know you'll get this shit handled quicker than me, and I'm the guy laying new carpet in here, maybe the hallway too. My tenant's on vacation, the apartment downstairs had water pouring through the ceiling this morning. Fucking plumbing kills me. My guy got this bitch under control. Good news, except I can't do the fine work like you. Tell me it's handled."

Liv took out her phone, speed-dialed Claire. "It's handled."

He grinned at her. "You're giving me thrills, kid. Thrills."

Two days later, Kyle's number panned across her phone, and she considered letting it go to voicemail, but answered instead. Knew she could use lunch as an excuse; Hoffman's wife had made lasagna, a green salad, and poured water into the glasses as Liv opened her phone. The stove and refrigerator like displaced refugees in one half of the dining room, a table set for three in the other.

"I want to take you out for drinks. You've done me some favors, and I want to talk to you about a few things. You up for some drinks this week?"

"I'll clear it with Claire, call you back."

"I like that plan. Talk soon."

Drinks at Zola, and she liked Kyle more all the time. They were in jeans, light sweaters, both of them taut, rangy, getting looks from every direction. They sat in the leather booth nearest the bar, on display in the alcove beside them, a nurse's cap.

"You been here before?" he asked.

"Sure."

"I love this place. Waiter's hopeless."

A soccer guy in a ringer T-shirt and black Adidas sneakers came over, knelt beside them. "Hey, Dad," he said. "The usual?"

"My oldest son. Bruce, this is Liv."

"Hey, Liv. How about I surprise you?" He stood without waiting for an answer. "Leave it to me."

Bruce brought them Scotch, a pitcher of beer, and four plates of samplers. On the stage, two girls with guitars threw their voices like darts.

"I'll make myself sick if I don't tell you what I'm thinking and get it out of the way." Kyle sipped his Scotch, flexed an eyebrow. "Yeah, that's working. Now, Liv, I got these twelve apartment buildings, and they are value for money. I know you like independent. I'm not trying to bind you to anything. But I see you're skilled, and I'm thinking like an investor. You with me? I'm thinking about investing in you."

She had a strange sensation that he was asking to be her corner man. "You want to manage me?"

He laughed. "I want to invest in you. You ever think about building on a bigger scale? Get the big equipment, and the big contractor jobs, and start building some shit that'll still be standing when Bruce is middle aged.

"You and me, we see the value in hardwood. We see that it's all in the craft. Plywood and the rest of this shit can smoke me. People want contractors that build a good, lasting product. You and me are partners in an S-Corp. I'm the investor, you run the thing, and we split the profit 50-50. You with me? Right in half. You're the one hires the crews, manages the jobs. I'm the guy keeps the equipment running smooth."

He paused, sipped his drink, stared at her. "What happens now if you get hurt? You make good money, I know you do. But for how long? Your body can't take this shit forever. You worked a crew before?"

"Yeah."

"How'd you like it?"

"I liked it. Running the whole operation, though, that's something else."

"Same concept on a bigger scale is all."

Liv shook her head. "You make everything sound easy."

"Take a little time with this. Think it over. You got a little kid now. Objectives shift when there's a kid, you with me?"

239

She was. She was with him. This guy she admired, offering to bank her. High maintenance, frenetic, but with connections, and capital: a pragmatic businessman. Bruce dropped by with another round of Scotch, crouched beside Liv, explained that he coached a co-ed indoor soccer team, that they were always short girls. Wondered if she'd be interested in coming to a game sometime.

"How old are most of the players?" Liv asked. She figured him for twenty-two tops.

"We have a guy that's twenty-five. He's like our best player. Just come to a game." He handed her a schedule. "Check us out, and then decide."

He cleared their plates, and Liv grinned as Kyle yanked at his hair, told him. "You two operate."

"Taught him everything he knows," Kyle said. "You give this offer some thought. Talk to your girl. I got time." He reached into his coat pocket, tossed some pictures on the table. "My kids when they were little. Fucking beautiful shots here."

Thirty-eight

With with-child, refrain

Simon watched trains running on epic tracks, crashes set to Thomas' theme music, video narration shot by eight year olds, and posted on You Tube. Occasionally he'd cackle with laughter, and Claire would glance away from the bank statement, enjoy her kid for a moment.

A key in the lock, and Liv let herself in, stomped snow from her boots, set the bags of food down to lift Simon, kiss him, inquire after his day.

"And how's Mommy?" Liv asked as she carried Simon, and the food, into the office.

"Mommy's cross," Simon said.

"Yes, she is," Claire said.

Liv laid boxes of Chinese on the desk, took some bowls and napkins from the top drawer of one of the filing cabinets. "Why cross?"

"I'm doing the bank reconciliation, and it isn't reconciling. Something's wrong with the last payroll, or something."

Liv handed Simon a bowl of fried rice and a spoon. Claire helped herself to a mix from each of the cartons, served Liv as well.

"You'll sort it," Liv said.

This was true, Claire knew, but not the same as commiseration. "Eventually," she allowed.

Simon told Liv about the mouse he'd seen in the parking lot. How Bailey had said it must live on pastries. Claire gave him another scoop of rice, and some lemon chicken.

"Did they get off alright, the Napa expedition?" Liv asked Claire.

241

"They were like little kids on their first adventure. Julia came by here for Bailey. She'd bought Travel Scrabble to play on the plane. It was kind of sweet."

After pulling a bottle of white wine from the walk-in, Claire offered Liv a glass.

"Not for me, thanks," Liv said, wishing for a beer.

Claire poured milk for both of them, sipped at her wine, and said, "Sophia asked if she could drop in on us this weekend. I guess she's anxious when she's alone."

"What happened to the boyfriend?"

"They split."

"That sucks."

"Bailey almost called the trip off. She's that worried."

Simon brought his plate over to the desk, stood at the edge in order to eat with them. Nobody ate rice like Simon.

"I'll take Simon back with me," Liv said, "if you think you'll be here awhile yet."

"I'd love that. Did you get your car seat back from Bailey?"

"No. How about, I'll take your car, and change the oil in it tonight?"

"In the freezing dark?"

"In the heated garage."

"Wow, are you in the running for some award?"

"Darling," Liv grinned. "You know I'm a compulsive overachiever."

"Compulsive," Claire laughed, "is half right."

Snow dusted them on the walk to the car, sticking already to the parking lot. Claire strapped Simon into his seat, kissed him good night, anticipating a long evening's work ahead of her. Liv had started the car, and half-finished clearing the windows.

"Thanks for dinner," Claire said.

"Anytime, beautiful." Liv kissed her, waved goodbye.

Sated and reinvigorated, Claire returned to the office, and finished the reconcile forty-five minutes later. While checking the locks, before she put out the light, or set the alarm, she heard a knock at the door.

Anxious, in spite of herself, certain the pink-haired girl had returned, maybe with a weapon, she backed away from the door, and edged toward the heavy pans. Then she heard a key in the lock, and the door swung open.

"You said you'd be here late," Sophia said.

"Jesus, you scared me." Claire crossed to the girl, and bolted the door. "What's happened?"

"I'm sorry to come here like this, but I can't be at home." Sophia dropped her bag on the floor. Her eyes and nose were wet. "I freaked myself out watching *X-Files* reruns. I don't know what I was thinking." She burst into sobs, her arms around her belly in one last attempt to hold herself together.

Claire held her, murmured, "Honey, honey."

"I don't want to be pregnant anymore. It's so hard. I'm sore, and tired, and a crybaby, and I'm frightened all the time. I'm scared of everything. I've never been so frightened." She choked, and hiccupped, and kept sobbing. "I wasn't supposed to be doing this alone. I can't do this by myself. Help me. Please help me. This poor kid. He's going to hate me."

Claire rubbed her back, hummed, held on.

Claire had the truck's wipers on high, and still had to wipe the windshield to see. "I can't believe you drove around in this," she told Sophia. "The *X-Files* scared you more than a blizzard?"

"It wasn't snowing this hard when I left, and you told me you'd be working late, so I just focused on getting there before you left. Besides, I took Bailey's Subaru—new snow tires and four-wheel drive—I didn't even notice the snow."

Sophia had asked Claire if she could stay with them until Bailey got home. Claire could remember being frightened like this when she was pregnant. Sometime in that last miserable month, her aunt had found her, weeping in the shower, and she'd climbed in—boots and all—to hold Claire while she cried.

Claire followed Fourteenth to Maple, along the bus route, since they'd plow bus routes first. Half a dozen cars on the road, each one crawling along, and leaving as much space as possible in every direction. The truck fishtailed at the stop sign on Walnut.

"Fuck," Claire said, throwing the emergency brake. "I love winter."

Once they were off the hill, they both relaxed perceptibly.

"I think he feels my anxiety. He's freaking out." Sophia unfastened her seatbelt to stretch forward, and massage her belly, flex her back. "You know what I miss? Sleeping on my back. I really miss sleeping on my back."

"I missed sleeping on my belly. After Simon was born, I still couldn't because I was breast-feeding." She laughed. "I thought I'd been uncomfortable before …"

"How long did you breast-feed?"

"Ten months."

"God, that's amazing. It wasn't hard?"

"It was wicked hard. My nipples bled for days, and ached for months. I would have kept going, but he bit me so hard that last time I told him we were done." She adjusted the heater. "Anyway, he'd already acclimated to sippy cups by then."

"He never had a bottle?"

"Sometimes. I'd pump so Dee could feed him from a bottle while I napped."

Claire thought she heard a sniff, and glanced at Sophia. The girl had bent so far forward she looked like she was trying to kiss her own belly.

"Are you OK?" Claire asked.

"Yeah," Sophia breathed. "He just kicked me really hard. He's got hiccups. I don't think he likes hiccups."

"Me neither. We're almost home," Claire said, reaching out to her. "There's the bridge up ahead, and we're the first right."

Through the snow, two deer ran into the headlights.

The pounding at the kitchen door startled Liv from her magazine. She hopped up and ran through, anxious that Simon not wake. Claire on the doorstep: blood smeared over her right eye and down her cheek, the sleeve of her coat ripped and bloody, her jeans and boots slick with mud. Liv took this in without moving, said, "What's happened? What have you done?"

Claire stood, silent. Blood in her hair, and from one of her ears, and all at once Liv's brain unlocked her body, and she seized Claire, brought her straight through to the bathroom, sat her on the toilet, and turned the shower on.

"What happened?" She couldn't tell if the cuts were serious. "Claire, where are you hurt?"

Claire trembled. Liv could hear her teeth chatter. Kneeling, she peeled off Claire's boots, and coat. Tore her shirt away to avoid pulling it over her head, eased it past Claire's torn hands. "Tell me what happened." She had the most trouble with Claire's jeans, had to brace Claire's body with her head and shoulder in order to yank them down.

"Claire," Liv said, forcing her voice to be sensible, soothing. She stripped her own clothes off, grabbed Simon's step ladder from the pantry, and shouldered Claire from the toilet seat to the highest step of the ladder. "Claire, can you tell me what happened?" Liv used her own body to keep Claire from toppling into the tub, and poured water over her head, rinsing away the blood and dirt.

"Simon's asleep," Liv said now, digging into Claire's hair to pull several pieces of glass from her scalp. "We read a couple of stories, and then he fell right to sleep. I figured I'd give you another hour before I called. Thought I'd wait until ten to interrupt you." Claire's ear was cut, and her right eyebrow. Neither was deep, though they bled easily. Already her torso, along her ribs, as well as her right knee and thigh were bruised.

"Claire, were you in an accident?"

Once she'd been rinsed off, the cuts were obviously minor; even on her hands, she'd only cut a couple of shallow lines in her palms. "Claire, did you hit your head?"

She talked while Claire shivered. She kept the water hot, rubbed at Claire's arms and legs. When the chattering seemed to be louder, Liv pulled Claire from the shower, toweled her off, and eased her into Liv's own pajamas before leading her to the sofa and cocooning her in blankets. Liv grabbed sleeping bags, and a heating pad, and propped Claire between the arm of the sofa and a battery of pillows.

"Claire?" Liv said. "Should I take you to the hospital? Your injuries look superficial—the ones I can see anyway. Does your belly hurt, or your head?" Starting at her feet, Liv pressed her fingers gently into Claire, hoping a hidden injury would evoke some response. She'd worked up to Claire's face, pressing into her temples, when she realized that she'd never heard the truck. "Claire? Did you have to leave the truck someplace?"

Should she wake Simon, drive to the emergency room in a blizzard? In the bathroom again, she grabbed Claire's clothes and jacket and boots, and took them through to the laundry room. She didn't know for sure what had happened. If she found the truck, though, if she found the truck she might know more. She grabbed clothes from the hamper, and Claire's boots, and put them on.

Liv returned to the living room with an ice pack, and held it against Claire's head. "Claire? Can you talk to me?" She'd stopped shivering. "Were you in an accident? Did something happen to the truck?" Out the bay window, the snow seemed to fall more heavily still. Her tools were in the lockbox in the bed of the truck. If the truck were on the road somewhere between here and town, at night, in the middle of a blizzard, she'd have to leave sooner rather than later, if she hoped to find it.

"Listen, Claire, Simon's asleep. He's in his room, sleeping." She turned the television on, found a nature show. "I'm going to run out for just a minute, OK? I'm going to run out and see if I can find the truck. I'll just walk along the road for fifteen minutes, that's all."

Claire pulled her legs up, drew the blankets tightly around herself. "Claire? Can you talk to me?"

Claire was staring at the TV when she whispered, "By the bridge."

"What?"

"I lost Simon," Claire said. "He had hiccups and I couldn't find him."

"No, honey. Simon's in his room. He's asleep. Don't you worry about him. You just need to rest. Do you think you can rest?"

"You have to go," Claire said. "By the bridge."

"That's right." Liv kissed her several times on the forehead, and mouth. "You'll rest here; and I'll take care of everything. Keep this on your head." Liv adjusted the ice pack. "And I'll see if I can locate the truck and figure out what happened."

Liv set the cordless phone on the couch, and kissed Claire again. "I'll be right back."

Liv's flashlight barely penetrated the snow. She pulled her cap lower on her face, zipped her coat up so that the metal pressed into her chin. She could still see Claire's footprints, and followed them to the road, along the road to the bridge, and then began to look for tire treads.

Ten yards from the bridge, she saw tracks run away to the left, and followed these. The truck had hit a maple tree, and rolled at least once, sliding on the passenger's side into another tree. Claire had pushed, or kicked, through the windshield. Both doors were locked. Amazingly, Liv's tools were still in the lockbox she'd built in the truck bed. Her poor truck—essentially intact, though—and far enough from the road to remain for the night. She walked around the far side of the truck and stood looking at a pair of legs.

Liv vomited twice. She had blood on her hands—she'd pulled off her gloves to get a better grip—and had smacked her head on the truck so hard that she'd cut herself. She wiped blood from her eyes. Sophia lay supine, her left arm and shoulder pinned under the cab of the truck, the rest of her upper body buried deep in snow. Liv had stood, staring at the legs, trying to puzzle the incongruity, legs beside her wrecked truck in the woods. She'd tried to make them animal legs at first, despite the lace-up shoes. Her mind had pulled together slowly. And then she knew everything.

She'd checked for a pulse, and found a slow one, though Sophia's skin was blue. She'd tried to shift the truck. Tried to dig Sophia out. Finally, she'd run back to the road, and called 911, given directions for an ambulance, learned there was a pileup on the freeway, and it would be twenty minutes before anyone could get to her.

Liv ran back to the truck, pulled blankets and a tarp through the broken windshield and tried to cover Sophia. The snow had not let up. Liv called the house phone. It rang and rang and no one answered.

She heard a siren in the distance, and ran back to the road. The fire truck stopped beside her, killed the siren, but kept its lights flashing.

"She's this way," Liv said. Crying now, stumbling. Two of the firefighters lifted her, turned back toward the fire truck.

"You're bleeding," one of them said. "We can see your truck all right."

They guided Liv to the fire truck, sat her down, wrapped her in a blanket, working around her as though she were injured. She could only cry.

"We're taking you in," a voice said. "You've sliced your head open." The sirens started again.

"Don't leave her," Liv said. "Don't leave her."

"It's OK." The same voice. "It's OK. We've got her. We've got her too."

Thirty-nine

A sound woke me

He called her several times before her eyes opened. They closed, and he called her again.

"Mama."

"I'm awake."

"Mama."

"What is it, baby?"

"A sound. I heard a sound."

He'd heard a shriek like a pterodactyl, and found his mother's bed empty. Down the long hallway, he thought maybe they'd been eaten. In the living room, his mother slept in a nest of blankets, on television a commercial for pet supplies.

"I want to sleep with you," he said.

"OK."

"Mama."

"I'm coming."

He came and stood beside her. She followed him down the hallway—leaving the light on, the television—crawled into bed, and tucked him against her. Sleep broke over them.

Five stitches. They had to shave a patch of Liv's hair to clean and stitch her scalp just to the left of her part. Wrapped her forearm too, the skin sliced and bleeding from the broken windshield. Sophia in emergency surgery, they said. Trauma, they said. Trauma not word enough for that girl's body.

The police officer found Liv in the waiting room, and led her to a cubby of an office down one of the wings. A huge, scrubbed guy in a button-down shirt and suit jacket, no tie; he had two cups of coffee, and held one out to her.

"How's your head?"

She shook it. This guy looked like he might cry too. They sat side by side; he'd turned in his chair to observe her. The coffee tasted like silt.

"We found deer tracks," he said. "Along the roadside where you swerved. You hit one of them with the truck—we found it on the other side of the road—then the truck hit the tree, and then it rolled."

Her eyes burned, her jaw from clenching it.

"It could have happened without a blizzard," he said. "We notified her parents—found her cell in her bag, and called them. They're driving up from Ritzville." His voice was subdued, as though to lull her to sleep, and she wanted to be lulled to sleep. "You were driving?"

Liv stared at Claire's boots, the torn knee of her jeans. "Yeah."

"She was in the passenger's seat?"

"Yeah."

"Was she wearing her seatbelt?"

"I don't remember."

"Where had you been, before the accident?"

"Sophia's house. She and her boyfriend just split up." Liv choked, coughed. "Her housemate is in Napa. I've tried to call her, but I just get voicemail."

A knock at the office door, and the officer stood, stepped outside. She looked at the bandage on her arm, a dark patch at its heart. Her coffee spilled, the liquid expanding across the floor. She tried not to think of blood. He came back into the room, shut the door, knelt beside her.

"She's fucking dead," Liv said. "She's fucking dead, isn't she?"

The cop said yes. A shudder escaped before she could seal it off. "And the baby? Her little boy?" Liv saw legs in the snow, her body half buried, and blue. Nothing could survive that. Nothing.

"I'm sorry," he said.

"Fuck," she said. "Fuck." She crushed the Styrofoam cup with

Claire's boot. "I'd gone over there because she was frightened to be alone. I was taking her back to my house, and then—"

She could not swallow the wail; it tore from her. Sophia would never have a little boy named Riley.

Simon played on the floor beside his mother's bed. He had made breakfast, and drunk milk, and gone back to the kitchen later for raisins, and a banana. Still she slept. And so he'd brought his trains into her room, set up a track along the floor to the chest of drawers.

When he heard the kitchen door open, he ran down the hallway, and launched himself into Bailey's arms.

"Hey, sweetheart," she said. "Where's your mama?"

He climbed her, clutching her neck and shoulders, and buried his face into her throat.

"I've got you," she said, squeezing him. "I've got you."

"Mama's sick," he told her.

Bailey jostled him in time with her heartbeat. "It's OK," she said. "We're going to be OK."

Forty

Those are my boots

Coffee going cold in the mugs they held, Liv's mother and father sat at the kitchen table at Claire's house. On her way to class, Drake had dropped off bagels and apples, but no one could eat. Liv stood at the counter, beside Bailey, and tried to remember the police officer's name. Watts, she thought. Could a cop be named Watts?

He was even bigger here, impossibly large in this kitchen. He kept his voice soft, she noticed, to minimize his size. Today he wore a tie, a blue suit. Officer Watts, she tried it in her mouth.

They'd buried the mother and child three days earlier, another item in the paper. The night of the blizzard, twenty-four people had died in accidents, most of them in the freeway pileup. She got a sentence in the lead article the morning after, the young pregnant woman killed in a collision on Government Way.

The police had taken photographs of the scene, measurements, asked Liv for a voluntary blood sample that night at the hospital to rule out any question of impairment. They had investigated thoroughly because of the death involved in the crash. The death involved in the crash. He had explained all this to her, this detective. Today, in the kitchen, he assured them that the case was closed, the accident officially accidental, and no charges would be pressed.

Claire came into the kitchen, holding Simon's hand. They sat at the table, and Simon crawled across into Susan's lap.

Bailey had shaken Claire awake that first morning, told her that something terrible had happened, and that she needed to get up.

Nauseous, aching, Claire had tried to sit. "I feel awful," she said.

252

"Simon said you were sick."

"Where is Simon?" Claire asked.

"He's here. Claire, you need to get up. Something's happened."

"I had a dream," she said. "I couldn't find him. He was lost. I looked everywhere, but I couldn't find him." Simon had been lost in the woods. It was so real. But here he was on the floor playing. "My head. Something's wrong with my head."

"Is it the flu?" Bailey asked, glancing at her, as she grabbed jeans and a sweater from the bureau. "Do you want some ibuprofen?"

"You're in Napa, aren't you?" Claire said. Why was she wearing Liv's pajamas?

"We came back early from Napa." Bailey laid the clothes out on the foot of the bed. "Claire, you have to get dressed. I'm sorry to drag you out of bed when you feel rotten. I don't know much yet, but Julia—" Her phone rang and she looked at the display. "I have to take this; it's Julia." She left the room, with Simon tailing along behind.

Her head ringing, a pain in her belly whenever she breathed, Claire pushed up from the bed. She discovered the bruises when she undressed, examined them in the mirror, pressed her ribs as she breathed in and out. After dressing, she found them in the kitchen, Simon in Bailey's arms, his head tucked, eyes closed.

"There's been an accident," Bailey said.

And then she explained that Liv had hit a deer in the blizzard, and rolled the truck. She said that Sophia had been killed. Claire touched her ear, asked if Liv had been hurt.

The detective stepped toward Liv, and she started. He'd said something, she realized. "I'm sorry, detective. I didn't catch that."

"Would you walk me to my car?" he asked.

Liv smiled, the idea of protecting this mammoth man, the first amusing thought she'd had in days. "Sure."

He held the door for her, and she led down the steps, and along the path through the snow to his unmarked car. Once she reached the car, she turned to face him, waiting.

"It's good your family's here with you," he said.

She stared up at him, his earlobes the size of half dollars.

"A time like this." He shaded his eyes to see her better. "We closed the case, but that doesn't mean things will resolve for you. I know how hard you worked to help your friend—your tracks were all over the place. I know you worked desperately. I know you did. And to find her, in the woods in the dark after an accident, to try to help her, to call for assistance, Liv, you did everything you could. Remember that."

"Stop," she said. His kindness hurt her. "Please."

And so he stood quietly with her beside the police car, the sun refracting off the snow.

In the kitchen, Bailey brewed tea. A house full of people, and nobody had anything to say. The day after the accident, while they waited for Drake to bring Liv home, Bailey had played trains on the floor with Simon, while Claire sat on the sofa, her head splintered.

Simon woke her, crying Liv's name. When Claire stepped into the kitchen, she saw Liv on her knees, holding the little boy. Her head shaved just back from the forehead, stitches showing in the patch of scalp. Her eye and cheek were bruised.

Drake said she'd brought some groceries, some things to make sandwiches, in case anyone was hungry, and asked if Bailey and Simon would help her bring the bags in. They put the child in his snowsuit, and headed outdoors.

"Those are my boots," Claire said.

Liv sat down at the table, rested her head in her hands.

"Liv, what happened last night?"

"Sophia died."

"Bailey told me you were driving."

Liv went to the sink, poured a glass of water. Outside, Simon hit one of the women with a snowball. They heard his ecstatic, *Gotcha!*

"You were driving?" Claire asked. Just standing in the doorway hurt. And breathing.

"What do you remember?" Liv asked, her back to the room, to Claire.

Claire could see the deer in the road. They hadn't had time to scream. She'd woken in Liv's pajamas with black, livid bruises. "What happened to your head?"

"I hit it on the truck."

"You weren't in the truck," Claire said. She'd cut her palms crawling through the windshield. She stared at her hands. "Liv?" Sophia bent forward trying to kiss her belly. "Liv," she said again. The baby hated hiccups. "Look at me."

A snowball splattered against the window above the sink. Liv stared at it. "The truck pinned her," she said. "Threw her and pinned her." Liv drank the water, poured another glass.

"You weren't driving," Claire said. She knew this. "I was driving. A deer ran into the road, and we hit it." Two deer in the snow, and they'd hit one.

"She's dead," Liv said. "They're dead."

"I don't understand you." Claire crossed to the sink, leaned against the counter because it hurt less than being upright. "Why have you done this? It was an accident. I hit a deer."

"And left an injured pregnant woman in the snow." At last, Liv turned to face her. The white of her eye was bruised too. "And you never said a thing. Not a fucking word about Sophia. I found her. Buried in the snow where you'd left her."

Claire stepped back. "Things were—" she looked around the kitchen, "confusing."

"Oh, confusing," Liv sneered. "Well, that explains everything."

In the dark, Claire had stumbled in the woods, had tripped and crawled and dragged herself up. She'd been looking for Simon. No, not Simon, Sophia. She'd been looking for Sophia. The snow—drifts of it, and the blizzard—and she hadn't seen anyone. She didn't know how long it had taken her to find the road, or how long she'd been in the truck before she'd kicked her way out. She'd only known that she had to get home. That if she got home, she'd be safe. She looked at Liv's stitches. "Why didn't you take me to the hospital?"

"Is that what I should have done?" Liv asked. "Tell me what I should have done."

"I don't—"

255

They heard Simon, on the stairs, his shrill voice asking for hot chocolate. Then they were all in the kitchen: Bailey and Drake hauling groceries, Simon flushed from cold and pleasure, holding out a bag of animal crackers. "Look Mommy, we got these cookies. They're my favorite."

Bailey brought her tea to the kitchen table. "I'm going to work tomorrow."

"That's a good idea," Dennis said.

Susan brushed her fingers through Simon's hair, watched the kitchen door. They didn't know what to do with Liv and the cop outside. What couldn't he say to her in front of them? Hadn't she been through enough?

Without designating anyone in particular, Claire said, "If you need me, I'll be in the office."

A field guide to skeptics and martyrs: no one suffers like you do. Claire's bruises hidden by her clothes, her cuts by her hair, she'd smuggled herself past them, and they'd never suspected. They'd never noticed. No one stopped her when she left the kitchen.

Forty-one

Suspended like this

That inexhaustible winter, Spokane had snow in May, unusual, even in the Pacific Northwest. Spring flowers would bud and die in a single afternoon, undone by the wet chill; Claire thought Government Way might be laced with snow until mid-summer.

Liv and Kyle had incorporated: Building Blocks, Inc. They ran their business out of the first floor of Kyle's apartment complex on Post Street—contracted a green-building project in Peaceful Valley, a windmill farm on the Palouse, and had half-a-dozen renovations on the bluff lined up for the summer. Liv slept more and more frequently at the office, said the commute to Claire's for four hours of sleep didn't calculate.

At the café, Bailey hired a baker from Seattle, and they finally extended the hours, opened seven days a week from 6 a.m. until 3:30 p.m. Claire worked on the books part-time at the café. Each month, their profits increased.

The last Tuesday in May, Claire wandered outdoors on the property with Simon, down to the river, pacing like one of those zoo animals that cannot pretend the confinement away any longer. Simon paced beside her, stepping from rock to rock, ambling as though his energy would never flag, four now, and protective of his mother.

They walked past the spot where Liv had stored her trailer, strangely deserted now; in March, they had hauled the trailer to the Palouse farm for the builder to use there. Dismantled, item by item, the life they had shared. Claire's closet, the shelves in the bathroom, all the cupboards had seemed bereft, so much less.

And then Claire had had a letter, forwarded by her publisher, from a professor at Cornell. A man known to her from conferences she'd attended with her aunt. He taught at the Department of Plant Pathology, and wanted her to contact him as soon as possible regarding a research project proposal that he had. For a week, she'd kept the letter in the pocket of her coat, reread it until she could see the words as a pathway, and then called Patrick.

"Sure," he said, "I know a phenomenal agent. I've used her a couple of times now. Why are you asking?"

She told him. Patrick kept quiet for a substantial time, so long that she thought perhaps her cell had gone dead.

"You still there?" she asked.

"Are you sure?" he said. "Certain?"

"Yes." Though she wasn't. Not of anything. And afterward, when Bailey asked this same question, while Claire packed Simon's toys in the office at the café, Claire could only shake her head.

"What will you do?" Patrick asked.

"I've been offered a research fellowship in New York."

"Researching?"

"Fungi."

"Oh," he said. And then, "You don't just want to rent the place?"

"No."

The agent had called Claire later the same afternoon, and the house had sold the first day it listed. For an amount that Claire considered absurd—she'd agreed to the list price as a final stall—to a retired couple from San Diego.

They would close in another week, and the movers arrived in the morning. Claire had explained all this to Simon. He'd listened without response, not even a flicker in his eyes.

Along the gravel drive, just before Claire and Simon reached the fence line, Liv's new rust-colored Toyota truck appeared.

"Liv," Simon hollered, running forward.

She parked, climbed from the cab, caught the boy. Thinner, and taller, he stretched nearly three-quarters of her length now. Liv had come for the last of her things.

Claire waved, but did not step toward her. They had never had another conversation about the accident after the angry abridgment in Drake's kitchen. Weeks would pass before Claire understood. She could never atone. Not for an accident she supposedly had no part of, a tangential death. Liv had re-written the story, and in Liv's version, Claire had no injuries, no guilt, and therefore, no suffering. Claire hadn't been in an accident. Hadn't woken sideways in the cab, disoriented, shaking, thinking, *By the bridge. By the bridge.* And then fought her way out of the truck, crawling and bleeding, through the dark, the forest litter and trees, the slick of snow, her breathing like an ice pick jabbed into her lungs as she searched.

Liv had meddled with the accident, and created a crime, hadn't she? Staged a murder to look like the accident that it always was. And now, they were beyond prosecution for recklessness or negligence. If the police were told, they'd suspect a conspiracy, a cover-up, one lover protecting another. A suspicious death. This silence, this unvoiced, unacknowledged guilt, even the grief, were nothing to Claire, nothing compared to Liv's punishment: Liv's slow, inevitable vanishing.

"Liv," Simon asked, "want to play trains with me?"

"I have to take some boxes to the truck," she said. "Do you want to help me?"

"OK."

Claire kept her eyes on the tree line. At dusk the last several nights, she'd seen a bull moose. He'd walked to the river, then returned to stand at the edge of the meadow, as though he were waiting.

Simon carried something each trip: a small bag, or some towels, a handful of books. Claire stayed on the deck. She could not assist with this anymore. Could not be party to Liv's leave-taking.

When the tailgate slammed shut, the sound shook through her. Several minutes later, their voices nearby, Simon's plaintive, and Liv said that she would. They went indoors.

At four, the moose came. Picking through the meadow as though he'd lost something, and then, on his way back, he stopped in the open, and looked toward Claire. He could not see her, though he probably smelled her.

259

Liv came out again eventually, lit a cigarette on the deck. Said that Simon had fallen asleep on the couch. Asleep. For him now, Liv's last visit would be a prelude, a dream. Claire stared at the field where the moose had been.

"I liked New York," Liv said.

Claire nodded, held onto the rail of the deck.

"I hope you and Simon will be happy there."

"Me too."

Claire pushed off the deck and walked toward the trees, she could manage no more.

At Bailey's, their last night in town, Claire stayed in the room with Simon until he'd fallen asleep, and then came out for beer, and some pizza Bailey had baked.

"What do you think of the new girl?" Claire asked.

"She's always bitching at me about labeling my receipts. You never did that."

"I knew what your receipts were for."

"Yeah. She's not you."

"Thanks." Claire picked the mushrooms off the pizza, ate them first. Remembered a trail through the woods, her aunt crouched beside small white parasols of matsutake.

"I've got tickets to visit you next month," Bailey said.

"Have you?" Claire had never imagined this.

"Enough time for all your boxes to be empty, and your guest room comfortable." Bailey opened another beer, handed it to Claire. "I'll miss you. You get that, right?"

"I'll miss you too."

"Julia wants to go to Prague this summer. Does that sound like fun to you?"

"I've never been to Prague."

"I've been pushing for Holland."

"I've never been there either."

"God, Claire, we've got to get out of this town."

"I am."

"Right. Maybe Holland and Prague." She plated another piece of pizza. "Where will I get my kid fix with Simon gone?"

"I guess you'll have to visit a lot."

"Now you're getting it."

Claire laughed, patted Bailey's foot rested on the chair beside her.

Liv sat up, pulled from her sleeping bag, and slid her jeans back on. Outside, the rain fell thin and light. A block away, she heard a girl call out a name, and then laugh. The streetlights blinked red through downtown. She walked up Monroe, crossed at Tenth, down toward the bluff, to Bailey's sleeping house. She'd tried, once, to pick up a girl, and had abandoned the scenario the moment the girl responded. She could not bear anyone else's hands.

With four jobs going at once, she'd started to forget to eat, had dropped weight she couldn't afford to lose. In the afternoons, she'd walk down to the river, fling rocks into the water, ache for Simon, for summer, for those nights on the deck drinking wine. While she stood on the sidewalk outside Bailey's house, smoking half a pack of cigarettes: the rain stopped, the sky lightened, the crows squawked.

Kyle had connections, and enough jobs lined up for the summer that she'd need to hire another dozen people to work her crews. She could fill her life with this. She could. She had to. Love like this would ruin her. She'd claimed that girl in the snow without hesitating. She'd meant to save the girl, believed she could, but she hadn't saved either of them—not the girl, or Claire. She'd played savior, and written a story neither could tell—an accident she hadn't experienced, couldn't know, had only judged from its aftermath: a dead woman, and Claire to blame. Crime-spree Claire.

A guy in a suit climbed into his car, two women ran past with their dogs. And then Bailey's door opened and Simon came outside, dragging his tiger backpack. He waved to Liv.

Behind him, his mother stopped on the stairs, said something to Bailey. Claire followed Simon down, Drake and Bailey behind her. Claire opened the backdoor, stowed the last two bags. Liv hugged

Simon, loaded him in his car seat. Bailey and Drake kissed them both goodbye.

Liv held Claire. Stepped back, wiped her face. Claire climbed into the car and started it, rolled down the windows, pulled away; Simon calling, "See you tomorrow."

Epilogue:

Twelve years later

His mother is tense. This alone keeps him from sulking, dragged to Spokane for a funeral in the middle of term. He will miss two soccer games, and has had to lug all of his books with him, scribble his assignments on the food tray during the flight over, and—Calculus, an interminable misery—back to Ithaca.

In the rental car now, the day bright and warm just to spite him, his mother announces they're on the South Hill, and nearly there.

"Lovely hill," he says. She laughs, and his mood slides away, just like that. "It'll be good to see Bailey."

"Yes. Bailey is always good."

He hasn't been back here since they left. Twelve years. They pull up in front of a Cape Cod, the dormers like raised eyebrows. He doesn't remember this house, wonders if he's ever been here.

"I'll get the bags," he says.

She thanks him, climbs from the car, and stands in the street, looking up and down the block, and finally at the house.

"Hey," his mother says, arm extended in greeting.

Bailey has sprung from the house, and is going to kill herself on the stairs. He steps toward her, hands raised against calamity, and she catches into him, pulls his mother into their embrace as well. The both of them crush him, murmuring and crying. Here less than two minutes and already they're crying.

"Oh, Bailey," she says, "I'm so sorry."

"I can't believe you're here. I thought you wouldn't come." Bailey releases his mother, but strains backward to stare at him. "Jesus, you're bigger every time I see you. How's that possible? Your mother's so little."

"Hey," she objects, and swats Bailey.

"Thank you for coming, Simon. I'm sorry you're missing your games."

"It's OK," he says. "I don't mind." He wants to say something consoling, but can't. He's taller than she is now, and can see that her blond hair has washed grey. All these years of Bailey's visits, the pile of loot she never fails to bring him, and this is the first time he has thought of her as old. She links her arm through his mother's and they walk ahead of him to the house.

Inside, the hardwood floor, and each step on the stairs, creaks as Bailey guides them to the guest rooms. Something delicious—croissants, he hopes—is baking. The house is rich with it: cinnamon and dough.

He takes longer washing up than his mother does, and interrupts them in the kitchen. His mother's tension has increased.

"Do you drink coffee, Simon?" Bailey asks.

"Sure."

"Latte?"

"Sure."

He loves the sound of steam. A timer dings, and she turns from the espresso machine to remove a bunt-cake pan from the oven. Not croissants, then. His mother is standing in the threshold, with the exterior door opened, her coffee raised to her lips as though she might rinse her face with it. Morning light makes her ageless; it wings from her glasses, and the door's pane. She'd brought a pile of student papers with her to grade on the plane, complaining, as always, of lax scholarship. She didn't sleep on the flight, as he had. Yet she doesn't seem fatigued now, but wired, expectant.

Bailey sets his coffee beside him, and sits at the table. "We'll eat as soon as it's cooled. I have fruit too, mango."

Bailey's in jeans, a pale green sleeveless sweater, striking by any standard, long-legged with veiled eyes and an easy manner. And he's aware of this—her desirability—in a sorrowful way, as though it were not a gift.

264

"I never thought I'd see your mother in this town again." Bailey says this to him, though his mother must hear. "Do you remember this house?"

So he has been here before. He stares around him, the kitchen a marvelous room of copper pots and china, spices in uniform jars displayed in steel baskets, a large painting of an umbrella tipped back like some struggling insect on the wall above the table. Nothing jars his mind.

"No," he says, wishing he could.

Up again, she takes a knife, and plates, to the stove. "Are you hungry, Claire?"

His mother crosses to Bailey, wraps around her. He wants to be elsewhere, and here observing, simultaneously. This intimacy shames him, this grief.

"Yes," his mother says at last, and picks up a plate.

He wants to ask about Drake, finds himself listening for her voice. He is so used to them—Bailey and Drake—that he forgets.

His mother hands him a plate with a sort of battlement on it—the bricks of a castle wall rolled in cinnamon—beside slices of mango.

"Monkey bread," Bailey says, in response to the hesitant poise of his fork. "You'll love it."

"You always say that," he grins. He bites into a chunk, and finds himself kneeling on a kitchen chair, a helmet on his head, his mother across from him eating cantaloupe, her leg propped on the chair beside her. She is impossibly young—without glasses—her hair dark and shorn, one strap of her white tank top has slid down her arm. And then, another woman leans into his mother, and kisses her. The woman is like his mother—a twin, he thinks—and then knows that she is not, that his mother and this woman are not twins, not like-nesses, but dualities, light and dark, the two of them, bowed into one another and then looking across at him, their voices bright with laughter.

In Bailey and Drake's kitchen—just Bailey's now—his mother has raised her head, alert to the sound of boots on the stairs, the rap of knuckles at the kitchen door.

265

Another bite: his helmet tipped back on his head, the kiss, and laughter. This is what he remembers, the story he tells himself.

The woman who comes into the kitchen now is slight and rough, his mother's shadow rather than her twin. But she was never her twin.

"Claire," Liv says, her voice as rough as her work boots. Liv has had twelve years to think of something elegant to say. Twelve years dreaming the river, a boy with a boat, Claire in her arms—always in her arms. She wants to say that she leaves that stone house, Claire injured and disoriented on the couch, bleeding when Liv leaves her, always leaves her, closes the kitchen door, walks into the blizzard, only to find herself back in the living room, leaving, again, the woman on the couch. Wants to say it is fresh each time, the hurt in her. But, "Claire," is what comes out. "Claire."

At the table, Simon takes another bite, and his gesture draws her focus. She turns toward him. He is so familiar that she finds herself grinning.

"Simon," Bailey says. "You remember Liv."

"Hey, Liv," he says, and grins back at her. "Have some of this monkey bread. You'll love it."